BOOK FIVE

DRAGONKEEPER

SHADOW SISTER

Carole Wilkinson

D0925296

black dog books

First published in 2014
by **black dog books**,
an imprint of Walker Books Australia Pty Ltd
Locked Bag 22, Newtown
NSW 2042 Australia
www.walkerbooks.com.au

This edition published in 2015.

The moral rights of the author and illustrator have been asserted.

Text © 2014 Carole Wilkinson
Cover Illustration © 2014 Sonia Kretschmar

National Library of Australia Cataloguing-in-Publication entry:
Wilkinson, Carole, 1950- author.
Shadow sister / Carole Wilkinson.
ISBN: 978 1 925126 32 7 (paperback)
Series: Wilkinson, Carole, 1950–. Dragonkeeper; bk. 5.
For children.
Subjects: Dragons – China – Juvenile fiction.
A823.3

Bee illustration in internals © 2014 Sonia Kretschmar
Typeset in Adobe Caslon Pro
Printed and bound in China

Contents

· Map of Luoyang Region ·

· Map of China in the Sixteen Kingdoms Period ·

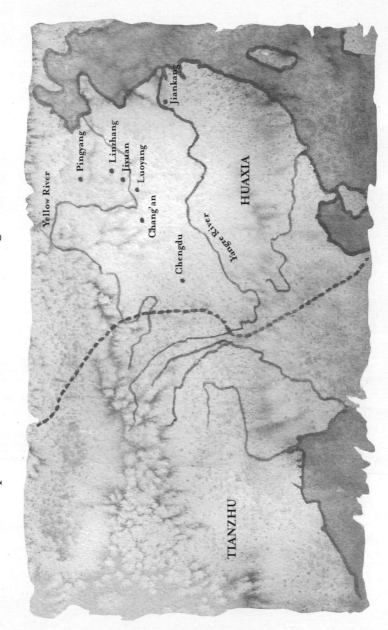

· Luoyang 325 CE ·

Mang Shan

Zhao Garrison

Broad and
Boundless Gate

Great Xia Gate

Jilong's
Quarters

Heavenly
Purple
Palace Gate

Palace

Establishing
Spring Gate

Ruins

West
Brilliance
Gate

East Sunlight Gate

White
Horse
Temple

Huan
House
Ruin

Bronze Camel Street

Broad and
Sunlit Gate

Clear and Bright Gate

Luo River

Gate of the
Sunlit Ford

Manifest
Sunlight
Gate

Peace and
Prosperity Gate

Opening to the
Morning Sun Gate

Chapter One
BELLYACHE

The dragon groaned. "My stomach hurts."

He had been slow-moving all day, insisting on stopping often to rest.

"Let me see your tongue."

The dragon sat on his haunches in front of the boy. Tao had grown a little in the weeks the two had been travelling together but, when sitting, Kai was still head and shoulders taller. He was imposing, even when his scales were dull and the spines down his back were drooping. He obediently stuck out his tongue. It was long, narrow and ended in a point, like a snake's tail. A grey snake.

Tao knew that a dragon's tongue should be a healthy red, not grey. Also it should not be covered with a thick, greenish coating. Tao prodded it with a twig. "It doesn't look good."

Kai groaned again. "I think I am going to be—"

He retched. Tao stepped back but he wasn't quick enough. A stream of dragon vomit spewed onto the ground and splattered all over Tao's straw sandals. It formed a grey puddle, thick and slimy, containing dark yellow lumps and several squashed insects. It smelled putrid.

"That is disgusting," Tao said, wiping his sandals and feet with leaves.

"Feel bad," Kai moaned. He held a large rusty nail in his left forepaw.

"The cockroaches I gave you to eat might make you feel sick, but they still could stop the iron from hurting you."

The dragon opened out his paw. Blisters had formed where the nail touched his pads. Kai threw the iron nail into the forest and then retched again, adding to the pool of vomit.

Tao moved to where he could breathe in fresher air. He drank from his water skin. Then he consulted a list scrawled on a piece of bark and crossed out an item with a stub of charcoal.

"That rules out cockroaches," he said.

"Insects with shells are bad. I told you that," Kai said, or at least those were the words Tao heard in his head.

Tao recited a sutra for the dead cockroaches and prayed that their next life would be better.

"I ate some beetles when I was small," Kai continued. "They made me sick too."

Tao spent a long time searching for the nail in the undergrowth. When he finally found it he scooped up a handful of wet earth and squeezed it around the nail. He wrapped a length of leather around the clump of earth and put the bundle in his bag.

It was Tao's fault that the cockroaches had died. He felt guilty, but he was eager to discover how to protect Kai from the effects of iron. Dragons reacted badly to contact with anything made of that metal. Just having iron nearby made them lose their strength. If it touched the belly or the hide around their ankles, where there were no protective scales, weeping sores formed. Prolonged contact with iron resulted in sickness and awful welts. Tao had seen it himself. It also weakened their eyesight.

It was impossible to avoid iron while they were travelling in the realms of men. The poorest peasant had some sort of iron implement for the field or the kitchen. Even a piece of iron as small as the nail, buried in earth and wrapped in three layers of leather, seemed to make the dragon lethargic. Tao hoped they would eventually reach uninhabited lands but, while they were still near human settlements, Kai's sensitivity to iron was a serious handicap.

"We need to get going, Kai."

"Am too sick to walk," the dragon said. "Want to stay here."

"It's mid-afternoon. We can't stop yet."

The dragon crouched down and pulled all four paws under him, which meant he wasn't going anywhere.

"And I will not eat the other things on your list."

Tao leaned on his staff. He was tired too. For six weeks he'd been walking up and down mountains with the dragon. The idea of stopping early was tempting. He looked at the sky, or at least the patches of it visible through the trees. It had been overcast for weeks, but hadn't rained. They didn't really need shelter, but Tao still preferred to spend his nights with a roof over his head, or at least a cliff at his back.

To ensure that they didn't run into bands of nomads, Kai had chosen a path that was no bigger than a goat track. Nomads were men from the tribes beyond the Great Wall who had invaded Huaxia. They were skilled horsemen who could ride anywhere they wished, but they were used to wide plains where their horses could gallop. Nomads didn't like the mountains with their tall trees and narrow hemmed-in paths. Tao hoped that if they were careful, they could avoid being caught up in the chaos of the time. Most of the conflict took place in the cities and the towns, where rival nomad tribes fought over the ruins. There was little left in the towns for nomads to plunder, but there was nothing at all in the mountains. That's what Tao hoped anyway.

"Let's keep going for a little while. There might be swallows nesting in an overhang around the next bend in the path."

The thought of having his favourite food for his evening meal encouraged the dragon and he got to his feet. Tao was pleased he'd managed to get Kai moving again. Now all he had to do was convince him not to abandon the iron project.

The idea had come to Tao when they were climbing up a particularly steep path and he was wishing he could fly – or at least that Kai could. He had remembered the yellow dragon Sha, a dragon old enough to have wings. Tao had given her a scroll of precious sutras that he had rescued. He was wondering if she had fulfilled her promise to carry them to safety. When Tao had first seen Sha, she was a captive of the Zhao nomad general Jilong. He had given the dragon a potion to make her aggressive – a foul brew of tigers' blood mixed with scorpion tails, cockroaches, snake tongues, bat droppings and cinnabar. Tao had noticed that when Sha was in battle rage, although iron blades wounded her the same as any creature of flesh and blood, proximity to iron did not make her sick or weak. He had concluded that one of the ingredients of the potion must have made her immune to the effects of iron. The tigers' blood was the main component. Tigers were one of the few enemies of dragons, and Kai was sure that the blood of an enemy would be what made the shy dragon aggressive. In fact, it had turned her into a killer.

Tao was quite proud of the experiment he had devised

to discover which of the other ingredients had given Sha immunity to iron.

Scorpion tail had been the first item on the list. Kai had refused to cooperate, so Tao had no choice but to find a scorpion on his own. His conscience troubled him sorely – a Buddhist should not harm any creature – but he had overturned every rock they passed, searching for one without success.

One night a few days earlier, Tao had made a small fire to cook some taro root.

"Iron is not a problem," Kai had complained. "Most people have moved south."

It was true, they had hardly seen a soul since they'd left Yinmi Monastery. Anyone who was able to make the journey had fled from the nomads to Jiankang, a city in the south. Tao had insisted on conducting the experiment anyway.

"We might run into nomads," Tao had said.

Nomads carried many weapons – spears, swords, daggers, arrow tips – and they were all made of iron.

As he'd poked the taro root to see if it was cooked, he saw a sandy-coloured scorpion sitting on one of his firestones. It edged closer to the fire, warming itself.

"Kai! There's a scorpion. Catch it!"

The dragon moved his head slowly from side to side. "I will not."

Tao was sorry to disturb the creature, but he managed to trap the scorpion under the melon gourd he used as a bowl. While he was wondering what to do next, the creature had escaped and stung him. Kai came to Tao's rescue and squashed the scorpion with a large stone. The dragon consented to taste it. After he roasted it over the coals, he actually enjoyed eating the scorpion, and added it to his list of favourite delicacies.

The scorpion bite made Tao sick for three days. He accepted that it was karma for killing the creature.

Snake tongue was even more difficult to locate. Kai felt a kinship to all scaly creatures, and wouldn't kill a snake. Tao couldn't contemplate killing one himself. It was by chance that they startled a hawk in the process of eating a small snake. The bird flapped away and dropped his meal. Tao was relieved that he wasn't responsible for the snake's death. He cut out the dead reptile's tongue and Kai ate it raw. Since small creatures like scorpions and snakes were so difficult to catch, Tao was very glad that they didn't need to capture a tiger for its blood.

The previous night, Tao had made Kai eat the cockroaches as the next phase of the experiment and now Kai was still groaning about their effects on his stomach. Tao tried to take the dragon's mind off the pain.

"You haven't recited a poem for a while," he said.

"You do not like my poetry."

"It's improving," Tao said, though he didn't mean it.

Tao had grown tired of Kai's riddling and one day, after twenty-five riddles in a row, he'd put his fingers in his ears and refused to listen to another one, let alone answer it. Kai had sulked for a *li* or two and then started reciting poetry of his own composition.

Kai didn't need a lot of encouragement now.

"When my insides ache
And make a gurgling sound,
The contents spurt
All over the ground."

Tao could have been critical about the metre of the poem, not to mention the subject, but he kept his thoughts to himself.

Kai stopped walking again. "I need sweetie berries to settle my stomach."

"I'll search for some wolfberries if we can keep walking until sunset."

Kai reluctantly trudged up the mountain track, groaning as he went. Tao tried to do some walking meditation to distract himself from his blistered feet and aching calves, but his meditation skills had deserted him. This wasn't the life he'd imagined when he'd decided to go on an adventure with Kai. His mind was full of thoughts. What would they have for their evening meal? Where would they sleep that night? And, more importantly, where were they going?

Tao had spent seven or eight happy years being a devout novice at Yinmi Monastery, with the full expectation of living the quiet, contemplative life of a monk for the rest of his days. But then one night Kai had turned up at his monastery, and Tao found himself on an adventure, breaking every rule Buddha had set down for novices. He'd expected that the adventure would end, and his life would return to its normal measured pace but it hadn't. He abandoned his dream of becoming a monk and left his monastic life to travel with a dragon.

Although Tao had failed to be a good novice monk, he was trying hard to be a good Buddhist. He still followed the novice's precepts as best he could, refusing to eat the flesh of animals. He did now allow himself to eat after midday, and he'd given up straining the water he drank to rescue any tiny creatures living in it. He no longer wore monk's robes and he didn't carry an alms bowl to beg for food. As a novice, Tao had relied on the charity of others to feed him. Now he was learning how to forage for his own food, since Kai's idea of a tasty meal wasn't always to Tao's liking. It had taken hours of meditation and much careful consideration before Tao decided that it was all right for him to sacrifice the lives of a scorpion and three cockroaches for the cause of saving Kai from pain and discomfort, perhaps even death.

Their journey had started unexpectedly when they fled

from the monastery where the evil monk Fo Tu Deng was about to take control from the abbot. Monks were permitted only five possessions, and Tao had less than that at first – the clothes he wore, his staff, a vial of yellow oil, and a shard of purple stone. He was no longer a novice monk, but Tao had been determined to have no more than five possessions. He couldn't survive with the traditional possessions of a monk; instead he would carry his own five unique belongings. He'd added a water skin to make up the five. Then he'd realised that he wore a wolf tooth on a leather thong around his neck. Instead of discarding it, he sharpened it and used it for cutting. That meant he had six possessions. And he needed to cook food, so he'd found a melon gourd and firesticks. The nights got colder and a blanket became essential. Nine possessions, not five. Then there was so much to carry; he'd woven a bag from willow twigs. Ten possessions, and that wasn't counting his bark list and charcoal. It was not an auspicious start.

Tao had enjoyed their wanderings at first, letting the fall of his staff decide which direction they went, but his feet were sore and he needed a purpose. He wondered if he'd made a mistake abandoning his dream to be a monk for this uncertain life of wandering.

Kai poked him in the arm with a talon. "You won't find any sweetie berries if you allow your thoughts to keep wandering."

Tao ignored the dragon. He didn't want to lose his train of thought.

"When we left Yinmi, you said we were going on a quest," he said. "We've been labouring up and down mountains for weeks and I still don't know what our quest is."

"You did not like any of my ideas."

"Hunting for bears because they taste good is not a quest for a Buddhist who doesn't eat meat."

"I had other suggestions."

"I'm not interested in searching for hidden treasure either. I have no need of treasure."

"I am waiting for heaven to suggest an appropriate quest."

Ever since Kai had announced that Tao was a dragonkeeper, his dragonkeeper, Tao hadn't known where his life was heading. His and Kai's destinies were entwined, he was sure of that, but he wished he knew what being a dragonkeeper meant. So far Kai had been rather vague about what it entailed. The dragon had also said Tao couldn't become a true dragonkeeper until he had accepted the bronze mirror that had been owned by Kai's previous dragonkeeper – and by his father's dragonkeepers before that. It was confusing. Tao was honoured that the dragon thought he was worthy of such a role, but he was only fifteen. It sounded like the job of a much older, more experienced person.

Somewhere to the west, on the top of a mountain, far from humans, was a place Kai called the dragon haven. This was where the other members of his cluster lived. Kai was the leader of that diminishing band of dragons, or so he said, but he had left his home when he became bored with life on a remote mountain top. That was where the dragonkeeper's mirror was kept.

"We need a proper quest, Kai," Tao said. "Shouldn't we be heading towards the dragon haven?"

"That is where I am going. But it will be a long and slow journey. We cannot get there before you are ready to take up your role as dragonkeeper."

"I am ready." Tao didn't mention the doubts that were nagging him. "I've left behind everything I've ever known."

"Like a craftsman, first you must learn the appropriate skills."

"Yes, but what are they? You haven't told me yet. And how far is it to this dragon haven exactly?"

"No more speaking," Kai said. "My stomach still hurts."

That made no sense at all to Tao, but when the dragon wasn't in the mood to talk, there was no point pressing him further.

Tao knew that he was descended from Kai's previous dragonkeeper, a young girl called Ping. There were three characteristics that marked out a dragonkeeper – using the left hand, being able to interpret a dragon's sounds, and having second sight. Kai had said that Tao was the first of Ping's descendants to have the characteristics.

He glimpsed the drooping branches of a wolfberry tree not far from the path. There was one thing he had learned about dragons – they loved the fruit of the wolfberry tree. He pushed through the undergrowth to get to it. Birds and animals had long since stripped most of the tree of its fruit, but he searched each branch and managed to find a few of the red berries, now darkened and wrinkled. He found more that had fallen to the ground. There were mushrooms growing at the foot of the tree and he picked some for his evening meal.

"Here, Kai," Tao said. "I've found you some sweetie berries."

Kai took the berries. Tao was expecting him to grumble that they weren't fresh, but he didn't. He ate four and put the rest behind one of his reverse scales, and then set out along the path again. Tao followed him.

One thing had changed since Tao met the dragon – he had developed what Kai called second sight. The visions were difficult to unravel, like puzzles, but he had learned to interpret them – eventually. That gave Tao confidence that he really was a dragonkeeper. He hadn't called up a vision since they left Yinmi. He didn't want to squander this gift. For all he knew, the number of visions could be limited.

"I would like worms for dinner," Kai announced. "I wish they were not so hard to find."

"Worms are easy to find!" Tao was tired of listening to the dragon complain. He pointed at the damp earth. "You can see where they've burrowed into the earth."

Kai dug holes in the soft earth, grumbling when he still couldn't find any worms.

"You're pretending they're hard to find, so that I'll do it."

"I am not!" Kai said, digging an even bigger hole and flicking dirt into Tao's eyes.

"You're doing it wrong," Tao said. "You don't need to dig, that scares them off. This is what you do."

He laid his hands flat on the ground. "You can feel them below the earth."

"My paws are always in contact with the earth." Kai was getting annoyed. "I never feel worms."

Tao waited patiently with his palms on the damp soil. Before long worms emerged and Tao put them in the gourd. More creatures were about to meet their end because of him.

"Hmmph," Kai said. "I suppose there has to be *one* thing you can do better than me."

A few months earlier, Tao's life had been filled with holy pursuits – meditating, transcribing sutras and learning Sanskrit. Now it was all about finding worms for a lazy dragon.

The sky was dark and heavy, the landscape was colourless and the sun hadn't shown its face all day. Night had been reluctant to leave the land that morning, and all day darkness had been lurking not far away, eager to shroud the world again.

Tao didn't have the energy to continue. He could see a rock face with a slight overhang not far away. It was probably the closest thing he would find to shelter that day.

"Let's stop here for the night," he said.

Kai didn't object. He went off to hunt, while Tao did some meditation.

When Kai returned with two mice and a squirrel, Tao was sitting next to a pile of twigs and sticks, neatly set to make a fire.

"I suppose you'd like to cook those."

"Of course I would," the dragon replied, a little perplexed.

"Go ahead."

Tao looked smugly at the dragon.

"Could you light a fire?" Kai asked.

"I could," Tao replied.

"*Will* you light a fire?" Kai said. "Please."

"I will."

Tao reached for his firesticks. He was pleased there was more than one thing he could do better than Kai.

Chapter Two
UNSEASONAL WEATHER

The next morning, Kai was walking slowly, head down, studying the path. He had eaten all the worms Tao found the day before. What the dragon failed to mention was that eating worms made him fart. Tao was keeping a good distance between them.

"Where are you going?" he said when Kai wandered off the path to examine the foliage of the undergrowth and low-hanging tree branches. "I don't think we should stray from the path."

"I will only be a moment."

Tao was glad that at least the dragon was no longer feeling sick.

If Tao was a dragonkeeper, as Kai said, then his job should be more than running around finding him worms and wolfberries to eat, things that a full-grown dragon could manage perfectly well on his own. Tao had no intention of being a dragon servant. But if he could find a cure for the dragon's iron sickness, then he would be worthy of calling himself a dragonkeeper.

Unfortunately, so far none of the ingredients they had tried lessened Kai's reaction to iron. However, Tao noticed that they had other effects. Kai had stepped on a large thorn and had been complaining for days about how sore his paw was, but after eating the scorpion tail, the pain disappeared. It made sense that the other ingredients in Sha's brew had some medicinal purpose too. The day after Kai had eaten snake tongue, Tao noticed that he was having trouble keeping up with the dragon. He'd concluded that eating it had given Kai speed.

Kai was still fossicking around in the bushes.

"Hurry up," Tao said.

The dragon took his time, picking up some stones and sniffing them thoughtfully before returning to the path.

"You said you weren't going to take long. We've been in this same spot for at least half an hour."

"Humans are so impatient," Kai said, as he finally set off again. "I was speaking in terms of dragon time."

Tao followed him, trying hard not to be annoyed.

"Did you notice any effect from eating the cockroaches?" he asked. "Apart from the vomiting."

"It is too early to be sure, but I believe that the cut I had on my tail is healing very quickly."

"Cockroaches must have healing properties." Tao was

pleased. His hypothesis was proving correct. Each of the ingredients of the tigers' blood potion had a useful effect on the dragon.

"I do not care what they do. I will not eat so much as a cockroach feeler again."

Tao was undeterred. "There are two more things on the list – bat droppings and cinnabar."

Kai groaned again.

"Bat droppings shouldn't be too hard to find," Tao said. "I don't know about cinnabar."

"I am not eating bat droppings. I would rather suffer pain."

As far as Kai was concerned, that was the end of the subject.

There were breaks in the clouds and through them Tao could see blue sky. The sun showed its face for the first time in more than a week.

Tao stopped. "I thought we were heading west."

Kai kept walking. "We are."

Tao didn't have a good sense of direction. He had never been able to read the stars like other novices could. Fortunately, the only journey he'd had to make alone was from Yinmi Monastery to his family home twice a year, and that was always by day and along a good road. When he'd got lost, he could usually manage to work out which direction he was facing from the position of the sun.

"But the sun rose over there." Tao pointed to his left. "That means we're walking south."

"The road west is not always straight," Kai said.

Tao closed his eyes. The dragon's lack of information about their journey was starting to annoy him and although he was no longer a novice monk, he didn't like to get angry.

"Yes, but we're going the wrong way."

Kai was several *chang* ahead.

"We must avoid the main roads," he called back as he disappeared around a bend. "We do not want to encounter nomads."

Tao hurried to catch up and nearly ran into the dragon. He had stopped at the edge of a village, hidden by trees until they were upon it. It was in ruins. All the houses were destroyed, smashed to pieces as if they'd been trampled. The houses would have been fragile to begin with, made from saplings, thatched with twigs and rotten from being in a place that was dank and wet for most of the year.

"This is the work of nomads, I'm sure," Tao said. "Though why they would be in such a remote part of the mountains and attacking poor peasants, I don't know."

Tao had visited many mountain villages while collecting alms for the monastery. This one should have been busy with the bustle of village life – chickens flapping as they passed, perhaps a pig blocking their way, children playing, old women sitting mending by the side of the path, enterprising villagers trying to sell them dumplings or rice balls. Tao's stomach rumbled at the thought.

Kai didn't say anything, but he overturned stones and snuffed the strengthening breeze.

"What are you doing, Kai?"

"Looking for tracks."

"Surely the village was attacked long ago."

The rotting timbers of the ruins were already decomposing into the forest.

"Not so long."

As Kai searched, Tao realised they had not come across any bodies.

"There is no tomb, no grave cairn," Tao said. "If nomads attacked, where are the dead?"

"Perhaps no one was killed," Kai said. "Perhaps the people moved to a better place."

Among the ruins there were cooking utensils, shoes, a split sack of grain.

"They must have left in a hurry," Tao said.

He hoped Kai was right and the whole village had moved south. But the place had an eerie stillness that made him uneasy.

Kai picked up a bronze bowl. "This will be useful," he said, filling it with damp grain.

"We can't take that. What if the people come back?" As he said the words, Tao had a feeling the villagers would never return.

There was one building that was undamaged. It was a small temple on the edge of the village, crudely built from mud bricks, almost hidden by the trees. Tao knew it was a temple and not a house because of the crooked little mud-brick pagoda leaning against it. A breeze stirred the single lopsided bell that hung from one corner of the moss-covered roof and it made a tuneless ding. The sound saddened Tao. He imagined the people who had done their best to build a house for Buddha with their simple skills and whatever materials they could find.

"We could stay in the temple tonight," Kai said. "You will feel at home. I will go and see if it is dry."

It was late afternoon. Tao needed reassurance that they would be safe before he agreed to stay. Even though there was a building with a roof on it, a Buddhist temple, he had a sudden desire to leave the village and never come back. Kai had already disappeared into the temple, but there was another way that Tao could seek advice.

He took something from his bag – a small vial made of pink quartz, which had once belonged to his mother. He sat down cross-legged and removed the stopper from the vial and allowed a few drops of yellow oil to drip onto his palm. It was the mixture of sesame oil and dried safflower that his mother had rubbed on his brother Wei's useless limbs, hoping it would make them work again. Tao smeared it over his hands, closed his eyes and started to chant a Buddhist sutra. The words calmed him as they always did, leaving him relaxed and at peace with the world. He wanted to know if it was safe to spend the night in the village. It took a while to clear his mind of his annoyance with Kai and his awareness of his painful feet, longer still to ease the sense of disquiet he'd been feeling. He put his hands together to form a shallow bowl, opened his eyes and allowed them to relax until the smear of yellow oil on his palms became unfocused. An image took shape. He saw a cliff face with a large dark spot on it. The vision was clear and stood up from his palms as if it were actually there.

Tao's contemplation of the vision was disturbed by sounds from the forest. Tree branches shook and he could hear large feet trampling the undergrowth. Birds took off squawking. A small, terrified animal, a weasel perhaps, darted out of the undergrowth and through Tao's legs so fast all he saw was a blur. He had his answer without attempting to interpret his vision. The village was not safe.

"Kai, are you all right? Is it a tiger?"

There was a loud animal sound, halfway between a screech and a roar. It was not the sound of a tiger. It was like nothing Tao had heard before.

"Kai, where are you?"

Tao was terrified. Had the creature attacked Kai? Surely, the dragon would have cried out. Tao hid behind a large log that had once been part of a house.

The disturbance faded into the distance. The creature, whatever it was, had gone. The log that Tao was crouched behind started to shimmer. Its dark brown bark turned greenish. Tao looked away. When he turned back, the log had turned into a dragon.

"Kai! Why didn't you tell me you shape-changed?"

"I was being quiet. Wild animals often have very good hearing."

"You could have put words in my mind without making a sound."

"I forgot."

Tao sat down again, waiting for his heart to stop hammering. "What happened?"

"I disturbed a creature." Kai was trying to appear calm, but he was making a sound like scraping knives, which meant he was afraid.

"What sort of creature?"

"I do not know. A bear perhaps. It has gone."

Tao had heard a bear roar before. It was nothing like the unnatural screech that had echoed through the forest. Kai was peering into the undergrowth. Whatever the creature was, it made him uneasy. Tao picked up the bronze bowl and the grain.

"We must leave this place. Now."

The sky had darkened. Not because night was approaching, but because a black cloud had appeared in the sky. Tao could feel the air change. It was suddenly chilly and heavy with moisture. There was going to be rain. Heavy rain. Tao knew he had to expect colder weather as winter approached, but summer was the time when it rained. Autumn should gradually become drier and drier until, in winter, there was no rain at all.

"Tell me what you saw in your vision," Kai said.

"A cave in the mountain." That much had been clear.

"The village is not safe," Kai said, echoing Tao's thoughts. "Your vision is showing you a place for us to shelter. Where is this cave?"

That was not at all clear. Tao closed his eyes and tried to recreate what he had seen on his palms.

"There was a large character carved into the rock above the entrance to the cave. It should be easy to recognise. And inside, I saw glowing embers."

He was worried that the remains of a fire meant that someone else had been there before them. But his visions had never led him into danger before. He needed to trust his second sight. A fire would warm them, and it would also keep wild animals at bay.

The sky was getting heavier. There was the sound of distant thunder.

"It's going to pour. We need to find that cave, Kai, before the embers go out."

But it didn't rain.

Instead it began to snow.

Chapter Three
REFUGE

Snowflakes settled on the sleeves of Tao's jacket. He scanned the sky. There was still a single black cloud in the grey sky, but it had doubled in size.

"This will not last long," Kai said, pointing to a break in the clouds to the south, but Tao could tell he was also feeling uneasy.

The snow fell more heavily. The chilly breeze of a few moments earlier seemed like mid-summer compared to the biting wind that was now blowing. Normally, it didn't snow until the depths of winter, and then only on the highest peaks. The black cloud grew as they watched.

"What else did you see?" Kai said.

"Just the character above the cave."

"Which one was it?"

"It was the character *fu*," Tao said. "Good luck."

"We will need more than just luck to find this cave before the weather gets worse." Kai's optimism had disappeared with the last chink of blue sky in the distance.

"We must go down the mountain."

"No." Tao had to shout to be heard over the wind. "We must climb."

The gentle snowfalls at Yinmi Monastery were brief and left a pretty dusting of white. Now all Tao could see through the thickly falling snow were the faint shapes of snow-covered trees. He felt his way towards Kai and grabbed hold of his beard.

"We must trust my vision." He gently tugged the dragon's beard. "The cave is higher up. I'm sure."

The dragon allowed Tao to lead him.

Tao stumbled up the mountainside, through the driving snow. This latest vision had been clearer than those he had experienced previously. And there was something new – an indescribable sensation that indicated a higher altitude. He was sure he was right: the vision had told him to climb the mountain. He wished it had been more specific and told him which way to go.

Tao's toes were numb. The snow on his sleeves was almost an inch thick. Kai's beard felt like frozen straw in his hand. He clung onto it, glad he could feel the dragon's breath on his fingers, glad he wasn't alone. The path had disappeared beneath a foot of snow and he couldn't see a handspan in front of him. As they climbed, the trees became sparser. He had no way of knowing if he was heading in the right direction.

Tao bent into the wind. The snow stung his face and got into his eyes. He could see nothing. How would he ever find a cave? He stumbled into a rock wall that rose up sheer above him. They had reached the end of the path. To go any further up the mountain, they'd need wings.

"Kai, what can you see?"

"Nothing."

Tao felt his way along the blank rock, hoping to find the cave. Something swooped past his eyes, a blur of black. Then another, so close it scratched his face. The black shapes disappeared into the snow.

"Bats," Kai said.

Tao felt talons grab his sleeve. He couldn't see Kai in the blizzard, nor hear him above the roar of the wind. He guessed he was making the scraping knives sound he made when he was anxious. Thankfully, he could hear the voice in his head as clear as ever.

"This way. My eyesight is better than yours. Hold on to my tail."

Tao grasped the dragon's tail and allowed Kai to pull him along, scrambling over rocks that had fallen from the mountain peak, always keeping the cliff on their right. When Tao was sure he couldn't make his frozen feet go any further, a black hole appeared in the rock face. Kai disappeared into it. Tao staggered in behind him and collapsed onto the cave floor.

They both sat breathing heavily, their breath forming white clouds.

"How did you know where the cave was?" Tao asked.

"Bats," Kai said. "I followed the bats."

There were flapping noises above them. As his eyes got used to the dim light, Tao could see small black shapes swooping overhead.

"My vision said nothing about bats. And where are the glowing embers?"

"We can seek another cave if this one does not suit you."

"No. No. That's not what I meant. This is a wonderful cave." He touched the dry rock. "I thought I was getting better at interpreting my visions, but it didn't help me find the cave at all."

Tao heard a sound like tinkling wind chimes, the sound Kai made when he was happy.

"*Fu*," the dragon said. "*Fu* is also the name of these creatures." He pointed at the bats swooping into the cave then disappearing into its depths. "Bats do not usually go out during the day, but the sudden darkness must have confused them."

Tao covered his mouth and his nose. "It smells awful in here."

"It is the bats. The smell of their urine and droppings."

"The stench is worse than any bats I've smelled before."

Tao was annoyed with himself for thinking the cave

would have a character carved above it. He should have known that his visions were never that straightforward.

"But it wasn't the character for 'bat' that I saw, it was the character for 'good luck'."

"It is like a word puzzle," Kai said. "Danzi, my father, once wrote directions for Ping so that we could find a place where many dragons lived." He made the sad sound of a cracked bell tolling as he remembered that time. "He did not want anyone else to know where it was, so he wrote the instructions in a secret code. He used characters that were pronounced the same, but had different meanings. Your vision did help."

"Yes, but it was you who worked it out, not me. And there are no embers here."

"Patience. Second sight for dragonkeepers is never easily acquired."

The cave was not as comfortable as Tao had hoped. Rocks and roots made the cave floor uneven, and there was the awful smell, but at least they were out of the foul weather. There was no dry fuel for a fire, so he couldn't cook the grain from the village. He found a dried persimmon at the bottom of his bag. Kai produced a dead mouse from behind one of his reverse scales. He had cooked it days before and kept it for an emergency. Tao watched in fascinated horror as the dragon crunched the blackened rodent.

"I think there might be swallows in this cave as well as bats," Kai said. "In the morning, I will hunt swallows."

The storm lasted into the evening. Finally, it died down and the bats were able to follow their natural instincts and go out into the night to find food.

"I think my vision brought us here, not only for shelter, but also to enable us to test the next ingredient of Sha's potion." Tao scraped some of the bat droppings off the cave floor with a stick and pushed a small pile towards Kai.

The dragon refused. "I will not eat bat droppings!"

"Just a morsel. It can't taste any worse than a week-old dead mouse."

"It might make me sick again. I need dragon food."

"You must make do with the mouse and the wolfberries behind your reverse scales."

"I already ate them."

"All of them?"

Kai nodded.

Tao pointed to the bat droppings. "Please. This could be the ingredient that cures the iron problem."

The dragon reluctantly scraped up a small amount of the bat droppings, no bigger than a rice grain, on the tip of a talon. He put it on his tongue and swallowed. Then he dug himself a shallow hole, scattering rocks and roots as he did. He turned around three times before he settled himself into it.

Tao found the least rocky patch and spread out his thin blanket.

"Kai is cold," the dragon said plaintively. "Lend me your blanket."

Chapter Four
BONES

The sound of returning bats woke Tao before dawn. They chittered and screeched as they flew over him, hundreds of them. He had been exhausted the night before, but he'd still found it difficult to get to sleep because of all the stones and roots sticking into him. The terrible smell in the cave, along with the sound of a snoring dragon echoing around the walls, hadn't helped. Also he couldn't stop worrying that the creature that Kai had disturbed in the forest would find them and kill them as they slept. When he did finally drift off, his sleep was haunted by a terrible dream. He heard voices calling to him for help, but he couldn't find the people because he was blind. He stumbled forwards and felt cold breath on his face. He knew it was the creature from the forest, about to attack him. He'd woken with a hammering heart. It was a long time before he'd been able to get back to sleep.

The sky was starting to lighten. In the pale first light, he could see the stragglers flying to the back of the shallow cave, but he couldn't see where they were roosting. Then Tao realised that he couldn't hear snoring. Not even breathing.

"Kai, where are you?"

"Sssh." The sound of tinkling wind chimes came from the back of the cave. "I am hunting swallows for breakfast."

"How can you see them in the dark?"

"The bat droppings did not stop the iron pain. I took out the nail while you were sleeping. But eating the droppings has been beneficial. My eyesight is better than usual. My eyes can penetrate the darkness. I can see where the swallows have nested and hunt them while they sleep."

Tao didn't consider that sneaking up on sleeping birds could be called hunting, but he kept that thought to himself. Kai was a beast, not a monk, and he needed to eat.

Something hard was sticking into Tao's back. He knew that he wouldn't get back to sleep so there was no point in lying there. He remembered the mushrooms he had found the previous day. A morning meal seemed like an excellent idea. One thing that he did like about his current life was being in charge of his own food.

Outside the cave, Tao was glad to find that the air was still and the usual temperature for that time of year. The sky was still overcast, but the black cloud had gone. He filled his lungs with fresh air, free of the horrible smell in the cave. A small drift of melting snow and a scatter of fallen branches confirmed that the snowstorm and the ferocious wind had been real, not one of his nightmares.

The sun appeared in the narrow band of clear sky between the horizon and the clouds. The rays warmed his face. It was a good omen. He collected some twigs and was about to light a fire when an anguished cry came from the cave – it sounded like someone banging copper bowls together.

Tao ran into the cave. "What's wrong, Kai?"

"Can you not see?"

All Tao could see was the after image of the sun rising. His eyes slowly adjusted to the lack of light in the cave, but he still couldn't see much. The dragon was turning in a slow circle, staring at the floor of the cave in horror.

"The round objects half-buried in the earth," Kai said. "They are not stones."

A ray of dawn light had crept into the cave, and Tao could see the lumps and bumps on the cave floor that had made the night so uncomfortable. He peered at the round rock closest to his foot. There were tufts of hair attached to it. Kai was right. The round objects were not rocks. They were skulls. Human skulls. Tao shuddered. He picked up the twig that he had used to scrape up bat droppings. It was paler than wood and harder. It wasn't a twig. It was a bone. A human leg bone. He let out a yell and dropped it. He looked around the cave. The hollow that Kai had dug wasn't full of roots and rocks, it was full of bones. Now that it was a little lighter, Tao could see the cave floor was littered with half-buried human remains. There were three arched ribs; a skull with black eye sockets; finger bones reaching up, as if a skeleton was trying to escape from an underground prison. He took a step back and stumbled over a small jawbone with two tiny front teeth. Scraps of cloth, the remains of clothing, poked out of the earth among the bones. He could see a half-buried shoe.

"They are corpses," Tao whispered. "We spent the night on a grave pit."

He realised the smell in the cave hadn't come from the bats. It was death. He clamped his hand over his mouth and nose, but he had to breathe. Death and decay were entering him with every tainted breath, seeping up through the soles of his feet. He wanted to run out of the cave, but his legs wouldn't move.

The bodies had been thrown into a large shallow hole without care. They lay strewn in all directions. Some earth had been carelessly scattered over them, but not enough to cover them completely. There were the remains of at least twenty people. It was hard to know how long the bodies had been there. Most of the flesh had decomposed, but fragments of rotting black stuff still clung to the bones in places.

"There are so many." Kai was as horrified as Tao.

"It's the villagers," Tao said. "Someone buried them here, someone in a hurry."

Tao thought it was his turn to be sick. He managed to get his legs moving. He staggered out of the cave, sucking in gulps of mountain air as he leaned against a large rock for support.

Kai followed him.

"I have seen the aftermath of nomad attacks before," the dragon said. "They do not take the trouble to bury the dead, even in this careless manner."

"Then who was it?"

Kai had no answer.

Tao didn't believe in ghosts, but he sensed a presence, unearthly, deadly. "We have to get away from this awful place. I never want to see it again."

Kai didn't argue.

They walked away as fast as they could, but they hadn't travelled more than two or three *li* before Tao had to stop.

"I feel dizzy."

"You need to eat," Kai said. "You have not had a good meal in days. And I do not want to waste these."

He held up two dead swallows. Eating was the last thought on Tao's mind, but his legs were weak, whether from fear or lack of food he didn't know.

They walked a little further until they came to a stream and a small clearing. Kai fetched water while Tao collected some wood and lit a fire using his firesticks. The damp twigs he'd collected smoked, but no flames emerged. He used the edge of his blanket to fan the few glowing embers. Kai leaned closer to inspect Tao.

"A bat scratched your face last night, and your hands are cut from holding on to my tail."

Tao glanced at his hands. They were covered in small cuts and scratches. Kai reached behind one of his reverse scales and pulled out a folded leaf. He opened it and handed it to Tao. It contained a dollop of something slimy and red. Tao guessed that the substance was chewed red cloud herb. He scooped up a little of the healing ointment and rubbed it into his cuts. It stung.

"I collected it when we were at Yinmi and you were busy bathing," Kai said.

That seemed like a very long time ago.

A small flame licked up from the smoking twigs. Kai was impatient for his breakfast. He threw wet leafy twigs on the fire, making it smoke even more.

"You should wait for the fire to burn down to embers," Tao said, "if you want the birds to roast nicely."

Kai couldn't wait. He skewered the birds on a twig and threw them on the fire. The smell of burning feathers filled the air. He barely left the birds long enough to sear before he pulled them from the fire.

"Smoked swallow is also good."

He produced some bat droppings from another reverse scale and sprinkled them on his food.

"I thought you didn't like bat droppings."

"I have changed my mind. They taste quite good as a garnish for meat."

Kai ate one of the swallows whole, crunching the bones and making appreciative noises. Then he stuffed the other bird in his mouth. Tao concentrated on cooking his grain and toasting his mushrooms to avoid seeing the blood running into the dragon's beard. He felt sick at the thought of eating, but he knew he had to. He ate slowly, one small mouthful at a time. It was the best meal he'd had for several days, but there was no enjoyment in eating it.

To take his mind off the horrors of the cave, Tao thought about his iron experiment.

"If my theory is correct and one of the ingredients in Sha's tiger-blood brew stopped her reacting to iron, then it has to be cinnabar. I don't know what it looks like. Do you?"

"I have seen cinnabar. It is a mineral in the form of red crystals. Humans dig for it in mines."

"How will we find some?"

"I do not know," the dragon said. "Perhaps we can purchase some. Herbalists use cinnabar, and magicians."

"It is most unlikely that we'll run into a herbalist … or a magician, but if we do, we don't have gold or anything to barter with."

Tao felt better after he had eaten. His vision had served more than one purpose. It had led them to shelter, showed them where to find the next item on Tao's list, and provided food for Kai as well. But he couldn't shake off the feeling of uneasiness.

He recited a sutra to help calm his mind, but before he was halfway through, his thoughts wandered back to Yinmi. At that time of day, the novices would all be in the Meditation Hall listening to their abbot instruct them on the meaning of one of the sutras.

"You are thinking about your monastery," Kai said.

"How do you know?"

"Sometimes your thoughts leak through to me."

Tao sighed. Not even his thoughts were his own.

"Do you wish to return to your monkish life?"

Tao allowed himself to imagine living at the monastery again – the peaceful rhythm of each day with a simple monastic routine, a complete lack of surprises and no decisions to be made. Part of him yearned for that safety and certainty.

"I couldn't bear to be in the same monastery as Fo Tu Deng."

Tao realised that the monastery he had been imagining no longer existed. Now that Fo Tu Deng was there, it would not be the same. He'd probably made himself abbot by now. The monk from Tianzhu had fooled Tao at first, convincing him that he was a venerable and holy man. But he was a fraud, a selfish man using the words of Buddha to benefit himself. In order to save his own skin, he had been happy to side with the nomads. He didn't deserve to be called a monk.

"You could find another monastery."

"No. That is not my destiny," Tao said. "I don't think I met you merely to share breakfast on a mountain. I have to face my future and be your dragonkeeper."

The boy and the dragon finally left their camp and walked in silence for some time. Clouds covered the sky again. It was not a cold day, but Tao felt chilly. He couldn't erase the images of the corpses in the cave, the bits of clothing still hanging on the bones. And his dreams hadn't entirely left him – the cries of the terrified villagers lingered in the corners of his mind.

"We swore a blood oath. We are bonded as brothers," Kai said suddenly. "But you are not yet my dragonkeeper."

Tao stopped walking. Now that Tao had left everything he knew and loved behind, had the dragon changed his mind?

"You cannot be until I hand you the dragonkeeper's mirror." Kai clapped Tao on the back with his forepaw. "There is no need to be melancholy. In the meantime, I will oversee your training."

Tao turned to the dragon. "What training?"

"A dragonkeeper needs many skills, and you have not yet mastered your *qi* power."

"*Qi* power? What's *qi* power?" Kai had never mentioned training before. "Did you make that up?"

"I did not! As you know, *qi* is the spiritual energy that exists in all creatures. Dragonkeepers, and dragons, learn how to increase their store of *qi* and then to harness it."

Kai had told Tao about the second sight that all dragonkeepers had, but he hadn't mentioned other powers.

"Dragons have unusual skills – you have your shape-changing and mirage skill," Tao said. "But I didn't know dragonkeepers also had powers. How do they use this *qi* power?"

"In many ways. Usually it manifests in strength. I have heard of a dragonkeeper who could throw with deadly accuracy and speed, and one who could leap long distances. Your ancestor Ping had powerful *qi*."

Kai often spoke about the young girl who had been his first and only dragonkeeper. She had cared for him since the moment he hatched, and she had been like a mother to the orphaned dragonling. Tao knew he could never live up to Ping's memory, but as well as his own *qi*, he also had his brother's. As he was dying, he had poured his *qi* into Tao's body. And Wei had been a very special person. His *qi* was powerful too, Tao was sure of that.

"What was Ping's *qi* power?" Tao asked.

"She was able to focus it and defend herself from blows and weapons."

"I have my staff for that."

"Once she killed a man with a bolt of *qi*."

"I won't be using Wei's *qi* to hurt anybody."

Kai was quick to defend Ping. "She was protecting Danzi. That was her job."

"Are you sure I have *qi* power?"

"All dragonkeepers do," Kai said. "Some have potent powers as Ping did. Others have powers that are less … significant. One could boil water by holding the pot in his hands, so I heard."

Tao thought that sounded like a useful skill.

"How can I find out what my *qi* power is?"

"Perhaps it is some small skill you already have, that you can enhance," Kai said. "What can you do?"

Tao thought hard. "I can memorise sutras."

"I suppose you could bore our enemies to death."

"I can whistle." That was the one thing he'd been able to do better than the other novices.

"Your *qi* power might be an ear-splitting whistle that will make people's ears bleed."

Tao was horrified at the thought of doing something so cruel. "I can light fires."

"All humans can do that. But perhaps you will develop the ability to light fires spontaneously."

Tao didn't mention his skill at finding worms. He wasn't in the mood for more dragonish jokes at his expense.

When Ping unexpectedly became a dragonkeeper, Kai's father, an old and wise dragon, had trained her. In dragon terms Kai was young, and he had spent more than four hundred years living in the confines of the dragon haven. As far as Tao knew, Ping was the only dragonkeeper Kai had known, so his knowledge of them was scant.

"Your *qi* power may take another form," Kai was saying. "It may need a little time to develop."

"I suppose when you say 'a little time' you're talking in dragon terms and that means ten or twenty years."

"Perhaps fifty."

Wei had given his *qi* to Tao for a purpose. What purpose, he didn't know. He owed it to his brother to find out.

"But I can't feel my *qi*. How can I access it?"

"Your *qi* is dormant. You will need to do some exercises to help wake it."

Kai demonstrated some *qi* concentration exercises – focusing on an ant crawling across a rock, counting the leaves on a tree. Tao tried them. After years of meditation, those things were not difficult for him.

"After you have located your *qi*, you must learn to harness it, to bring it forth when you need it."

Tao sat on a rock and stared at the distant mountains. "How far is it to the dragon haven?"

Kai thought for several minutes, as if composing a long answer, but when he eventually spoke, his reply was short. He pointed to high mountains in the distance.

"It is many *li* from here."

The mountains were a long way away.

"But we're closer to it than when we left Yinmi, aren't we?"

"Much closer," Kai said. "But we cannot travel through the mountains in the winter. I could do it, but you would not survive."

Tao wriggled his toes. His straw sandals were already coming apart and they weren't suitable for a winter journey.

"We have plenty of time for a quest," Kai said.

The dragon continued along the path, snuffing the earth like a dog following a scent, and then he stopped to scrape up the wet earth with his talons.

Tao knew Wei's *qi* was inside him, but he couldn't find it, couldn't feel the beginnings of any sort of power. When Kai wandered off the path to examine some leaves, Tao repeated the concentration exercises Kai had shown him. Then he picked up a stone to test his throwing skills, hurling it as far as he could. The stone flew lazily into the air and then plummeted down almost immediately.

He heard a sound like small bells ringing. "You throw like a girl." Tao hadn't realised that Kai was watching him.

Apart from his sister Meiling, there was the only one

other girl Tao had ever been friendly with – the nomad, Pema. She had a good throwing arm. He wished he could throw as well as she did.

Tao's shoulders sagged. "Throwing isn't something you learn in a monastery."

"Do not concern yourself. You will harness your *qi* and find your *qi* power … eventually."

"I don't want a power that will hurt anyone," Tao said.

"What sort of *qi* power would you like to have?"

Tao thought for a moment. "I'd like to have the power to bring peace to Huaxia."

"A dragonkeeper's *qi* power must benefit dragons."

Tao hadn't considered that.

"Kai, we must stop dawdling. We've hardly made any progress since breakfast."

The dragon blew a stream of mist through his nostrils. That usually meant he was annoyed.

"You've eaten well today. Now isn't the time to be hunting."

Kai was still sniffing the path.

"I am not hunting, I am tracking."

Fear suddenly gripped Tao. "Tracking what? Not that creature we heard in the forest yesterday?"

Kai didn't answer.

"We shouldn't be following it! We should be getting far away from it."

"The only thing I am following is the path, but I keep finding unusual paw prints." Kai pointed to a mark in the earth.

"That could've been made by any number of animals."

"No other creature has such big paws."

"Well, it's yours then, isn't it?"

Kai pushed one of his paws into the earth. "This is my paw print."

Tao looked at the marks left by the pads of Kai's paw, surrounded by the imprints of his four toes and talons. The other paw print was longer and narrower than Kai's, and it had three toes, the middle one the longest.

Kai poked through a pile of leaves and picked up a brown sphere about the size of a plum.

"There is also dung."

"Dung?"

He held it out for Tao to examine, but Tao didn't want to touch it. It was hard and brown. Tao realised that what he had seen Kai pick up earlier wasn't stones at all. They were animal droppings.

"I'm not interested in animal tracks … or dung. Can we please get going again? We're still not far enough away from that awful cave."

Kai continued along the path, reciting a poem about his tracking skills.

"No one can evade me,
Not man nor beast nor bird.
However clever my quarry,
I will track it undeterred."

"We need to walk faster," Tao said.

Tiny midges started swarming in the air in front of Tao. More and more joined them until thousands of the insects formed a black cloud barring his way. Tao was trying to wave away the midges without harming them, when Kai suddenly stopped in his tracks.

"What's wrong?" Tao asked.

"I feel …"

"Feel what?"

"Unwell."

"Is it the bat droppings? Are you going to be sick again?"

Kai was rubbing his eyes with a paw. "My eyes are sore."

Tao got down onto his hands and knees so he could crawl under the cloud of insects. He caught up with Kai.

"Did you hear that?" Tao said. "I thought I heard something. It sounded like …"

The forest suddenly ended and they found themselves in a clearing. Tao felt exposed without the shelter of surrounding trees. The sun broke through the clouds and Tao was dazzled by bright light. He squinted. The sunlight reflected off metal objects – all sharp, shiny and pointed in their direction. There in front of them was a band of mounted nomads, at least twenty-five of them. They were armed with swords, spears and arrow tips all made of iron. Their saddle blankets bore the rearing horse emblem of the nomad tribe called the Zhao. They blocked the path, staring at Kai who hadn't had time to shape-change.

"We have found them," one of the men called over his shoulder. "A boy and a dragon."

The leader of the nomads broke through the line of horses. He was a small, skinny man who looked like a child astride a horse, except that he had wrinkly, leathery skin. All the happiness dropped out of Tao. The man was dressed in the saffron robes of a monk, but he wore a fur hat and fine leather shoes as well. He was also wearing a broad grin. It was Fo Tu Deng.

"Ha!" he said cheerfully. "We've found you at last!"

The monk was high on the list of people Tao never wanted to see again. Questions crowded Tao's mind. Why was the monk searching for them? What was he doing with the nomads? And why wasn't he back at Yinmi?

Tao and Kai glanced at each other.

There was only one thought in Kai's head. "Flee!"

Chapter Five
BLACK

Tao turned and ran back the way they had come. Kai was on his heels. An arrow flew past Tao's ear.

"Don't harm the boy, you idiot!" Fo Tu Deng's voice rang out. "I need him captured alive. The dragon too. And remember, he might not be in the shape of a dragon. Capture anything that moves."

Tao could hear whinnying, stamping hoofs, and riders berating their mounts as the horses jostled for a place on the narrow path. Nomad horses were used to galloping on open plains, not creeping along cramped mountain paths hardly wide enough for a goat. The confusion gave Tao and Kai a head start. Tao allowed himself to believe that they would lose their pursuers, but the sound of a horse behind them soon burst that small bubble of hope. One nomad had got control of his mount and won the contest to be first after them. Over his shoulder, Tao saw Kai swipe the man with his tail, knocking him from his saddle.

They kept running. When another nomad came up behind them, Kai pulled back a branch and let it go again, startling the horse. They left the path and ran into the trees, zigzagging to lose any other nomads who might be behind them. Tao had to stop to catch his breath.

"Get onto my back," Kai said.

Tao did as the dragon said. He clung on to Kai's mane as the dragon ran through the forest, weaving between trees, leaping over rocks.

They broke out of the trees and onto another path. Tao hadn't thought about where they were going, but somehow they had wound their way back to the same path. They were at the mouth of the cave. It was the last place Tao wanted to be. He jumped off Kai's back as he was about to run into the cave.

Kai was making his agitated scraping knives sound. "Into the cave!"

Tao didn't move. "We'll be like birds in a snare."

Kai pushed Tao into the black cave. Tao covered his mouth and nose, trying not to breathe in the fetid smell. He couldn't believe he was back in this dreadful place, after vowing he would never go near it again.

Kai pulled an arrow from his tail.

"Are you all right, Kai? Let me put some red cloud herb on the wound."

"No need. My tail is tough."

The nomads gathered outside, their horses snorting and stamping.

"Go on then!" Fo Tu Deng shouted. "Go after them!"

"In there? But it's dark and cramped," one of the nomads said. He sounded terrified. "It's the horses. They won't go in."

"It's not the horses I want to go in, you imbecile. Get off your horse and use your legs!"

Tao could see one of the nomads dismounting. Kai pulled Tao to the rear of the cave. The nomad stepped inside the cave and sniffed the putrid air as his eyes adjusted to the light. Then he saw the bones and he backed out of the cave.

"It is an evil place of the dead!" he said.

There was a murmur of panic.

"The dead won't harm you!" Fo Tu Deng shouted. "They're just bones. I will report your cowardice to Jilong."

Tao tried to make sense of all this. Kai had already worked it out. "Fo Tu Deng is working for the Zhao," he said. "He must still be claiming the visions you had were his own."

Tao understood now why Fo Tu Deng wanted to capture them. The monk had pretended he could work miracles and see visions given to him by Buddha, but he had no second sight, no visionary powers of his own. When they were imprisioned by the leader of the Zhao, Shi Le, the monk had passed off Tao's visions as his own in order to impress the nomads. Now it seemed Fo Tu Deng was in the service of Shi Le's cruel nephew, Jilong.

"He needs you," Kai said. "How can he pretend he can see into the future without your visions?"

The nomads were still refusing to enter the cave.

"You are more cowardly than the boy and his beast!" Fo Tu Deng shouted.

"We'll wait," one of the nomads said. "They'll have to come out or starve to death."

"He's right, Kai. We can't hide in here forever." Tao could make out the mud nests of the swallows on the cave walls. "*You* can eat the swallows, but I can't. And even if I was driven by hunger to eat the birds, there isn't any water."

"When I was hunting for swallows, I noticed an opening at the back of the cave that leads to a narrow passage. Can you see it?"

"No."

"The bat dung I ate this morning has started to take effect. I can see it clearly," Kai said. "The bats do not roost in this cave, they go deeper into the mountain, through that opening."

Tao didn't want to go into the dark passage, but he could hear Fo Tu Deng ordering the nomads to set up camp outside.

Kai grunted and puffed as he squeezed himself into the

hole. "There may be another way out."

He appeared to make himself longer and thinner. Tao could hear the dragon's muffled voice. "Come."

Tao took a deep breath and crawled in through the hole. He was expecting the narrow passage to open out into a cavern on the other side, but it didn't. It was only just wide enough for him to scramble through on his hands and knees. Crawling was difficult, as he had his bag over his shoulder and his staff in one hand. He could hear the dragon in front of him, his scales scraping along the sides of the passage as he threaded himself through the tight space. It was pitch black. Panic overwhelmed him at the thought of the dragon getting stuck in the passage, unable to back out. Tao's instinct was to stand up, turn around and run, but all he did was bang his head on the rock ceiling. His heart was hammering. Sweat ran off his body. The stench of the cave was being replaced by the less unpleasant smell of bats. His breath came in ragged gasps, as if he were still running. He reached out for Kai but his groping hands couldn't find the dragon's tail. Then his lungs refused to work at all. Sparks of light appeared in front of his eyes. His ears started ringing. He was about to lose consciousness, when the dragon's tail hit him hard in the face.

Tao heard the dragon's voice in his head. "This is not a time for fear."

Tao gasped and sucked in a mouthful of foul air. Kai wrapped his tail around Tao's staff and Tao felt himself being pulled along. The smell of the bats grew stronger, but at least it wasn't mingled with the odour of death. He tried to picture something pleasant, but his mind was filled with darkness. And he was cold. His elbows and knees scraped against the rock. He was glad that he could feel the pain, smell the bats and hear the dragon's grunting. He couldn't see, but at least his other senses were working.

Panic no longer filled Tao's heart, but there was no hope either. He stopped crawling, resigned to being stuck in the dark until he starved to death. He felt for the shard in his bag. Its smooth rounded surface gave him courage. A little speck of something entered the darkness. It wasn't light, it was nothing he could see or hear. It was a sensation. In his blank mind he saw the faintest image of his brother's face, his slow, dribbly smile. Tao made his hands and knees move again.

Then he could feel space around him. The tunnel had ended. He cautiously got to his feet. They were in a cavern, but it was still pitch black.

"Kai, where are you?"

"I am here." A dragon paw touched Tao on his shoulder.

"I can't see anything."

"I can see a little, thanks to the bat droppings. It is as if it is a dark night with only a slender moon," Kai said. "This is a wider passage. I can feel a draught of air."

Tao tried to guess how big the cave was from the way the dragon's sounds echoed off the walls and the ceiling. He could smell the bats and hear their screeching. He felt his scalp creep. The bats were hanging not far above their heads.

Kai's talons hooked into Tao's jacket. "Walk alongside me."

Tao was shivering. The sweat on his body turned icy as the cold penetrated his bones. He had spent years living on a mountain wearing threadbare robes throughout winter. He should be used to the cold. Why was he suddenly chilled to the bone?

Kai kept walking. The passage was wide enough for them to walk side by side. Tao stumbled along, tripping on the uneven ground, banging into the rock walls. His teeth were chattering from cold and fear. And then he felt icy fingers brush his arm and cold breath on his face. It smelled like death.

"I want to go back," Tao whispered.

"Into the arms of Fo Tu Deng?"

"There's something else here with us."

"There is nothing else here. How could there be?"

Tao still didn't move. "I felt something touch me."

"The darkness is confusing you." Kai said. "I can see, remember? There is no one here but you and me."

"No one alive."

"Hold on to my mane. Let me lead the way. I am not scared of the dark."

Tao grasped a tuft of the dragon's mane in each hand. "*You* are not in utter darkness like me."

He looked back, hoping to see a trace of daylight behind them, but there was none.

"We should go back while we can still find the way, or we will roam in the darkness until we die of starvation."

The dragon kept moving forwards. "I can feel a faint breath of air. I am sure there is another way out."

The blackness overwhelmed Tao. It wasn't like the dark of a moonless night, when faint shapes and the stars above could be seen, and the touch of familiar things gave assurance the world was still as it should be. He longed to see a grey sky again.

The cold penetrated Tao's thin jacket and trousers like freezing wind.

He could see nothing, he could hear nothing. He felt icy fingers touch the back of his neck. He spun round, waving his staff to fend off whoever, whatever was there. He foolishly let go of Kai's mane. He reached out again, this time searching for the dragon. He wanted to call out to Kai, but his jaw was clenched shut. He couldn't utter a sound. He tried to transmit words from his mind, but they froze half-formed. One thought entered his head. The ghosts of the dead from the cave had followed them. They wanted to punish him, even though their deaths were no fault of his.

Tao banged his head on something. He reached up to feel what it was. A huge icicle pierced the blackness above. He moved away from it, but tripped over another icicle protruding from the cave floor. Tao didn't know how icicles could grow upwards. Whichever way he turned he ran into another. They were like teeth. This wasn't a cave; it was the giant mouth, the living entrance to the underworld. The frozen, prodding fingers of the ghosts had driven him into its gaping jaws. Soon the teeth would close behind him and he would never be able to get out.

The sharp fingers gripped him on both arms. They turned him to his left and propelled him forwards with unexpected force. The ground disappeared from under his feet, and the fingers let go. He fell, tumbling down a steep slope. Cruel, jagged points of rock dug into his body, first his arm, then his back, then his knees. What little breath he had was knocked out of him. He crashed into hard rock. He had reached the bottom of a pit. The black had swallowed him completely. He knew he should try to find Kai again but he had lost the will to move. He tried to call out, but no words came out of the dry hole that had once been his mouth. He tried to stand, but he had not escaped the cold fingers. They had hold of him again.

They clutched at his body, dug into his flesh so that the cold entered his stomach, his liver, his heart. He wanted to weep with despair, but his blank eyes couldn't make tears. In this world of rock, he felt as if he were turning to stone himself. He knew where he was now. He had entered the realms of hell.

Chapter Six
LOST THINGS

The novices at Yinmi Monastery had a game they played to frighten newcomers as they lay on their pallets in the dark, missing their homes and families. They had memorised the many dungeons in the sixteen realms of hell.

"Which would you rather endure?" they asked. "The dungeon where you must kneel forever on bamboo splinters, or the dungeon where you are forced to drink liquid dung?"

As the night progressed, the tortures they described grew worse.

"Would you rather the dungeon where you have to walk across five-pronged forks, or the one where demons scrape your flesh from your bones?"

They reserved the worst till last.

"Would you rather the dungeon where your brain is removed from your skull and replaced by a hedgehog, or the one where crows peck out your heart and lungs?"

By that time the new novices were either sobbing or

screaming. When the monks came to see what the noise was about, the older boys feigned sleep.

Tao wasn't a bad person. He wouldn't be going to one of the worst realms of hell. But he remembered from those night-time stories that the entrance to the first realm of hell was very dark. There was a special place in that hell for monks who had done bad things – a dark dungeon called the *Puqingshuo* where devils with black and red faces suspended bad monks by their feet for all eternity. Tao knew what his sins were. First he had broken every one of the novices' precepts. Then he had abandoned his vows. Finally, he hadn't given a thought about offering prayers for the dead in the cave. When he had realised it was a grave, he had been concerned only for himself, too busy thinking about his own discomfort to consider his duty. Now he was paying for that neglect.

The souls of the dead villagers had become ghosts, hungry ghosts. Lost and angry, they had not passed into their next lives. They were lingering, longing to get revenge for their violent deaths, for their inadequate burial, for the lack of prayers to send them into their next life. They had latched on to Tao, the person who had ignored their silent plea for release, and pushed him into the mouth of hell. They blamed him, and he deserved their blame. He should have prayed for them. Unless he corrected this error, he would continue his journey in darkness until he reached the *Puqingshuo*.

He called out to Kai with his mind, but there was no response. If he could just get back into the world, he could put everything right. But how could he do that? Perhaps he could summon a vision, despite the darkness. He reached for his bag. He felt around him. All he could feel was his water skin over his shoulder. The ghosts had taken his bag. He couldn't attempt to call up a vision without the mixture of sesame oil and safflower. They had taken back the bronze bowl Kai found in the village, and with it all his other possessions. Those things could be replaced; even the vial of yellow oil was replaceable, if he could ever find a place in Huaxia where such treasures as safflower and sesame oil still existed. But there was one thing in his bag that could never be replaced – the shard of dragon stone. The shard was precious to him, and he had only just begun to understand that it had powers of its own.

His ancestor Ping had used the dragon-stone shard to help her find lost things. After centuries, that precious tool had found its way to Tao. And what had he done with it? His frozen lips bent into a bitter smile. He had lost it! Even without ghosts to steal from him, he had always been good at losing things. He needed Kai. But he had lost the dragon as well. He remembered that you were permitted to take nothing with you into the realms of hell, nothing but the sins you committed. That explained why the ghosts had taken his possessions.

There was no use lamenting the loss of the shard. It was gone. He had nothing to aid him. Then he remembered. There was one thing that he still had. One thing that the ghosts could never take from him. He had Wei's *qi* – all of it – his brother's dying gift. Tao still didn't have a clue what his *qi* power was, but whatever its form, it might be useful to him now. He searched within, trying to locate the knot of Wei's *qi* inside him. It was small, no bigger than a peach stone, but he knew that it was concentrated enough to last him one lifetime at least if he was careful and didn't squander it. He needed it now. If he died in that cold, dark hole, then Wei had sacrificed his life for nothing. He searched inside himself. He made a promise to the ghosts. If he ever got out of the darkness, he would offer prayers for them. He would make a proper memorial to their passing.

Tao located Wei's *qi*. It was in his heart. Of course. Where else would it be? But it was frozen solid, like a large hailstone. He needed to thaw it out. He tried to think of something warming. He remembered his dear brother, who had never been able to walk or speak. They'd experienced many happy times together when they were young. But Tao's brain was frozen as well. He couldn't recall a single image of their shared childhood. Not an image of his brother's face, so like his own, and yet so different.

A holy thought then. There had been times when, deep in meditation, he had felt the radiance of Buddha shining on him like sunlight. He recalled one of those moments, but the Blessed One's glow didn't reach him. It was as if he were watching himself from behind a sheet of ice. An image flashed into his mind. Not of his brother. Not of the glory of Buddha. Not of a brush swollen with ink creating a perfect character on a fresh page. It was Pema. Pema the wild nomad girl. He remembered the touch of her lips on his cheek before she had turned and walked away into her own future. That unholy happiness was not what he had been seeking, but it was exactly what he needed. The spot on his cheek burned hot.

The warmth spread in a rush of pleasure and guilt. His heart started to thaw a little. So did Wei's *qi*. A thin strand of it began to flow, slowly like honey in winter, gradually moving into his limbs. The ghost fingers fell away.

He hurt all over, but none of his bones had broken in the fall. And at least he wasn't numb. He could see nothing, but he was no longer afraid of the dark. His hand touched something smooth and wooden. It was his staff. He used it to struggle to his feet. His instinct was to crawl back up the slope he had fallen down, but the *qi* flowed to his legs and his feet turned him round. He walked in the opposite direction along another tunnel, further away from the cave where they had entered the mountain. He didn't resist. He had to find Kai. And with his brother's help he could do it.

He focused his mind and spoke to Kai with his thoughts. *Where are you?* There was no reply. Tao still couldn't see, but his other senses were beginning to thaw. He could hear water dripping. He could feel the whisper of air that Kai had mentioned. He took tiny steps, his staff held out to alert him to any obstacles. He felt more of the huge icicles hanging from the cave ceiling and protruding from the cave floor. They were thick and slippery with moisture, but now that his body had thawed, he realised they were not as icy cold as he had thought. He licked his fingers. They were wet with water that tasted of minerals. He realised that they were made of rock, not ice.

Tao could hear a faint sound in his mind. It reminded him of his father sharpening his wood-carving tools on a stone. The sound grew a little louder. It was mixed with the low toll of a cracked bell. Tao moved towards it. He felt his way through this strange forest of stone. He could hear water dripping from the ceiling. He felt the drips on his face and hands. He was beginning to understand the world of the blind.

His foot struck something soft. He heard a different sound. "Ooof." And there was a new smell. A faint whiff of salty fish mixed with plums on the turn.

"Kai." He kneeled down and ran his hands over the

dragon's scales as if they were smooth and soft, like satin, not rough and scratchy. "Are you hurt?"

"Frozen." The dragon's voice was faint in his head.

Tao felt the shape of the dragon's great body. He was lying coiled in a knot, his nose buried beneath his back paws, his tail drawn up through the centre of the coil.

"Hungry ghost," the dragon whispered.

"It's okay, Kai. The ghosts won't hurt us."

"Trip. Freeze."

"Yes, but they did this to us because they want us to help them into their next life."

Though dragons had no religion, Tao knew that Kai had more faith in the old beliefs than in the words of Buddha. He didn't believe that after death a creature's soul moved into a different body and began another life. He believed that the souls of the dead lingered near their graves. If these souls didn't get offerings of food and a comfortable place to spend their afterlife, they would turn into hungry ghosts. They would punish whoever they thought was responsible for neglecting them. That's what the people of Huaxia had believed before they were shown the way of Buddha.

"Underworld," Kai said.

"I thought I had fallen into the realms of hell. But we are not in the underworld, just lost in a cave. If we promise to fulfil the wishes of the dead from the ruined village, they will let us go. We cannot help them while we are trapped in this place. They know that."

"Not many ghosts. Only one. Gu Hong."

Kai had spoken about this dragon before. She was an old one who had died while Kai was still at the dragon haven. This was no time to debate religious differences, no time to press him to follow the way of the Blessed One. If Kai believed he had been visited by the ghost of a dead dragon, then that was what Tao would use to convince him to move.

He felt for Kai's ears and stroked them. They were small and unscaled, velvety to touch. The dragon's breath grew more even.

"What is it that Gu Hong's ghost wants from you?"

"She wants me to accept my responsibility, to tend her grave and lead the dragons."

"As soon as we return to our own world we will pray for her and honour her as an elder. You must promise that you will lead the dragons as she wished. Then, when we eventually reach the dragon haven, we will make a commemoration for her, ensure that offerings are made and the dragons speak her name so she is never forgotten."

Tao felt Kai pull his nose out from under his paws. "Cannot see," the dragon said.

"That's because the effects of the bat droppings have worn off. Use your other senses, Kai. I can feel that draught of air you mentioned. We must find its source."

Tao could hear the scratchy sound of the dragon nodding in agreement.

"That's it." He tickled the dragon below his chin.

Kai got up onto all four paws.

"Can you feel the draught?"

"Cannot."

"Let me lead you."

Tao took hold of the dragon's beard and gently led him into the darkness. With his other hand he held his staff before him to find a path through the stone icicles. He still bumped his head and stubbed his toes, but he did himself no harm. Kai followed. The drips of water were more numerous now. They were finding their way towards each other and forming a trickle.

The ghostly fingers no longer had hold of him, but Tao could feel icy breath on his face, so he knew the ghosts were still with them. His body was bruised, his legs heavy and slow. The darkness threatened to wear down his new resolve, to chip away at his confidence, but he withstood it, fortified by the *qi* within him and the memory of his brother's smile. Then he thought he saw a faint green glow, but he was sure his eyes were playing tricks on him. The sound of trickling water was getting louder. He rubbed his eyes, which were heavy and tired from straining to see through the darkness, but the glow was still there, faint as the light from a flame consuming the last drop of lamp oil.

"Do you see anything, Kai? I can see a glow. Is it real?"

"I see it too."

Then Tao felt space open up around him. He couldn't see its extremities, but he was sure they had entered a cavern. As they walked towards the light, Tao knew it couldn't be daylight, but he wasn't afraid. The sound of flowing water was growing louder. Then he caught his breath as he saw the source of the greenish glow. All those trickles of water had run together to form a lake. They reached the edge of the underground lake. Tao could see that it contained many thousands of specks of light.

"What are they?"

"Perhaps they are tiny creatures," Kai suggested.

Tao looked closer. The specks of light were darting around. The light they gave off was very faint, but it illuminated the greenish water. After so long in darkness, his eyes drank it in.

He turned to the dragon and smiled. "It is good to be able to see you again, Kai, even though you are faint."

Tao could make out the outline of the cavern. It was huge. But that wasn't the wonder of it. He could see the stone icicles that he had only felt before. Hundreds of them hung from the cave roof around the edge of the lake, glowing palest green, like eerie decorations for an underworld festivity. Others grew upwards from the cave floor. Tao and Kai stood in silence, listening to the liquid sound of trickling water echo around the cavern. This was not one of the realms of hell. It was more like a fairy world.

Tao suddenly realised how thirsty he was. He'd emptied his water skin long before.

"Do you think the water is safe to drink?"

Kai dipped a talon into the green water and let a drop fall onto his tongue. "It tastes like the green pool at the dragon haven. It will not harm you, but it might make you sleepy."

"That's okay," Tao said. "Water and rest are what I need most."

They both drank from the pool. It was cold but it didn't chill Tao. He found a dry place at the edge of the cave. There was a thin layer of moss, brought there by some animal. He lay down. It was like lying on a bed of silk floss.

Chapter Seven
DAYLIGHT

Tao woke. He had slept soundly, for how long he couldn't tell. Kai was still snoring. He knew exactly where he was. He was trapped in an eerie green underground cavern, with his only friend in the world, and he'd eaten nothing for a long time. Yet Tao felt confident that everything would work out well. He'd had no nightmares, just one dream where he was in his own bed at his family home, covered by a thick quilt of silk floss pulled right up to his chin.

As he lay there remembering the childhood comfort and warmth, he realised the feeling was not fading. He still felt that delicious warmth, though he knew his blanket was lost with all his other possessions.

As if he had read his thoughts, Kai suddenly let out a cry. It was not one Tao was familiar with. It was a shrill sound, like the clash of small cymbals.

"Beetles!" the dragon said.

Tao opened his eyes. He *was* covered, but not by a blanket or a quilt. He sucked in a breath. He was covered from chin to toe in beetles – hundreds of them. Each beetle was about the length of his little finger, shiny black with white markings. They were all waving their antennae, which were striped with black-and-white bars and almost twice the length of their bodies. Tao felt strangely calm, not repulsed as he might have expected. He let out his breath and the beetles opened their wings and took off. They flew together in a cloud over the lake.

"Did they bite you? Were you terrified?" Kai didn't like beetles.

"No. They were friendly."

"How do you know?"

"I could tell."

Tao got to his feet and carefully brushed off two or three beetles that had been reluctant to leave.

"We must find our way out from under this mountain." Kai's stomach made a loud growling sound. "Or we will starve to death."

Tao watched the last beetles fly off into the darkness. "I think we should follow them."

It was Tao who saw it first as he kneeled at the lake's edge and filled his water skin. Kai was still drowsy. Something glittered in a recess of the cave wall. It was different to the green glimmer of the lake, so he knew it wasn't a pool of water. Tao went over to it. He couldn't believe his eyes.

"Kai, come and look."

It was a pile of treasure. A mound of precious things. Tao could see a gold necklace and a finely carved jade pendant.

"Some rich person must have hidden all his wealth here, so that the nomads couldn't find it."

"Or it might be the hiding place of a thief," Kai suggested.

Among the precious objects, there were things of little value – a length of blue ribbon, a piece of broken pottery with a pretty pattern, an iridescent bird's feather. Kai peered closer. He took something from the pile.

"I do not think a thief would bother to steal this." It was a worn shoe.

Tao picked up a lump of black crystalline rock.

"Let me see that," Kai said.

He held it up against the glow of the lake. It was not a single crystal, but a clump of smaller crystals. They were not symmetrical and polished like gems, but irregular shapes and dull. As he stared at the crystal in the dragon's paw, Tao began to distinguish some colour in it.

"It isn't black. It's more of a very deep red."

"I know what this is," Kai said. "It is cinnabar."

Tao took the crystal from him. "Is it?"

The dragon nodded. "But how did it get here?"

"It doesn't matter how it got here. Remember the glowing red embers in my vision? It was telling me we would find cinnabar here. I wasn't clever enough to work it out."

He handed the cinnabar to Kai. "You keep it safe. I'm afraid I'll lose it. I lose everything."

The dragon put the crystal behind his largest reverse scale. It was a tight fit.

"Perhaps it was a gift from the ghost of Gu Hong."

Kai still believed that it was the ghost of the old red dragon who had visited them in the cave. Tao didn't try to convince him otherwise. He was glad that the dragon was on his feet again and keen to find the way out.

"I must think of a way to thank her," Kai said.

"Why didn't you honour Gu Hong when she died?" Tao asked.

The dragon sighed. "She left the haven when she knew she was dying. She wanted to go to the place that she had decided would be our burial ground. She tried to fly, but she didn't get far. Hei Lei and Tun, other male dragons, carried her the rest of the way. The other dragons escorted them. Except me. I could not fly. Hei Lei came back to get me, but I was too proud to let him carry me. So I did not help bury her. I did not sing for her."

Tao was glad Kai couldn't see a tear roll down his cheek. He was beginning to understand that there were reasons why Kai wasn't in a hurry to return to the dragon haven.

They couldn't fly across the lake as the beetles had.

Instead they made their way slowly around its edge, zigzagging through the forest of stone icicles, until eventually they reached the other side. The cavern narrowed and then divided into two passages.

"Which one will we choose?" Kai asked.

"The beetles took the left passage." Tao was confident they would find a way out. "We will too."

Once out of sight of the lake, the green glow faded with every step. More darkness loomed ahead of them. Tao kept glancing back until the last faint glimmer of green disappeared and there was nothing but blackness again.

He could no longer rely on his eyes, but he knew he could trust his other senses. He reached out. His hands felt the shape and the texture of the passage walls on either side. They were hard, rough and cold. They were real. It looked as if there was another black wall in front of him, but when he reached out, his hands passed through it. It wasn't solid, it was darkness. He moved forwards. Kai followed. The dragon was silent, still contemplating what he believed had been an encounter with his dead leader. Their progress was slow. Tao had drunk more of the green water before they left the lake, and he needed to stop for a nap often.

"I can feel air on my face," Tao said. "Can you feel it, Kai? I think this must lead to another way out into the world."

The dragon didn't respond.

After a while Tao thought he could make out the faint uneven surface of the passage walls, imperceptible at first but becoming clearer. Finally, there was pale light. Not eerie green light, but warm yellow light.

"Can you see it, Kai? Light."

Tao took a step towards the light and stumbled over something. He thought he must be seeing things.

"It's my bag!" he said.

"How could it have got here, when you dropped it before we reached the lake?"

"I don't know."

He picked it up, feeling the coarse weave of the willow twigs that he had woven himself. It was real. He felt inside, smiling as he touched his few possessions – the vial of oil, his firesticks, gourd, blanket and the stolen bronze bowl. Then his smile faded.

"What is wrong. Is there something missing?"

"Yes, the most important thing. My dragon-stone shard."

Tao's brief happiness disappeared like mist in sunlight.

"The ghosts," he breathed. "They have taken it."

"Why would they steal your shard? It has no value to them."

"It is payment. They have taken it in exchange for the cinnabar, and for showing us the way out of the realms of hell."

The loss of the shard sapped Tao's energy and confidence, but Kai had found a new store of strength.

"We must get out into daylight," the dragon said. "Everything will make sense when we are out of the darkness."

The dragon hurried towards the pale light. Tao found it hard to keep up with him. Then there was a bright circle, too dazzling to look at. Tao shaded his eyes. It was daylight. They hurried to it and stepped out into the world again. The day was dull and overcast, but it took several minutes to get used to the glare of the light. Tao breathed the fresh mountain air, and his eyes drank in every detail of the world – delicate fern fronds, the feathers of a bird's wing, even the grey rock had texture and shades of colour that were beautiful to behold.

While Kai went in search of food, Tao considered how he could do his duty and honour the dead.

The villagers hadn't deserved to be slaughtered by nomads. There was no one left to say prayers for the souls of the dead, so they hadn't moved into another plane of existence, into new lives. Tao couldn't return to the site of the villagers' grave on the other side of the mountain, but he could create a memorial where he was. He selected the face of a large boulder, and although weak with hunger, he began immediately. Using the iron nail as a chisel and a stone as a hammer, he carved characters on the rock, commemorating the destruction of the village and the deaths of so many innocent people.

Kai returned. He had trapped birds, and found taro roots and mushrooms. Tao hadn't finished the carving, but he needed to eat. He collected firewood and lit a fire. He cooked the food and they ate in silence, each with their own thoughts about their own ghosts.

It was late afternoon, so they decided to stay where they were for the night. Tao worked on his carving until dusk. He wondered how long they had been underground. It had seemed such a long time, but now that he was back in the world again, he wasn't sure. It could have been several days, it might have been only one.

Kai ground a small crystal of cinnabar with a rock, mixed it in water and drank it. Tao put the finishing touches to his carving while Kai composed a poem in honour of Gu Hong.

"Scales the colour of cinnabar
Whiskers blue as the sky.
Gentle dragon, most wise by far
Now in heaven you fly."

They sat in silence, watching the sky turn dark, each contemplating their own commemoration of the dead. Tao couldn't meditate and recite sutras for seven days, as he had when his brother died, but he hoped the ghosts would be happy with his brief prayers. He turned to Kai.

"We should pray together for Gu Hong and for the dead in the cave. Our beliefs might be different, but we both wish the dead peace."

He kneeled and the dragon sat next to him, his head bowed. Tao prayed for the safe journey of the souls of the dead into the next life, where he hoped they would find peace and happiness and absence of hunger. He recited a sutra. Kai made a deep humming sound that didn't translate into words in Tao's mind. Tao prayed for the soul of the old red dragon as well. They sat in respectful silence for a moment. A sudden gust of wind stirred the tree branches. The wind grew stronger, swirling around them, whipping up dust and fallen leaves. It made a sad keening sound as it spiralled up. The current of air ruffled Kai's mane as it circled above their heads, and then the wind seemed to sigh before it died away completely. The ghosts had gone.

Tao had fulfilled his promise and helped the souls travel to their next life. But they had extracted a heavy price. He felt the loss of the shard like an unhealed wound.

Tao woke with new energy. He'd slept well and had bittersweet dreams of himself and Wei running through a forest as children. He hoped that in his new life, wherever he was, Wei's baby body was growing strong and that very soon he would indeed be able to run through a forest, as he never had in his life as Tao's brother. Tao stood in front of the commemorative stone. He was pleased. The characters were of an even size, the columns straight. This commemoration would stand the test of time.

"Give me the iron," Kai said.

Tao unwrapped the nail and handed it to him. Kai held the nail in one paw.

After a few minutes, Kai opened his paw. It was unmarked. He rubbed the iron on his stomach and on the soft hide under his chin. It had no effect.

"You were correct," the dragon said. "The tiger's blood brew did contain an ingredient that took away the iron pain. I am sorry I doubted you."

Kai hurled the nail deep into the forest, as far as he could throw it. This time Tao didn't retrieve it.

Tao smiled. He had solved the dragon's iron problem. He had done something worthy of a dragonkeeper. They would need more cinnabar, but for the moment the chunk that they had was enough. He felt the warmth of the sun on his skin. He had lost something precious, but his life had been given back to him.

"So which way is it to the dragon haven?" Tao squinted as the sun broke through the clouds.

"This is the way," Kai said, setting out along the path.

"How much of the journey have we already travelled?"

"It is a long way. A very long way. But we have made some progress."

Kai was thoughtfully snuffing the early morning air, reading the smells that it brought to him.

"What can you smell?"

"More than the fragrance of pine needles and the decay of autumn leaves," the dragon said. "I can smell urine."

Kai sniffed again and pointed a talon at a patch of damp on a rock.

"That's just morning dew," Tao said, not wanting the beauty of the morning to be spoiled.

"Smell."

Tao kneeled down and sniffed the damp rock. He screwed up his nose. It was the pungent smell of some sort of animal urine. "You're right. It smells awful. Even worse than yours."

"Fresh," Kai said.

He walked along the path, head down, sniffing. He stopped and pointed again, this time at the earth. There was another paw print.

"It is the same creature I was tracking before."

"But that's not possible," Tao said. "We left the monster on the other side of the mountain."

Kai nodded. "And yet it has passed this way not long ago."

"Did the underground passage wind back? Are we not far from where we entered?"

Kai shook his head and pointed at the sun still visible

between the clouds. "You can tell by the position of the sun that we have passed through the mountain to the other side."

The talk of urine had made Tao want to pee. He followed a small track to a place behind a rock and suddenly the mountain ended. Beneath his feet the rock plunged down to a plain far below. Though clouds were still gathered above the mountain, the sun was shining on the plain. It looked green and warm down there – and flat. His legs ached from all the walking they had done. He squinted into the distance. On the other side of the plain, far away, he could make out a walled city. His heart sank inside him.

"Kai!" he called out. "Kai! Come here!"

The dragon came up behind him. "Have you found something to eat? Do you want me to pee with you?"

Tao was still staring out over the plain. He pointed into the distance.

"It's Luoyang."

Chapter Eight
TOO MANY DEAD

Anger bubbled inside Tao.

"We're south of Luoyang. You've led us around in a circle. You told me we were heading west, getting closer to the dragon haven, but we haven't made any progress at all!"

Kai didn't say anything.

"Dragons are supposed to have a good sense of direction. How could you make such a mistake?"

Kai kicked a stone with his left forepaw and avoided looking Tao in the eye.

The truth was suddenly obvious to Tao. "You haven't been heading to the dragon haven at all, have you?"

If Tao had better navigation skills, he would have realised before.

A trail of mist issued from the dragon's nostrils. "Do not want to go to the dragon haven."

Tao thought of the many *li* he'd walked, all those uncomfortable nights sleeping on the cold ground, and the terrible time in the underground darkness. It had all been for nothing.

"We *must* go to the dragon haven! You are the leader of the dragons."

"Do not want to be leader."

Tao stood in front of Kai, so angry he had a strong desire to punch the dragon in the chest. He didn't, but that wasn't the point. He'd lost his temper and wished to hurt another being. Kai looked down at him. His bulk was probably five times Tao's. There was nothing Tao could do to force the dragon to do his duty.

He sank miserably onto a rock. "Then there's no point in us being together."

"You have nowhere else to go."

To the east, Tao could see the mountains where his old monastery was hidden among the trees. Fo Tu Deng was no longer there. He could beg to be readmitted.

"I could return to Yinmi. I could find another monastery. I could go to Jiankang and be with my family."

"You do not want to do any of those things."

Tao wished his thoughts were private.

"The dragon haven is a boring place," Kai said. "It is small. I could walk from one side to the other in less than an hour. There is nothing to do. Nothing to see but the same rocks, the same pools, day after day, year after year, decade after decade. I escaped from that prison. I do not want to return."

"But you have the other dragons. Your own kind."

"The other dragons were lazy and … boring. All they did was sleep, and hold meetings and talk endlessly about rules. The winged dragons could fly away and visit other places, but I was stuck there. There were no other young dragons like me, none who enjoyed adventure."

"But it's your home."

"You have left your home. So have I."

"What were you planning to do? Walk around in circles forever?"

The dragon sighed. A trail of mist rose from his nostrils and dissolved on the breeze.

"What about the bond we made before we left Yinmi?"

"We pledged that we would be brothers," Kai said. "I have not broken that bond. You are the one who is thinking about going back to your old life. On your own."

"What about your vow to the ghost of Gu Hong?"

"I promised I would go to the dragon haven and lead the dragons. I did not say I would go there immediately."

"You said we were going as soon as we escaped from the darkness."

"I was speaking in terms of dragon time. I will go. I will honour her every day. And I will take up my role as leader. But not now. Perhaps when I have wings like the others."

"But that won't be for another five hundred years!" Tao knew that dragons didn't grow wings until they were around a thousand years old. "I'll be long dead. You said you were going to give me the dragonkeeper mirror. Was that a lie too? You don't really want me to be your dragonkeeper, do you? You want me around to amuse you and … find worms."

Tao's legs ached. His feet were blistered. He was hungry, even though it was not long since they'd eaten. Tears filled his eyes. He wanted to weep like a child.

In the old days, people knew how their lives would unfold. Farmer, merchant, priest – they all had roles in their communities. Survival might have been difficult at times, loved ones died, crops failed, houses burned down, but at least folk knew what they were supposed to be doing in this life. Since the nomads had invaded, the world was not as it should be. Tao had tried to map out his life, but like so many people in Huaxia, it had slipped out of his control. He had no idea what he should be doing.

A sound broke the silence, interrupting Tao's thoughts. "What was that?"

Kai craned his neck, snuffed the breeze. "Nothing that can do us harm."

The dragon shape-changed into a boy the same age as Tao and they continued along the path. As they drew closer to the sound, Tao recognised what it was – a baby crying. He expected to discover an abandoned infant on a bed of moss, but around the next bend there was an old man with a baby in his arms and despair on his face. The man's eyes lit up with hope when he saw them. He held out the child to Kai who shrank away from the baby.

"I can't feed him. I don't know how." The old man looked hungry himself.

"I'll take him," Tao said, though he had no experience in caring for babies.

The child was a few months old and so skinny Tao could see its ribs. The baby kept crying. Tao still had some of the water from the underground cave and he poured it into his gourd.

"It isn't water he wants," the old man said. "He's had nothing but water for several days."

"This is special water," Tao said. "It should at least enable him to sleep while we work out what to do."

The water didn't seem special. In the daylight it no longer glowed. It just had a greenish tinge, like stagnant pond water. Tao managed to drip some of the water into the baby's mouth. He had seen starving babies before, in the villages near Yinmi, and they were usually listless, with death already in their eyes. This one still had some fight in him.

The baby did go to sleep. There was no urgent need to keep moving, so Tao suggested that they stay and help the old man. Kai didn't object. Tao remembered a woman who had lived in his family community who made a sort of porridge to feed to her infant.

"I need to light a fire. Kai, see if you can find some food – roots, mushrooms, anything."

The illusory clothes Kai wore while in his boy shape were old-fashioned, as they had been when Tao first met him, but the old man was too distressed to notice that there was anything unusual about Tao's companion.

Tao laid the sleeping baby on the grass while he collected wood and lit a fire so that he could cook the remainder of his grain.

Kai returned with wild roots and some sort of edible tree fungus. He also had a dead rabbit. If he'd been cooking it for himself, he would have flung it on the fire, fur and all, and eaten it half-raw. But he skinned the rabbit, skewered it on a stick and held it over the flames, turning it slowly.

As they waited for the food to cook, the old man told them his story.

"Our village was destroyed by a wild beast. Many people died."

"Is it on the other side of this mountain?" Tao asked. "Does it have a mud-brick temple and a little pagoda with one bell?"

"Yes, that's Shenchi, my village. I made that bell myself. I intended to make bells for all the corners of the pagoda roof, if ever I had spare metal."

"We passed through your village. We thought it had been attacked by nomads."

"No. It was a horrible beast that attacked us."

Tao glanced at Kai, remembering the roaring they had heard. "What sort of beast?"

"It attacked at night. No one saw it clearly, but it sounded huge and made a terrible noise. It destroyed our homes for no reason." The old man's lips trembled. "My son died, and my wife. The only survivors from my family were me, my daughter-in-law, a granddaughter and this baby. My daughter-in-law was injured, bitten by the creature."

"Bitten?"

"Yes. It was as if a snake bit her. Most of the dead were crushed when the monster destroyed the houses, but it bit several of the villagers too."

"And you buried your dead in a cave?"

"No. We fled and never returned."

"But we found bodies in a cave," Tao said. "There were no human remains in the village."

"Someone else must have buried our dead. I knew we should have done it ourselves, but fear drove us from our home."

"Where are the other villagers?"

"There were about twenty survivors. We tried to find a suitable place to build a new village, but nowhere on this mountain seemed far enough away from the beast. The bites festered and more died from these wounds, including my daughter-in-law. And then my granddaughter got sick. I didn't realise she had been bitten at first, she hid it from us." Tao saw tears in the man's eyes. "A man is supposed to favour the boys in his family, I know, but Baoyu was my favourite. So bright, so pretty. She was five, but she always looked after me, made sure I ate well. And she loved listening to my stories. She saw the monster attack her mother, sink its teeth into her flesh. She went to help her. Tiny little thing that she was, everyone else ran. That's when it must have bitten her too. She was the only one who saw it clearly, but she couldn't describe it. It was beyond her child's words."

The old man brushed away his tears.

"When I realised that she had been bitten too, I saw that it had taken off the end of her finger, but it seemed to be healing. The first ones to be bitten died immediately. Others took a little longer. The beast's venom seemed to lose its strength. Baoyu was its final victim. I hoped she would survive. But as the days passed, the wound turned purple and swollen with poison. Then it turned black and the flesh started to rot away. It left a festering hole. You could see through to the bone. She was in terrible pain."

The old man was stroking a worn child's jacket.

"And then we saw nomads. We knew of their attacks down on the plain. We had seen the city on fire several times over the years, but they had never ventured onto our mountain before. Yet there they were. The other elders said that the people of Shenchi no longer had a place in the north. I wasn't so sure. They decided to try to find the southern city, to go far away from nomads. Only the strong could go. They wanted to leave the weak behind – an old woman whose mind had gone, my granddaughter, myself and this babe who has no mother to feed him. The old woman didn't eat and died after a few days. I am not a hunter or a gatherer of food. I worked with metal. I made the tools for our village, though there was little ore or metal that came our way. I mostly refashioned broken things." His mind was far away for a while, back in a time when his village existed and his family still lived.

"The fever entered my granddaughter about a week ago. She cried out for her mother. In her child's voice she cursed the monster. She was the one who found food for us after her mother died. I know nothing about food gathering. But even if we had food, she wouldn't have survived. She died too. Yesterday, or was it the day before? In the end, it was a relief to see her at peace."

He held up the grubby jacket. "This is hers."

Kai pointed to a small pile of stones that Tao hadn't noticed before. It was a burial cairn, poorly built and surrounded by a circle of freshly burnt grass where the pyre had been.

"It is not our way to burn the bodies of our dead, but I didn't have the strength to dig a grave. That cairn was all I could manage."

He looked at the sleeping baby.

"When this babe dies, my entire family will be dead. There will be no point in me continuing to live."

"Your baby grandson is not dead yet, sir," Tao said. "Too many people have died. I will do everything I can to make sure he lives."

"But I can't feed him. I don't know anything about finding food and cooking. That is women's work."

"In difficult times, food is everyone's business. You can learn these skills," Tao said.

"But …"

"In Luoyang, there are many broken families. Girls learn how to hunt. Men grow vegetables. Women build houses. I used to be a novice monk. I had never prepared food in my life before I left my monastery. I've had to learn. You must too."

"The world is upside down," the old man said with a shake of his head.

He noticed the bronze bowl for the first time. "I mended that bowl. See the seam where it was broken?"

"We salvaged it from your village. We meant no offence. You can have it back."

"I have no use for it now."

Tao let the grain cook until it was mushy. He mashed a piece of the roasted taro root into the grain and added water, making a sort of soup. Kai poured some into the melon gourd. "That is for you," he said. "I will add meat to the rest. The old man needs it and so does the babe."

Tao didn't argue.

Kai took the rabbit from the fire and broke it into small pieces, adding some of the meat to the pot. He offered it to the old man who took it and was about to slurp the soup down, but Tao stopped him.

"Let it cool. You must eat a small amount at first – a mouthful of meat, a spoonful of grain." Tao knew something about starvation. Desperate villagers had come to Yinmi begging for food. And there were monks who fasted for many days. "If you eat too much, too quickly, it will make you sick. You will waste the food. And your body is frail. The shock of too much food could kill you."

The old man blew on the soup and took a sip.

The baby stirred as if woken by the smell of the food. Tao picked him up.

"He's old enough to eat other things besides his mother's milk." He curved a leaf to make a spoon, scooped up some of the grainy broth and let it trickle into the baby's mouth.

Tao and Kai spent the next two days administering small portions of food to the man and the baby, gradually increasing the amount. Tao walked with the old man in the forest, showing him where to find food, and which roots were edible. They left Kai to mind the baby, which gave the dragon a rest from shape-changing.

"Your friend doesn't have much to say," the old man said.

"That is his way," Tao replied. He didn't see any need to go into details.

After a few more days, the old man was finding food and cooking broth. The baby was starting to hold up his head and make gurgling sounds.

"Gradually, he will be able to eat more solid food," Tao said. "Make sure everything is well cooked. Chew his meat for him at first. And if you come across anyone with an animal giving milk, beg them for some. Look after yourself as well. He cannot survive without you, so you must keep healthy."

The old man's face fell. "But can't we stay with you? You have no family. We could be your family."

"No, we don't know where we are going." He glanced at Kai. "If you don't want to live a solitary life, you must find a community to live among, so that your grandson has someone to care for him, when …" The man was old. He would be lucky to see his grandson reach five years.

"Where will I go?" the old man said.

"You could take your chances in Luoyang." Tao pointed at the dark smudge of the city that was visible through the trees. "It has its dangers, but it is close. The monks at the White Horse Temple will help you until you find a home, and your skills as a smith will be welcomed."

"I would rather return to Shenchi."

"You can't. It is ruined, and the monster may still be there. Face forwards, not backwards. That is my advice."

"Heaven is angry with us because we did not care for our dead."

"They are buried in a cave. Not skilfully, but at least they are not out in the open. And I said prayers and made a commemorative carving for them. Your dead are at peace."

"Tell me where this cave is where my people are buried. I want to be with my people."

"They have all gone their separate ways into new lives."

The old man didn't seem convinced. Despite making the bell for the village temple, Tao could tell that he hadn't let go of the old beliefs.

"If you want to be with your people, then you should seek out the living, not the dead." Tao said. "Follow the other Shenchi survivors and go to the southern city. It is a long way, but you will meet travellers on the road. If you can find a party to travel with, you should be safe. If you do catch up with your people, you will have proved that you and your grandson will not be a burden to them. If not, I can give you the name of my family who have moved to the southern city. I do not know where they will be, but I feel sure that someone will know of them."

The old man nodded slowly. The baby was asleep, wrapped in his sister's jacket. "I will do it for him."

Tao was troubled by the poor state of the dead girl's cairn, which looked as if it would not withstand a strong wind.

"May I improve your granddaughter's burial cairn, sir?" Tao asked. "Could I recite a sutra for her?"

The old man didn't object. Tao collected stones to add to the grave. The old man dozed and when the baby woke, Kai amused him by shape-changing into a puppy, a bird and a butterfly. The baby laughed.

"He is watching you shape-change, but it isn't making him sick," Tao said.

"He still has the innocence of infancy," Kai said. "He has not yet learned suspicion and fear."

When Tao had enough stones, he carefully reinforced the young girl's cairn. As he worked, some stones collapsed, revealing a pale grey bone. It was so small and delicate. When he touched it, he felt a chill pass through him. It wasn't a cold night and there wasn't a breath of wind. He thought he heard someone crying, but decided it was a night bird. He recited a sutra. He seemed to be spending a lot of time tending the dead. He finished his work.

The old man woke from his doze. "Is she properly at peace now?"

"Yes. She is at peace. Her soul has departed to find a new body and a new life."

Tao and Kai walked with the old man the next day until they found the road that led south.

"Are you sure you don't want to go with him?" Kai said, as they watched the old man stride confidently into his unknown future. His baby grandson was strapped to him in a sling Tao had made from the dead granddaughter's jacket. "You could go south and join your own family."

Tao thought for a moment. "If you're not going to the dragon haven in my lifetime, then this is what I should do."

"What?"

"Help people. The people of Huaxia are in great need. The nomads mistreat them, and they don't have enough food to feed their children."

Tao was glad to have a purpose. The truth was he was just as scared of his responsibilities when they reached the dragon haven as Kai was. He had felt useful for the first time in a while. Helping people was something he knew about, something he could get better at. After seeing so many dead, he had enjoyed helping the living survive.

"What about you, Kai?"

"Our destinies are entwined. You were right; we must go to the dragon haven. I must give you the dragonkeeper's mirror."

"So you're not going to wait until you have wings?"

"We will wait, but only until spring. You cannot travel through the mountains in winter. You will die."

This time what the dragon said made sense.

"Until then, I will assist you as you help the people of Huaxia."

Tao smiled. "The world changes. Empires grow and then fade away. There is no reason why the role of a dragonkeeper should not change as well."

Kai made his happy wind-chime sound. "We will work together. This will be part of your training. People will tell stories of the dragon and the Buddhist who helped the poor."

The old man turned and waved before he disappeared around a bend in the road. Tao's blanket was rolled up and slung across the man's back.

"You will be the first Buddhist dragonkeeper," Kai said.

Tao liked the idea.

Chapter Nine
BEAST

Kai promised that they would go somewhere away from Luoyang. He found a new path and as they walked, they enjoyed the sunlight and the freedom and the lack of fear. The further they travelled from the underground caves, the more sensible it seemed not to rush off to the dragon haven immediately.

Tao felt a new sense of purpose, now that he could see the sky and they had a firm plan. The monks at Yinmi had always cared for the poor and the injured, and there was no shortage of such people who needed help in Huaxia.

"How will we find people to help?" Kai asked.

"They will cross our path, as the old man and the baby did."

They'd been walking for weeks and the man from Shenchi and his grandson were the only needy people they had come across for the entire journey. Tao decided to recite more sutras, to think more holy thoughts. Surely

Buddha would direct their steps towards those who deserved their help.

They walked all day and, after eating, Kai was snoring gently before Tao finished clearing his sleeping spot of rocks and twigs. A half-moon had risen. In its light, the trees cast shadows – looming shapes with outstretched limbs and sharp twiggy fingers. Earwigs and cockroaches were scuttling around in the leaf litter, going about their night-time business. Most people didn't like these insects, but Tao admired their industry. He noticed they avoided one particular patch of moon shadow which didn't quite match the shape of the dead tree stump that cast it. One shaft of moonlight shone right into Tao's eyes. Where Kai was sleeping, the forest canopy was denser and no moonlight found its way through. Tao got up and moved closer to the dragon, clearing away twigs and rocks for a second time. He lay down again, but he still couldn't get to sleep.

Tao shivered as they walked the next morning, even though the sun had frightened away all but a few thin strands of cloud. "It was cold last night."

"It was no colder than the night before, or the one before that," Kai said.

"You have a thick hide to keep you warm."

"You should not have given away your blanket to the old man. I said so."

"He needed it for the baby."

Tao had given the old man the gourd as well. He would have given him the bronze bowl from his village, but the gourd was lighter and served just as well as a cooking pot and a dish.

Kai was peering at the ground.

"Can you see signs of the beast again?"

"I have not seen any paw prints for some time."

"Good. I hope it's far away."

Now Tao knew that the mysterious creature was responsible for the deaths of the people of Shenchi, he didn't want to come face to face with it.

Kai had found nothing to interest him on the path, and was snuffing the breeze. "I can smell smoke."

The path, which had wound its way along flat ground for several *li*, started to slope down, soon becoming so steep someone had cut steps into it. Kai was about to start climbing down the steps when Tao grabbed his mane and held him back.

"I can hear something. It sounds like … laughter."

The dragon peered through the forest below them. He made a scraping metal sound.

"What do you see?"

Kai was pointing a talon at a clearing, not half a *li* away, partially hidden by trees. "I can see a patch of yellow, bright yellow."

"Is it a tree with yellow leaves?"

"It is brighter than leaves, brighter than flowers. It is cloth. Clothing."

Tao's heart shrivelled within him. There was only one person he knew in Huaxia who wore such a bright colour.

"It isn't Fo Tu Deng, is it?"

"It is. I can see him now."

Tao stepped off the path to hide in the undergrowth. "What is he doing?"

"He is shouting at the men, giving them orders."

The nomads' camp was on an unprotected vantage point, exposed on all sides. It had been chosen with the careless confidence of oppressors assured of their complete control over everyone and everything.

"They do not even have anyone keeping watch," Kai said.

"There was another path that led to the west a few *li* back," Tao said. "We should go that way."

Clouds were gathering again.

They retraced their steps, but before they had gone more than a few *chang*, there was a disturbance in the forest. It was the same sound that they had heard near Shenchi village – branches breaking, undergrowth being flattened, the thud of large feet. There was also an unholy screech that made Tao's insides turn to water. Below them, the nomads had also heard the noise and were picking up their weapons. Whatever was causing this disturbance was getting closer. Tao's instinct was to run, but Kai stopped him.

"Wait."

Kai shape-changed into a sapling. Tao hid behind a bush.

The weather suddenly turned bad, as it had when they were searching for the cave. An ominous cloud covered the sun. There was a rumble of thunder. The screeching cry was now coming from a different direction. The creature sounded big, but it was able to move with great speed. Then it was so close they could hear breathing between the cries. Something leaped out of the undergrowth and across the path. Tao caught a glimpse of it. It looked like a man with wild hair wearing some sort of headdress, except the creature he saw didn't have legs. The bottom half of it was a serpent's tail.

"Kai. What was that? Did you see it?" Tao began to doubt his mind. "I …"

The dragon had resumed his true shape. "I saw it."

"But it was half-human." Tao realised that he was grasping the dragon's mane like a child clinging to its mother. It wasn't very brave, but he didn't let go.

Kai pointed at a paw print on the muddy path. It was the same three-toed print that they'd seen on the other side of the mountain.

"It is the creature I have been tracking."

"That's not possible," Tao said. "The monster I saw didn't have feet. It had a serpent's tail."

This fact didn't seem to trouble Kai. "It is frightened, charging in all directions."

"If you knew you were tracking a monster, why didn't you tell me? Why didn't we go as far away from it as possible?"

"I thought I would be able to control it. I did not realise it was so dangerous until I heard the old man's story."

The dark sky was heavy with moisture. Large spots of rain dotted the path and the strengthening breeze carried the shrill voice of Fo Tu Deng shouting at his men.

"They're coming this way!" Tao yanked the dragon's mane. "We must run!"

"No. You cannot outrun the horses. We will stay here."

Kai started to shimmer, and Tao looked away. Watching the dragon shape-change still made him queasy. This time Kai took the shape of a rock beside the path.

"Hide behind me," he said.

Tao ducked behind the rock shape, still clinging to the dragon's mane. The sight of his arms disappearing into what seemed to be solid rock made him feel squeamish, but he didn't let go. Five or six horses laboured up the steep path and came to a halt right next to them. Tao was too frightened to breathe. He couldn't understand the nomads' language, but he could tell from the way they were glancing in all directions that they were as scared of the beast as he was. Fo Tu Deng must have ordered them to hunt it down, but they were reluctant to chase the monster. The monk, of course, had stayed at a safe distance. And even if the men had been keen to pursue the beast, their horses were refusing to continue along the path.

Tao saw the trees around him bend and sway as if they were being blown by a strong wind, and yet the wind had died. Then something crashed through the trees. The nomads, wide-eyed with terror, were turning their horses and about to gallop away, but their captain shouted orders and the men held their nerve. They drew their swords and bows, dug their heels into the horses' flanks and set off in pursuit of the awful creature. Tao was relieved to see their enemies disappear down the track.

The creature, still close by, let out a terrible shriek just as it started to rain heavily. Kai returned to his true shape and started off after them. Tao couldn't understand why Kai was determined to follow the nomads.

"Let them go!" Tao shouted. "Let them fight the monster."

Tao was still clutching the dragon's mane, now soaked by the rain. His whole body was protesting. His mind was telling him not to let go of the dragon, and yet his feet were refusing to shift. His sandals skidded along in the mud, until he was forced to move his feet or fall over.

Kai didn't follow the path; he strode through the trees until he reached an outcrop of rock, from which they could look down on the nomads. He took on the shape of a boulder again, the same texture and colour as the surrounding rock. Tao cowered behind him. Below, they could see the creature backed up against a cliff, surrounded by the nomads. A sudden clap of thunder made the horses rear, but they didn't bolt. Like Tao, their eyes were fixed on the monster. He had seen nothing like it, not in his worst nightmares. It hadn't been Tao's imagination. It *was* half-human. The lower half was serpentine, but the upper part was human. Its face was dark skinned and its head was covered in black matted hair. Glittering earrings hung from its ears and it had a ring through its nose. What Tao had at first thought was a headdress, he now realised was a part of the beast's living body. Seven snakes grew out of the back of the creature's neck and shoulders. These were cobras with hissing split tongues and small mesmerising eyes like shiny black pebbles. It was unnatural and terrifying, like a demon from the realms of hell. Some nomads stared in terror, others tried to turn their horses so they could escape from the awful sight. But the horses were mesmerised by the beast, their hoofs refusing to move as if they'd put down roots.

"What is it, Kai?"

The dragon didn't answer.

Though Tao's quailing heart was imploring him to run, he couldn't tear his eyes away from the monster, which was starting to shimmer. Tao was sick with fear. He couldn't bear to watch. When he looked back, instead of a demon, there was a huge seven-headed snake. Its monstrous snake body was as thick as a tree trunk and at least three *chang* long, twisting and coiling in the mud. The seven heads were held upright, their jewelled crests glittering. Each pair of eyes was full of hate and hunger. The seven snake heads opened their mouths in unison, revealing long, sharp fangs. The nomads, much closer to the monster than Tao and Kai, stood in the drenching rain transfixed by the apparition. One of them screamed and shook his head, as if trying to dislodge what he could see from his mind.

Then the monster began to change from one shape to the other in rapid succession. One moment it was the giant seven-headed snake, the next the half-human demon. A nomad raised his sword and charged with a cry almost as awful as the beast's. The creature stayed in its snake shape and the seven heads darted forwards, fangs bared. They dug deep into the man's arm and held on while the venom pumped into him. The nomad's war cry turned to a scream of pain and he fell from his horse. The horse reared up, turned and galloped away. That broke the spell the monster had on the horses. The nomads managed to control their mounts and turned their heads from the creature. Once the horses could no longer see it, they fled, galloping down the mountain.

"This is the beast that killed the villagers," Tao said. "The one we heard at Shenchi."

Tao pulled at Kai's mane. Now was the time for them to flee as well. The wet strands of the dragon's mane slipped through Tao's fingers. Kai changed into the shape of a tiger and prowled down a slope towards the creature.

"Kai, what are you doing?"

Tao was left crouching among the rocks, which were not big enough to conceal him. He was as exposed and vulnerable as a baby bird fallen from its nest. When the beast saw Kai approaching, it changed into its half-human shape. The seven cobras sprouting from its shoulders hissed and spat.

Tiger-shaped Kai stood in front of the beast, not making a sound. Tao thought he must be mesmerised, but then the dragon reared up on his hind legs and roared. The creature let out another shriek and the raindrops turned to hail. Before Tao's eyes, flaps of skin unfolded from the sides of each cobra head, opening out to reveal large white-ringed eye markings. The flaps overlapped to form a protective hood around the creature's human head. Kai stood as if offering himself as a sacrifice. The seven cobras loomed over him, each split tongue hissing, each set of fangs dripping venom. If Tao had his staff, he would have found the courage to rush down and defend Kai, or at least that's what he told himself, but it was out of reach and he was too afraid to move.

Chunks of ice the size of chicken's eggs started to fall from the sky. Tao had nowhere to shelter, but most of the hail was falling on Kai. The beast changed back to the seven-headed snake, but the dragon dodged out of reach of the venom-dripping fangs. A lump of hail, bigger than the rest, struck the dragon on the head, dazing him and opening a gash above his right eye. He staggered backwards and stumbled over the dead nomad's body. He turned back into his true shape. Tao knew why. He had felt the dragon's triumph change to fear. He couldn't stay shape-changed when he was afraid.

Kai scrambled to his feet, blood pouring from the wound and into his eyes. The beast reared back, surprised to see a dragon before him, but it recovered more quickly than Kai. It was ready to strike again before Kai had wiped the blood from his eyes. Tao had to do something. He picked up a large piece of hail and, with a yell, threw it at the creature. The hailstone didn't get anywhere near the beast, which changed into its half-human shape and lunged at Kai again. Tao found his courage. He picked up as many chunks of hail as he could carry and ran down the slope, hurling them. None hit the creature, but they distracted it and the cobra heads all turned to Tao. They glanced between Kai and Tao, unsure which attacker caused the greatest threat. There was a final crack of thunder. And the creature disappeared, as if it had winked out of existence.

The hail stopped. Tao stood still, a hunk of ice in each hand. He stared at the spot where, a moment before, there had been a vicious monster. Now there was only himself and Kai.

"I think we can be sure that your *qi* exercises have not improved your throwing," Kai said.

"How can you be so calm? Where did it go?" Tao glanced around frantically. "It might come back."

"I am sure it has gone."

Tao wiped the blood from Kai's scales with wet leaves. "You're lucky that thing didn't bite you."

Alongside them lay the body of the nomad who had been bitten by the beast.

"That's strange." Tao was examining the wound on the man's arm. "I saw the seven snake heads dig their fangs into him, but there is only one wound."

There were two puncture marks on the man's arm surrounded by purple swelling. One bite had been enough to kill him.

"The seven heads were an illusion. It has one head, the same as all creatures." Kai had pulled the red cloud herb from behind his reverse scale. "Please concentrate on my wound."

"Sorry," Tao said. He smeared the ointment on the cut above Kai's eye.

"We were lucky to escape. I hope we never see it again."

"We are going to search for it."

"Why would we want to do that?" Tao thought Kai was making a dragon joke.

"I am beginning to understand this creature. I think it is hungry."

"A hungry ghost?"

"No, a creature of the world, like you and me, but starving."

Tao realised that Kai was serious. "I don't care how hungry it is! It's responsible for the deaths of all those people – the baby's mother, his poor sister. It is merciless, an unnatural murderous beast that has no place in this world. We need to get as far away from it as possible."

"It is not unnatural."

"But you saw it! It changed from one thing to another and then it disappeared completely. It had no real body of its own."

"It is a shape-changer, like me."

Tao remembered how he'd felt sick whenever the beast took on a different form. He'd thought it was fear.

"I am sure that when it is not so hungry," Kai said, "it will be less dangerous."

"I notice you don't say 'harmless'," Tao said. "How do you know it won't kill us?"

"This is the beast I have been tracking. I learned from its dung that it eats caterpillars. I believe it has wandered from its natural habitat and cannot find the food that it normally eats. We must help it."

"But it would take a cartload of caterpillars to fill a creature that size."

"You are right. We need something larger. We must find woodworms. Lots of them."

Chapter Ten
WOODWORM

Tao was searching through rotting logs, muttering to himself. "This is not how I thought I would be spending my time when I left the monastery."

He pulled apart the crumbling log with his fingers and revealed a woodworm, the larva of a beetle that ate through the wood. It was larger than his thumb and a creamy white. Its body was divided into fat segments like beads strung together. He pulled it out of the wood and placed it in the bronze bowl, which was now full of larvae.

"I don't understand why we are trying to attract this monster," Tao said. "I'm glad it's disappeared. We should be running away from it."

"It is not a monster," Kai insisted. "It is just hungry. You will see."

"All the more reason to keep out of its way. It's killed many people."

From pools of disgorged food that he had come across, Kai had discovered that the beast had tried all sorts of *wuji*

– spiders, beetles, worms, all the creepy-crawly creatures without a backbone – but it had regurgitated most of them. Caterpillars were all the creature could digest, but they were small. Kai was hoping the bigger larvae would satisfy the beast's hunger. They had been searching for wormwood larvae for some time, but the dragon had only found three.

"Have you been eating them?" Tao said.

"No. There are not many."

"There are lots of them. Can't you hear them chewing through the wood?"

The dragon made a sound like small bells ringing. "I cannot!"

Tao didn't think this was a time for laughter.

Kai took his three larvae and put them down on a large leaf. Then he and Tao hid in the trees and waited. Nothing happened. The larvae gradually started to move. Unused to crawling, they lumbered slowly like small fat emperors.

Tao was ready to give up, but when he opened his mouth to say so, he found it stopped by a dragon paw. Kai was sniffing the air. He took his paw from Tao's mouth and pointed a talon into the forest. There was the sound of rustling leaves. Something was approaching the larvae. Something they couldn't see. Tao knew it was there because tree branches were moving, even though there was no wind. A twig snapped. Where the branches were moving, the trees looked a little smudged, as if it was part of a painting where the artist had smeared with his sleeve. Tao didn't want to come face to face with the monster. He was looking around for the best escape route, when one of the larvae started to move faster than the other two – and not along the ground. It floated up into the air and hung there unsupported. The air shimmered, as it did when Kai shape-changed. Tao knew he should turn away, but he had to know exactly where the creature was at all times. He felt his stomach churn as the creature began to materialise, and there was a bitter taste at the back of his mouth. He was expecting to see the seven-headed snake or the half-human half-serpent, but instead there in front of them was a four-footed beast covered in blue scales. It had only one head.

"It's a dragon!" Tao whispered.

Kai was entranced by the creature. "But like none I have ever seen before."

The dragon was four-legged, but smaller than Kai. It had bright blue eyes to match its scales, but its most remarkable feature was a single horn that reared up from the middle of its head. The horn was thick at the bottom and narrowed to its tip. It was more than a foot long and a creamy colour, like fresh bean curd. The horn was covered in beautiful markings in the shape of curling leaves or misshapen teardrops, as if someone had carved a pattern all over it. It was actually quite a pretty dragon. It had one paw raised and the larva was clasped between two talons. It had three toes on each paw and they were long and slender.

"You knew!" Tao said.

"I thought it was a dragon as soon as I saw its paw prints. I was sure when I saw it shape-changing."

Tao finally tore his eyes away from the blue dragon. "Why didn't you tell me?"

"I did not want to alarm you."

"I was already terrified!"

The blue dragon sniffed the larva suspiciously. It opened its mouth, revealing a row of sharp little teeth with a longer fang on either side. Tao knew they were the ones that injected the lethal venom into its victims. He thought of the old man's granddaughter and her little burial cairn.

The dragon bit into the larva. It chewed the insect cautiously and then swallowed it with a sound like a huge purring cat. Saliva dripped from its mouth. It put its head down and gobbled the other larvae.

Its blue eyes glanced around nervously, and it had excellent eyesight, just like Kai, so it saw where they were hiding. Kai made his tinkling wind-chime sound to show the dragon that he meant no harm, but it disappeared again.

"Invisibility," Kai said with admiration. "It is similar to my mirage skill, but much better." Kai could only change his scales to one colour at a time. And when he moved, the illusion was harder to maintain, so that it was still possible to see him if you knew he was there. "This dragon can paint a picture with its scales, and change them as it moves."

Now that Tao had seen the creature in its true form, he knew that Kai was right about the dragon being hungry. Although Kai was sure it wouldn't attack them if they provided it with more food, Tao couldn't forget its previous victims. Kai placed Tao's bowl of larvae in the clearing. They waited again.

"It must have gone," Tao said.

"A starving dragon would never walk away from a source of food."

After several minutes, the blue dragon reappeared and ate the rest of the larvae, grasping the bowl with its forepaws and burying its short snout in the food. It was very hungry.

"But it's a murderous beast," Tao said.

"I do not think it meant to kill the people," Kai said.

"How could it accidentally kill half a village?"

"It was searching for food. The houses in the village were very old. Every summer they were drenched by rain for months. They were all rotting. And what do you find in rotting wood?"

"Woodworm larvae," Tao said.

"It was ravenous and had finally found something it

could eat. It destroyed the houses as it searched for the larvae, crushed them and pulled them apart, without regard for the people hiding within. That is what I believe."

"I don't trust it." Tao was looking at the blue dragon's fangs. "How can you be so sure it didn't mean to harm the villagers?"

"Because it carried the dead to the cave and tried to bury them. It was repentant."

Kai moved slowly into the clearing, towards the blue dragon. Tao stayed hidden in the trees, his staff at the ready in case the creature attacked. He watched the two dragons observe each other. The blue dragon was almost half Kai's size, and more delicate. Its legs were shorter, its body thinner, but it had huge feet. Kai carried his tail low, but the blue dragon's tail was erect, like a banner. At the end of its tail the protrusions weren't sharp and spiny like Kai's, which could be used as a weapon, but soft and curly, so that it resembled a flower. The blue dragon had a long thin beard and a lovely golden mane, which ran from the base of its horn down its spine to the shoulders. The dragons circled slowly, never taking their eyes off one another. Tao held his breath, worried that the blue dragon would suddenly attack and sink its fangs into Kai, but it didn't. Instead, it lifted one of its back legs and peed on the ground. Kai did the same. Then they both sniffed each other's pee. Kai made soft wind-chime sounds. The blue dragon replied with a high-pitched hiss that sounded almost like the tweeting of a bird.

"What is it saying?" Tao asked.

"I do not know. His sounds make no sense to me."

"So it's a male dragon?"

"He is."

"Are you sure he won't turn on us?"

"I am sure," Kai said. "We must help him. There is no reason why we should only help people. In fact, it makes perfect sense that a trainee dragonkeeper helps a dragon."

Tao was still wary of the blue dragon.

"Show him you mean no harm." Tao heard Kai say in his mind.

"I think it's him who should be showing me he means no harm."

Tao felt Kai's snout nudge him, and he reluctantly stepped out into the clearing and stood at a distance. The dragon's blue eyes grew large when he saw Tao approach. And then he disappeared again.

"He is as frightened of you as you are of him. Did you notice that he shape-changes when he is most afraid? It is the opposite with me. I cannot stay shape-changed if I am fearful." Kai was fascinated by the other dragon. "If we are going to help him, he has to get used to you."

"I tamed wild creatures when I was a child – a squirrel, a snub-nosed monkey, a leopard cub. It takes patience."

Food was the answer. Tao spent hours collecting larvae. He placed a pile of them in the clearing. The blue dragon soon reappeared and ate them all. Kai stood back as Tao replenished the supply of larvae, so that the blue dragon saw he was the one who provided the food.

"It will take a long time to feed him up and win his trust," Kai said. "Many days. We need a place where we won't be disturbed by nomads."

"Somewhere that Fo Tu Deng doesn't know about," Tao added.

The tinkling wind-chime sound of a dragon pleased with himself rang out. "I know the very place!"

Chapter Eleven
HOME COOKING

"I don't know why I didn't think of it!" Tao said.

From a distance, the walled community around the Huan house looked the same as it had the last time Tao visited his family. The walls were still intact, the huge gate was still locked, but as they drew closer, the changes became obvious. There was no one working in the fields. The crops had been left to run to seed. The fruit in the orchards was rotting on the ground. And there were no guards on the walls. It was deserted.

It had taken them most of the day to reach Tao's old family home beyond the Longevity Hills west of Luoyang. Tao was still getting used to the idea that they hadn't travelled far, despite their weeks of wandering. It had been much closer than he'd realised.

They would have got there even quicker if the blue dragon wasn't with them. The problem of getting the creature to follow them was solved by braiding vines from the forest to make a rope. Tao distracted him with larvae and Kai managed to loop the rope around his neck. The blue dragon was a wild creature, he didn't like being restrained, but he could shape-change or make himself invisible all he liked, and he did, but he was still tethered by the rope. Tao had suggested tying a rope around his snout in case he tried to bite them, but Kai wouldn't allow it. He was sure that the blue dragon wouldn't turn on those who were providing him with food. The blue dragon pulled in the wrong direction, sat down, scratched at the rope and tangled it around bushes, but a steady supply of larvae had kept him moving.

Tao went up to the gate and pushed. It didn't shift. It was barred from the inside.

"I know how to get in," he said.

It was a long time since Tao had needed to sneak in and out of the walled community, but it didn't take him long to find the narrow tunnel under the wall. It had started as a rabbit burrow. When he was young, he and another boy had enlarged it, so they could get out into the fields to play and talk to the people farming the Huan lands. Tao had managed to keep it a secret from his all-seeing mother, and he had used it right up until he left home to join the monastery. The bramble bushes that hid the entrance had grown thicker since he was a child, and it took him some time to cut a way through with the help of his wolf tooth. He tore his jacket on the thorns, but eventually managed to burrow through. If he hadn't grown thin from his diet of wild food, he wouldn't have been able to fit. He wriggled through and emerged in what had once been a chicken pen.

Tao climbed over the fence and stood in a place that was very familiar and yet strange. He walked up the hill towards the house. Weeds choked the vegetable gardens. The doors of the huts where servants and farmers had lived hung open. There was no one there. Not a soul. Whenever Tao had returned from the monastery to visit his family, there were always children and chickens, pigs and puppies, and, in a little hut away from the house, his father patiently carving wood into what his mother had thought were useless objects – small statues of animals, ornate candleholders, decorative handles for spoons. This time the compound was completely quiet. There were no farm animal sounds, no children's laughter, no steady clunk of a hammer hitting a chisel.

Tao followed the wall around to the gate and tried to lift the huge bar that held it closed. He couldn't, but he didn't want to admit that to Kai. He did some of the *qi* concentrating exercises Kai had taught him, and then searched for the core of *qi* within him. It wasn't as hard to locate as before. He could feel its power. He tried again to lift the bar. He still couldn't do it. That ruled out superhuman strength as his possible *qi* power.

Then he heard Kai roar angrily. "The blue dragon has escaped. He chewed through the rope!"

Tao added finding a lost dragon to his list of problems. But before he'd come up with a solution for anything, he felt something bump him. He turned. The blue dragon was behind him. He could see his fangs. The dragon lunged forwards. Tao jumped back with a cry. But the dragon was looking for more food, trying to get his nose into Tao's bag.

"What is happening in there?" Kai said

Tao's heart was still hammering. "It's all right. He's here. He followed me."

Tao wondered how the dragon had squeezed through the tunnel. Perhaps that was another of his skills. There were only a few larvae left, but Tao had an idea for a way to put them to good use. He held one of the larvae enclosed in his fist and pointed to the bar, but the blue dragon didn't understand what Tao wanted him to do.

Tao heard Kai rumbling and complaining on the other side of the gate. "Why is it taking you so long?"

Eventually, the blue dragon understood, and using his snout he lifted the bar. Although he was weak from hunger, the dragon was far stronger than Tao. Tao opened his hand and the dragon gobbled up the larva. He went to the other end of the bar with another larva. The blue dragon nudged the bar out of its slot and snatched the larva from Tao's hand. Tao dragged the gate open wide enough to let Kai in.

"At last," Kai said, pushing the gate closed again and effortlessly lifted the bar back into place.

They walked up the hill and arrived at the gateway that led to the main house. The wooden lintel was carved with peach blossoms and characters that read "Huan Family Home". The carving was his father's work. Above the gateway was a neat little tiled roof with corners that turned up at the ends. Tao ducked through the gateway and stood in his family's private courtyard, where the still silence was even stranger. There were no shrill orders shouted by his mother, no servants scurrying to do her bidding, no singing or zither playing from Meiling's room, but it was the absence of his brother that made the place truly empty. Wei never uttered a sound, but the house and garden had always been filled with his presence. Every time Tao had returned, he'd felt it as soon as he'd walked through the gate, before he had laid eyes on his brother. Wei had been the heart of the house and the community.

Kai put the blue dragon in a goat pen.

"Shouldn't we tie him up?" Tao asked.

"The quickest way to the heart is through the stomach. We have saved him from starvation. If we can continue to provide food, he will not stray."

"But I've run out of woodworm larvae. Tie him up until we have a plentiful supply of food."

Tao was hungry too. Kai tethered the blue dragon, and

they went in search of food. The food chests, the grain sheds, the vegetable cellars were all empty. Kai made sad sounds, but Tao hadn't given up.

His family and the other occupants had taken the food stores with them when they moved south, but Tao knew his mother well. Though she was no longer the stern and bossy woman she had been before Wei's death, she had been reluctant to abandon the land that had belonged to the Huan family for many generations. In one room there was a large bed with ornate carvings and a canopy of dusty curtains.

He called to Kai. "Come and help me move this bed."

Kai used his body to push the bed aside, revealing a trapdoor. Tao pulled it open and smiled as he surveyed the contents of the cellar in the dim light. There were sacks of grain, beans and rice. He climbed down the steps to have a closer look and found jars of pickles, dried fruit, nuts and a small tin of the dried leaves of the tea plant.

"Was it a vision that told you there was food hidden here?" Kai said.

"No. Just a lifetime of knowledge of my mother. She believes that the time of the nomads will eventually come to an end and that the Huaxia will regain control, and my family will return." He smiled sadly. "I bet my mother never thought I would be the one to return."

"You miss your family."

"I only saw them twice a year, but I always knew they were here, if I needed them."

The dragon sighed.

"I did not know my parents. My mother died before I was hatched. My father flew away to the Isle of the Blest when I was less than a day old."

"But I thought Danzi died in captivity."

"He did not."

"But I was told …"

"The nursery stories you heard were not always true."

"I still have a lot to learn about dragons."

"Jujubes!" Kai's sharp eyes had spied his favourite treats in a corner.

Tao passed up the jar. Before he had a chance to object, the dragon had eaten six.

After their struggle to find every mouthful of food in the wild, suddenly they had all the food they needed. Outside in the vegetable garden there was squash growing and some green-leafed plants that had run to seed. Wrinkly pears lay beneath a tree. But the Huan house was perched on top of a hill that could be seen for many *li*. They had to be cautious.

"We can't risk lighting a fire in the daytime," Tao said.

Kai made disappointed sounds. "I was looking forward to a good cooked meal."

"You'll have to wait until it gets dark. And even then,

we must not show any light."

Tao explored his old home as they waited for nightfall. The rooms were mostly bare. His sister had left behind a few gowns and cosmetics. His father had left most of his carving tools. Tao's mother had changed after Wei's death. She became quiet and introspective. Mr Huan took over management of the compound and had no time for carving.

There was one room in the house that was as it had been when the Huan family lived there, and that was Wei's. Their mother had insisted that it be left as it was when Wei died. His bed was covered with an embroidered quilt, there were paintings of animals and trees on the walls and, on a shelf, a row of things Tao had brought back for his brother from his walks beyond the walls – a bright blue bird's egg, a pile of coloured river stones, a cast-off snakeskin. Their mother didn't like having these things cluttering up the house, but though he couldn't speak, Wei had a way of letting people know what he wanted. Tao's childhood gifts to his brother had stayed where Wei could see them.

As soon as it got dark, Tao closed the kitchen shutters to contain the light from a single lamp. He lit the stove and prepared a meal. When he'd finished, he let the fire die down and blew out the lamp.

Tao's cooking skills were limited, but he was able to produce a tasty dish of rice and vegetables. After so long eating with his fingers from a burnt gourd, Tao took delight in eating from a green-glazed china bowl with chopsticks his father had carved. His simple meal seemed like a feast. Kai sat up on his haunches, holding a bowl in one paw and chopsticks in the other and made appreciative sounds as he ate. Tao smiled. Ping had taught him good table manners. The blue dragon, however, wouldn't touch the food. He finished off the last of the larvae and then made a sad sound like a gate creaking. He was still hungry. There was no rotting wood in the Huan compound, no source of more larvae.

"I don't know why he's so fussy," Tao said. "You wouldn't eat rice and cooked vegetables if you were living in the wild, but you'll eat it now, even if it's not entirely to your taste."

"He is a very wild beast."

"If I was starving, I would eat anything, I'm sure."

"Including the flesh of animals?"

Tao didn't know the answer to that.

"Where are the jujubes?" Tao asked. "Perhaps the blue dragon will like them too."

Kai hung his head.

"You didn't eat them all, did you?"

Kai nodded. "Tasted very good."

After the meal, Tao had to settle the dragons for the night. Kai dug himself a hollow in the goat pen and filled it with straw from the stable.

"I can guard you better if I sleep out here," he said.

The blue dragon didn't dig a nest. He made his sad creaking sound again.

"Perhaps you could dig a hollow for him as well," Tao suggested.

"He would dig his own if he wanted one. He must sleep some other way."

Kai fetched more straw for the unhappy dragon and he eventually settled down.

Tao had decided to sleep in Wei's room. Thick cloud blotted out the stars and the moon, so he allowed himself a small oil lamp. He shook out the dusty quilt, turned over the silk floss-filled mattress and collapsed on his brother's bed with a sigh of relief. It had been his childhood bed too. Now it seemed like imperial luxury, compared to where he'd slept in recent months.

In the soft yellow light of the lamp, Tao could just make out a large spider in the corner above the bed. It was a huntsman and would have been the size of Tao's hand, if it hadn't had its legs tucked neatly together, four on each side. For as long as he could remember there had always been a huntsman above the bed. When he and his brother were small, they had lain there, watching one of the spiders as it shed its old skin and emerged with a bigger body to show to the world. When their mother had brushed it down with a broom, tears had poured from Wei's eyes. Tao had stopped his mother from squashing the spider, and Wei had stopped crying. Their mother couldn't bear to see Wei cry, so she had allowed the spider and its descendants to live.

The huntsman crept down the wall and settled itself on the headrest. Tao could see now that it had an egg sac. He was glad of the spider's companionship. It seemed like a lifetime ago, but it had only been two or three months since he had last lain alongside his brother in that very bed, trying to decide how his life should unfold. He knew that the spiders lived for a year or two, so this spider could well have been the same one that had looked down on them that night. The smell of his brother still lingered on the quilt – sesame oil and ginger and the faintest hint of Wei's skin. He was glad that there was no moon that night – and no moon shadows.

Tao rose early. He'd slept well, better than any other night since he'd left Yinmi Monastery. The truth was, he felt safe behind the walls of his family home. Both dragons were still sleeping. He didn't want to waste this peaceful time when there was no need to rush off anywhere or to hide from enemies, always glancing over his shoulder. Having time to himself was a luxury. He meditated on the words of Buddha. In the dawn light he did more *qi* concentrating exercises. He could feel Wei's *qi* within him. It was already strong, he knew that, but it was still trapped inside him. What he needed to do was learn how to control it and use it for good. Kai had described how other dragonkeepers made their *qi* flow out through their fingertips or feet, in the form of bolts of energy that moved objects or lifted the keepers off their feet. These bolts could kill people.

Did he want a skill like those other dragonkeepers? Or would he find another sort of power that was more suited to a Buddhist? Perhaps that was his problem. Most of the *qi* power that Kai had mentioned had the capacity to harm people. Other dragonkeepers, even Ping, had been willing to kill to protect their dragons. Tao's Buddhist training wouldn't allow him to use his *qi* in any way that could prove lethal. He was worried that, despite having a great quantity of *qi*, he would never be able to convert it into any sort of useful power.

The morning passed peacefully enough. Tao walked around the gardens, collecting fruit and vegetables, though they were wrinkled and past their prime. He discovered food that lay hidden beneath the earth – turnips, onions, ginger root. He hadn't known such freedom from duty since his childhood. But he did have to find something that the blue dragon would eat. He selected a variety of things for him to try – dried fish, nuts, pickled eggs. The blue dragon hungrily sniffed everything Tao offered him, but he wouldn't eat any of it. Whatever Tao tried to do, the creature was always at his heels, making plaintive noises.

In the afternoon, while the blue dragon had a nap, Tao swept the peony pavilion where Wei had spent so much time. It had been built with three sides open so that anyone sitting in it could enjoy the surrounding garden. He dusted the couch and swept the path made from coloured pebbles, but he couldn't bring himself to brush away the spider webs that festooned the eaves. Wei had enjoyed lying on his couch and watching the *wuji* – butterflies on the flowers, slaters and worms when the gardener turned the soil, ants marching across the ceiling. He'd also liked watching creatures that repulsed most people – spiders, cockroaches, millipedes.

Although it filled him with guilt, Tao collected some of the insects. If they were its natural food, it was not for him to interfere in the ways of the world. Tao offered them to the blue dragon when he woke, but he wouldn't eat them. Tao set them free again, relieved that they had been spared, but worried about how he would find something the hungry dragon would eat.

"We have to teach him to communicate with us," Tao said that evening as he cooked every combination of grain and vegetables he could think of.

"I have tried to make the blue dragon comprehend me, but though he may guess my meaning, he cannot understand my sounds," Kai said.

And when the blue dragon made his tweeting sounds, they meant nothing to Kai either.

"It is a waste of time," Kai said.

"But he's quick to learn. I'm sure eventually he'll be able to understand my words and your sounds."

"Maybe so, but that will take a long time. You have spent all day trying to get him to eat." Kai's stomach rumbled so loud that the blue dragon pricked up his ears. "Perhaps now you could prepare something for you and I to eat."

Tao was quite proud of his cooking skills. He would make the vegetables he'd cooked for the blue dragon tastier by adding ginger, and improve the flavour of the rice with spices. Since he had a stove, he decided to be more adventurous and attempt to make steamed buns. He'd watched the process many times when he was a child, and even helped the servants knead the dough. But cooking was more difficult than he'd ever realised. Keeping an eye on the buns, the rice and the vegetable dish all at the same time was impossible. He was about to call to Kai to come and help him when he heard footsteps behind him.

"Can you pass me the ginger, please?"

A hand reached out and passed him a piece of ginger root.

"Thank you."

It wasn't until he had chopped it up and stirred it into his vegetable stew that he realised the ginger had been passed to him not with a paw, but with a hand. He spun round, brandishing the chopping knife. A dark figure was standing in front of him, a sword in hand, dressed from head to toe in black cloth so that only a pair of eyes was visible.

"If I was your worst enemy and I had murdered your family, you wouldn't use that," the intruder said.

Tao dropped the knife, stepped back and knocked over a pot of cooked grain. He knew that voice well. Its owner shouldn't have been standing in the Huan kitchen dressed in such an outlandish way. But the blue eyes confirmed it. Tao's mouth hung open while his brain sorted through the possibilities. Was it a vision? A ghost? A figment of his imagination?

Kai came into the kitchen, making rumbling dragon noises that translated into complaints about how hungry he was. He stopped in the doorway. His rumbling was replaced with the sound of wind chimes. The blue dragon was close behind him, but as soon as he caught sight of the stranger, he disappeared.

Tao knew then that the figure in front of him wasn't a stranger at all.

"Pema," he said.

He couldn't think of another word to say.

Chapter Twelve
SWEETNESS

Tao watched Pema unwind the length of black cloth that covered her head and face. It gave off a faint smell of incense. And then revealed her smile. He knew he was staring, but he didn't care. Her hair was in an untidy knot on the top of her head, like a boy, but not even the scar on her cheek could detract from her lovely face.

"Whatever that is you're cooking, it smells very good," she said.

Tao filled bowls with food, and Pema and Kai followed him outside to the peony pavilion. The blue dragon suddenly materialised in front of them. Pema squealed.

"It's all right," Tao said. "He's harmless. Most of the time."

Pema kept her eyes on the blue dragon. "Where did it come from?"

Tao smiled. "He was here all the time. He can make himself invisible. He was frightened of you when he first saw you."

"He was frightened! So was I."

Tao handed her a bowl of grain and vegetables. He offered some to the blue dragon, though he knew it was a waste of time. The creature made a mournful creaking sound.

"He's hungry, but we can't find anything he likes to eat, apart from caterpillars and larvae."

Kai had spent several hours collecting grubs for him, but the blue dragon wolfed them down in the time that it took Tao to raise his chopsticks to his mouth. They weren't enough to fill him up. Tao offered him different *wuji*. Snails were acceptable and so were worms, though from the noise he made, he didn't like their taste.

"Can't Kai ask him what he wants to eat?" Pema said.

"No. Kai can't understand him either."

"Every time I see you, you've got a new dragon that you can't communicate with!" Pema said, through a mouthful of ginger-flavoured vegetables.

"What are you doing here?" Tao asked.

"Things didn't work out as I expected," Pema said. That was all she had to say on the subject.

They were all enjoying the food, except for the blue dragon, who refused to try it.

Pema, on the other hand, ate three bowls of grain and vegetables, as well as four steamed buns, even though they were a bit tough.

Tao was eager to hear what had happened to her since they parted company.

"Why aren't you in Chengdu as you planned? And why are you wearing trousers?"

Pema was a member of the Di tribe. There were many Di people living in Chengdu, and though she had no living family members, she had gone to live among her own people. After she had scraped her bowl clean with her last piece of bun, and then eaten a handful of nuts and some dried persimmons, she finally began to tell them her story.

"I reached Chang'an with the family I was travelling with, but the only people travelling on to Chengdu were merchants who weren't interested in having a girl tagging along. I tried travelling alone. It didn't work out well. I had nothing of value, but I lost count of how many times I was robbed. I didn't get halfway. In the end, I decided to go back to Chang'an."

"So what brings you here? How did you know where we were?"

"I didn't know. I've used this place as a hide-out from time to time since I returned."

Pema explained how she had found a place in the wall where there were footholds and climbed over.

"But I saw no sign of anyone else being here," he said.

Pema smiled. "I am more cautious than you. I didn't set myself up in the middle of the main courtyard. I sleep in one of the farm workers' huts and hide my sleeping mat whenever I leave."

Tao was pleased that she'd chosen his family home as a refuge.

"You were careful not to show a light or cook during the day," Pema said, "but I knew someone was here. I could smell the smoke from your stove on the wind. And when I got closer, the food smelled delicious. Then I heard Kai's cracked-bell sound, and I knew it had to be you two."

Tao wanted to know more about what she'd been doing, but she was more interested in the blue dragon which was nuzzling her hands, in the hope that she might have something edible hidden there.

"Be careful. He's wild."

She giggled. "His breath is cool. It tickles."

Tao smiled. It was a pleasure to hear her laughter.

Her blue eyes stared at him. Tao felt his cheeks start to burn.

"I know you disapprove, Tao, but I'm not the only one who's changed their plans since we last saw each other. You aren't wearing monk's robes, you are eating after midday – and you have some hair."

Tao ran his fingers through his hair, which was now more than two inches long.

"You aren't a novice monk any more."

"No."

"So why did you leave your monastery? Did nomads attack it?"

"No. When I got back, Fo Tu Deng was there. I thought he was going to take control. And I felt my destiny was with Kai."

"I heard that Fo Tu Deng was working for Jilong," Pema said.

"Heard?" Tao said. "From who?"

"I use the skills I perfected when I was living in Luoyang. There is no need to ask questions. I wander quietly among people and listen."

"You've been back to Luoyang?"

"Of course. How else would I get news? I could sit by the roadside out on the plain and hope someone would pass every week or two, I suppose, but Luoyang is the best place to get news – people gossip, traders come from afar, and there are nomads living there, some loyal to the Zhao, some to the other tribes."

Pema changed the subject.

"Now you must tell me what has happened to you since I last saw you. How did you come by *this* dragon?"

Tao sighed. "It's a long story."

Pema smiled at him. "Good. I haven't had any entertainment for a long while."

He recounted their journey since leaving the monastery, and Pema listened closely.

"Your adventures are better than any tale I've heard from travelling storytellers. None of them contained ghosts, invisible dragons and giant seven-headed snakes!"

Kai made a tinkling sound.

"It isn't a tale. It's … my life," Tao said. "I don't do these things so that I can have stories to entertain people with afterwards."

Pema patted the blue dragon and tickled him under the chin.

Tao wanted to ask her advice, what she thought of his plan to help people, if she considered he'd make a good dragonkeeper, but she kept quizzing him.

"Are you going to stay here? What will you and Kai do?"

He wished he had answers to those questions.

"I need time to think, and decide exactly what I am doing." Tao glanced at Kai. "What we are doing."

Pema studied the blue dragon, who had given up looking for more food and, with a long sigh, curled up next to the stove.

"He's very different to you, Kai," she said. "He must be a different type of dragon, just as there are different species of birds. That's why you can't communicate with him."

The blue dragon moved closer and closer to the stove, until he was almost lying in the ashes.

Different emotions were bouncing around inside Tao.

He was glad to see Pema, very glad, but he was annoyed that she had not done as she'd promised when they had parted and gone to live somewhere that was safe. He had told her everything that had happened to him, but she had said very little about her own adventures. She hadn't really explained how she came to be in the Huan compound, or why she was dressed the way she was. He was about to ask more questions, but Pema yawned.

"I'm tired. I need to sleep."

She said goodnight and went to whichever hut it was that she had chosen as her sleeping quarters. Tao was disappointed. He'd been looking forward to talking to Pema into the night. He wanted to know every detail of what had happened to her since they said goodbye, but he found it difficult to tell her what had happened to him. Recounting it all made him feel like he'd failed at everything. For the first time since he was seven, his life had no real purpose.

Kai settled down in the goat pen, and the blue dragon trailed after him like a lost child.

Tao wasn't in the least tired. He lay on Wei's bed, staring at the ceiling. It was covered in dark spots, hundreds of them, as if there had been a sudden attack of mould. He peered at them and realised what they were – baby huntsman spiders, each no bigger than an ant. The mother spider sat in her customary corner, keeping an eye, several eyes probably, on her brood. Tao was glad to have their company.

They didn't, however, help him get to sleep. He was wide awake. A shaft of moonlight shone through the window. It cast a moon shadow on the other side of the room, a replica of one of the rocks in the garden outside. The rock was irregular, tall and chosen by his mother for its craggy shape, so that it resembled a miniature mountain. As the moon made its way slowly across the night sky, the shadow moved across the floor towards him. Its edges began to ripple. Tao watched, unable to drag his eyes away as the shadow gradually changed shape, fraying around the edges. Tendrils lengthened and streamed out like ragged shreds of torn grey silk, until the shadow bore no resemblance to the rock that cast it.

Tao leaped out of bed, grabbed the quilt and ran outside. He didn't want to be alone. He wished he could wake Kai, but how could he explain his fear of shadows? He lay on the couch in the peony pavilion and pulled the quilt over him. The moon went behind a cloud, but there would be no sleep for Tao that night.

Tao was up well before the others. In the daylight, the events of the previous night seemed no more frightening than childish bad dreams. Turning his thoughts to breakfast, he crawled through his tunnel under the wall and walked through a field where grain once grew, towards the orchard. All he could find were some fallen apples, partly rotten, half-eaten by grubs. He picked up some of the fruit anyway, thinking that there was a chance the blue dragon might eat it as it was full of grubs.

As he walked back towards the walled compound, he heard buzzing. He followed the sound, which led him to a pomegranate tree. Bees were zooming in and out of a hollow in the trunk. When Tao was a child, his father had kept bees. Tao loved honey and enjoyed helping him collect it from the hives. He had spent hours watching the bees industriously going about their business. He had stood up close to the hive, still and silent, and they had taken no more notice of him than a fence post. He had marvelled at the way bees worked and worked until they died, all for the sake of their hive. The only time they became angry was when his father took away their honey. That was understandable. To prevent the bees from stinging him, his father had worn thick trousers tied at the ankles, goat-skin gloves and a hood fitted with a see-through mask of gauzy silk.

The smell of the honey was making Tao's mouth water. It would be a good addition to their food store. Tao stood as still as a stone and watched the bees returning to the hollow, their legs fat and yellow with the pollen they had collected. But the bees leaving the hive didn't ignore him. They didn't fly off into the trees in search of pollen and nectar. Instead, they came to him. He sensed they meant him no harm. The bees swarmed in front of him. One at a time they made their way back to the hollow, forming a long line. Tao was sure they were leading him to their hive. He followed the column of bees. He had no protection, but when he got to the hollow, he reached inside. He could feel the waxy honeycomb under his fingertips. This was the sort of thing that normally made the placid bees furious.

Tao had been stung several times by angry bees when he'd leaned too close while his father was stealing the honey. He knew how painful a bee sting was. Yet without any fear, he broke off a piece of the honeycomb and withdrew his hand. The honeycomb was sealed with wax, so Tao knew that it was full of honey. The bees flew off again and resumed their work. Tao stood with the honeycomb in his hand. The bees had allowed him to take their honey. They had given him a gift.

Back at the house, Kai was awake, but the blue dragon wouldn't get up.

"He is weak from hunger," Kai said.

Tao cut up the apples and gave them to the blue dragon, who pulled out the grubs and ate them, but wouldn't eat the fruit. The grubs weren't much of a meal and he was still hungry.

"That's all I've got, I'm afraid."

Tao carefully sliced the layer of sealing wax off the top

of the honeycomb with his father's knife. The clever bees had made a mass of hexagonal cells from their wax, and each one was full of honey. The cells were where the queen bee laid her eggs, and the honey fed them as they turned into larvae and then into baby bees.

Pema, dressed in black again, came to watch as Tao up-ended the honeycomb and let the honey drip into a bowl. He didn't stop her when she dipped her finger in.

"I have never eaten this before," she said as she licked her finger. "It is the most delicious thing I have ever tasted."

Tao agreed with her. He remembered how sad he and Wei had been when their mother had made their father sell the hives after she was stung.

He cut away the rotten and eaten parts of the apples and put the rest on a platter with nuts and dried persimmons. Tao felt guilty that he had food to eat while the blue dragon sat there whimpering.

"There won't be any caterpillars in winter. I'm beginning to think that we'll have to watch him die of hunger before our eyes."

"Perhaps not," Pema said.

She pointed at the blue dragon, who had found the honeycomb. As he chewed it, he drooled and made a purring sound.

"I think you have discovered something he likes to eat."

Tao mixed a spoonful of honey into a bowl of cooked grain and the hungry dragon ate every morsel. He ate another bowlful of grain and honey with the remaining apples chopped into it. The blue dragon had a sweet tooth.

The food had an immediate effect on the dragon. He was suddenly full of energy. They watched the transformed blue dragon as he ran around the peony pavilion six times, jumped over the pond and climbed a tree. He played a game where he made himself invisible and then reappeared in unexpected places. Then he went back for more food, belched, lay down and went to sleep.

"That was entertaining," Pema said.

Tao was glad that he didn't have to worry about the blue dragon any more.

They sat in the morning sun. Pema yawned, though she had told Tao she had slept well.

"Tell me again about the ghosts in the underworld," she said.

She was intrigued by this part of their story. Tao didn't like to recall those terrifying events, but he recounted it again.

"You never saw anything when you were in the underground cavern?" Pema asked.

"No, it was pitch black most of the time. We didn't see the ghosts, we felt them. They were cold and their icy fingers poked and prodded me."

Pema pondered this information. "I don't think there were any ghosts."

"You weren't there!"

"Which is why I can look at it more realistically. I have spent a lot of my life underground, but I would have been terrified if I was in darkness like that."

Tao didn't say anything.

"So what is Pema's theory?" Kai asked.

Pema couldn't understand the dragon like Tao, but she had learned to interpret the mood of each different sound, and to guess his meaning.

"I think it was him in the cave. He was following you."

"The blue dragon?" Tao said.

"Yes. He has long, thin bony toes, like fingers, and his talons are sharp. His breath is cold. And he can make himself invisible."

Kai made a slow clinking sound like someone striking a bowl with a spoon. It was the sound he made when he was thinking hard.

"That makes sense," he said. "It would explain why I found his tracks on both sides of the mountain."

"But you said you were tracking him." Tao didn't want to be proved wrong. "How could you have been tracking something that was following you?"

Kai looked at the snoozing blue dragon. "He is clever. Much more clever than I thought. He must have made himself invisible, so he could occasionally make a few paw prints ahead of us on the path."

"You think I'm right, don't you?" Pema said to Kai.

Kai nodded. The blue dragon was snoring contentedly. He was the one who could confirm Pema's theory, but none of them could communicate with him.

Tao wasn't ready to concede.

"But the ghosts left us a gift. The cinnabar."

"I have been thinking about that," Kai said. "That pile of 'treasure' in the cave did resemble a dragon's hoard."

"So you think the cinnabar belonged to him?"

"It is the sort of glittery mineral that dragons admire."

"But you believed that the ghost of Gu Hong was haunting you."

"I did, but when I was finding food for the old man and the baby, I wondered why I kept finding piles of half-eaten insects that some creature had regurgitated."

"You suspected the monster was following us, even then?"

Kai was unwilling to admit that he had been wrong about his ghost.

"But why would he follow us?" Tao asked.

"It makes perfect sense," Pema said. "He was following another dragon, his only hope of finding food."

"But he pushed me down into the *Puqingshuo*."

"Perhaps he didn't." Pema was pleased with her powers

of deduction. "Perhaps he was trying to show you the way out. Perhaps he was prodding you so you would go in the right direction."

Tao and Kai looked at each other, both feeling foolish for believing in ghosts.

"There were no ghosts!" Pema announced.

Chapter Thirteen
DRAGON FOOD

Tao spent the rest of the morning digging the vegetable gardens and planting seeds. He carefully set aside any worms or slaters he came across, so they weren't injured by his spade.

"Unless you're going to stay here, you're wasting your time."

Pema had come up behind him, unheard, as she had a habit of doing.

"Wei loved being out here, enjoying the garden. It gives me pleasure to return it to how it was when he was here. And anyway, Kai and I have a plan."

He told her about his plan to help the people of Huaxia.

"This compound would be a good place to live. Kai and I could go out into the countryside, find people in need and bring them back to safety behind these walls."

The more he thought about it, the more Tao realised he wasn't quite ready to leave humanity behind and go to the dragon haven. He wondered if he could enlist Pema to be part of their plan. If she were involved, the scheme would be perfect. She could use her skills as a spy to listen for news of people in need. But he couldn't find the courage to ask her.

"Your new friend is undoing all your work."

Pema pointed. The blue dragon had dug up the seeds that Tao had just planted. He was playing with the worms that Tao had saved.

"Don't do that!" Tao clapped his hands to shoo the dragon away.

The dragon slunk off, his usually erect tail hanging like a wilted chrysanthemum.

Tao had found that the blue dragon would eat almost anything if it was mixed with honey. He wasn't sure how the creature fitted into his plans, but he was confident that its arrival would prove to be useful. The Huan compound would be their secret hide-out, a place to rest and plan, a place to grow food, so that he could distribute it to those who needed it most.

Tao had cleaned the house, tended the vegetable garden, recited many sutras, but there were still several hours until it got dark. It was pleasant sitting in the garden in the autumn sunlight, but he couldn't possibly do that all afternoon. Pema had sat with him for a while, but she had dozed off. He spent some time doing his *qi* exercises.

Then he placed a pear on a wall and tried to get the *qi* to shoot out of his fingertips and knock it off. As usual, he was unsuccessful.

He went to the small hut that his father had used as a workshop. His carving tools were hanging neatly from hooks. When Tao was young, his father had taught him how to carve simple things. He tried to think of something he could carve now. He didn't need a spoon or a bowl, there were enough of them left around the house. Then he realised he had the perfect project in his hand. His simple staff had once been a Zhao lance and it had served him well since he commandeered it, but the wood at the top was split and broken. Tao decided he would saw off the broken top and carve a new one, something decorative.

Half of the workshop was taken up with bits of wood of all shapes and sizes that Mr Huan had collected. He'd picked up fallen branches as he walked in the nearby countryside. Whenever the trees were being trimmed, he would sort through the prunings. If a chair or a bed broke and it couldn't be fixed, he salvaged any wood he thought might be useful. There was one piece in particular that caught Tao's eye. It was a tree branch with a sudden bend, like an elbow. Tao recognised the dark gnarled bark. He knew that it had come from an old cherry tree that used to grow in the courtyard.

One of his ancestors had planted the tree a thousand

years ago, on the hill where the Huan house now stood, or so Tao's father had told him. The tree's branches had been gnarled and bent this way and that, like an old man's limbs. They were so thick and heavy that they were supported by props, preventing the branches from breaking under their own weight. It had been the home of birds and small animals, and many *wuji*. Tao had tried to climb the tree when he was small, reaching a branch almost ten *chang* above the ground. Tao remembered Wei's delight. But their mother had shrieked with horror when she saw Tao up in the branches, making him slip and almost fall. One of the servants had to climb up and get him down. After that, Tao was forbidden to climb any trees. He had vowed that, when he was a little older, he would practise climbing the tree when his mother was away, but he never did.

Despite this memory, Tao had always loved the tree. So had Wei. In winter, its crusty trunk and dark branches had loomed over the courtyard, but Tao had never been afraid of it. In spring, the tree's branches were covered with pink blossoms and in summer it bore sweet cherries. One night during a storm a branch had blown down and fallen on the chrysanthemum bed near the peony pavilion. Though Wei loved the tree, their mother had decided that it was too dangerous and insisted it be chopped down. Wei and Tao were only six at the time, and they had both cried when their father felled the tree.

With the cherry tree gone, there was a large bare area left in front of the peony pavilion. Mrs Huan had decided to design a garden especially for Wei.

"He'll like this," she said as the gardeners worked on it. "It'll be like a corner of the imperial garden in the painting in my room."

The new garden had clumps of bamboo and chrysanthemums. It also had tall slender rocks that narrowed at the top and were arranged so that they resembled a mountain range seen from a distance. To replace the old tree, a small weeping cherry tree was planted. It had inedible fruit no one picked and that got squashed on the path. Every winter, it was pruned back so that it didn't grow tall enough to climb and never spoiled the symmetry of the garden design. Wei had enjoyed seeing the flowers change with the seasons, but Tao suspected he'd never liked the garden as much as he'd liked the old tree that was always so full of life.

Mr Huan had kept all the wood from the tree and made handsome pieces of furniture from its lovely reddish wood. The family had taken the furniture to the south. This branch, too small and crooked to be turned into anything useful, was all that remained. As soon as Tao saw it, he realised that a carving was already embedded in the piece of wood. He hadn't carved anything since he'd become a novice, but he had his father's tools. He started carving the wood immediately. In a few minutes it began to take the shape he had seen within it – a dragon's head. The elbow of the wood was the top of the dragon's head and there were two lumps that he would turn into ears. One angle of the branch formed the neck, the other the dragon's jaws.

Tao spent the rest of the afternoon shaping the ears and a wavy mane.

Kai appeared in the doorway. He had been hunting in the fields. Tao didn't want to know what was in the bag that contained his catch.

"That is very good," Kai said. "I did not know you could carve."

"It's to go on top of my staff. I don't know what to do about the horns though. This piece of wood isn't big enough to carve long branched horns like yours. I could carve them separately and fix them onto the head, but they'd break off."

"It does not need horns. It can be a young dragon, less than five hundred years old."

Kai had come up with his own way of passing the time.

"You must not eat meat. I understand that," he said. "But dragons need meat. I would like to cook my own food tonight. A meat dish if you will permit it."

Tao didn't object. "I'm sure Pema and the blue dragon will also enjoy a meat dish. I can make something for myself."

It was dusk. Kai disappeared into the kitchen to start preparing his meal. Tao sat on Wei's couch in the peony pavilion. He'd worked hard in the garden and on his carving, but he still felt a little guilty having time to relax.

The pavilion was open on three sides and the couch had been placed facing west so that Wei could watch the sunset. The drift of clouds turned different shades of pink. The warmth of the day faded with the light. Pema came and sat next to Tao, and they watched the sky like scholars studying a painting. Except that this work of art was changing as the cloud shapes altered, and the pink deepened and turned purple.

Large moths were fluttering around them. Or around Tao at least. He held up his arm to shield the bright rays of the setting sun from his eyes. His sleeve slid back and some of the moths settled on his bare arm. They were large moths. They opened their wings, which were almost a handspan wide, coloured in soft dusty brown shades and marked with purple eyes that matched the colour of the sunset. Tao liked their furry bodies and their many branched antennae, which looked like tiny leaf skeletons. They would make a reasonable snack for the blue dragon, but Tao couldn't bring himself to catch them. He stood up and raised his left hand so that his other sleeve slipped back. More moths settled on that arm and on his head. Pema and the blue dragon watched in amazement as if he was a street performer. As the orange disc of the sun finally slipped below the horizon, the moths all took off together and circled around Tao's head in the deepening orangish light. Tao muttered a fragment of a Sanskrit sutra and the moths flew off.

As Tao spoke the last line of the sutra, the blue dragon was suddenly alert and made his hissing tweets, interspersed with pretty melodic sounds, like notes from a flute.

"I think he's trying to speak to you," Pema said.

"What do you mean?"

"He understood what you were saying in the language of Buddha. He's trying to communicate with you."

The blue dragon continued to chatter away.

Kai had been watching from the kitchen door. "I believe Pema is right."

Tao was still bathed in the glow of the sunset and the pleasure he had felt when the moths settled on him. It took him a moment to understand what they were saying.

"You think he understands Sanskrit?"

"Yes," Pema said. "Say something else."

Tao was suddenly flustered. "I learned Sanskrit so that I could read it, so that I could translate sutras. My teacher didn't converse with me in Sanskrit. I can't speak it."

"But you *can* speak it. You just did."

"I recited part of a sutra I had memorised."

"So you know some words. Say something."

Tao had only ever thought of Sanskrit as a language for communication with the Blessed One, not for chatting to dragons. He had learned strings of words that someone else had composed. And they were all about the stories of Buddha. Tao searched his memory for some words that would be suitable to say to a dragon.

"The sun has travelled to the end of the endless sky, the fruits of the trees await us. Will you eat?"

The dragon's blue eyes grew wide as rice bowls. He made more flute sounds and ran over to the kitchen door.

"He does understand you!" Pema said. "What did you say?"

"I asked him if he was hungry."

Kai stopped him from entering. "It is not ready yet."

The blue dragon made a mournful sound.

Kai didn't need much help in the kitchen. Two of the talons on each of his forepaws worked like a human finger and thumb, so when he sat on his haunches he could hold a spoon to stir a pot, and he could use a knife to chop things, though he held it high and let it fall like an axe. He did need some help to lift pots on and off the stove, but Pema was willing to assist with that and Tao could stay out of the kitchen.

"I think the blue dragon must be a *naga* from Tianzhu," Tao said. He and Pema were waiting for Kai to finish his cooking.

"I didn't know there are dragons in Tianzhu."

"They are creatures in the stories of Buddha," Tao replied. "They don't look like dragons. They are sometimes described as half-snake, half-human, sometimes as seven-headed snakes. I should have realised before! That is what the blue dragon transforms into when he shape-changes. In the Buddha stories, the *nagas* must have always been shape-changed. When the texts were translated into the language of Huaxia, *naga* was written as dragon."

"So someone must have known that *nagas* were dragons."

"Yes. One of the monks who brought the stories to Huaxia long ago. Perhaps one of those who founded the White Horse Temple in Luoyang."

Using his few words of Sanskrit to communicate with the blue dragon, Tao discovered that he was indeed a *naga*. He had lived with many other *nagas* in a huge forest that had been home for so long his ancestors had sat at the foot of Buddha. In this forest, it rained often and the trees grew tall. Discovering these three facts took more than an hour of stumbling Sanskrit and guesswork. Tao tried to find out if the *naga* had a name, but he couldn't make the blue dragon understand what he meant.

"I will give you a name. There are many *nagas* in the sutras." He tried to remember their names. "Pandaraka. Samkhapala. Mucalinda."

"Those names are too hard to pronounce," Pema said.

"Give him a simple name. What is Sanskrit for blue?"

That was a word that Tao did know. "Sunila."

"That's a good name," Pema said.

Tao patted the *naga* on the head. "Sunila. That's what we will call you."

The blue dragon was unaware that he had a new name. He was more interested in the strange smells emanating from the kitchen.

"Kai's been in there a long time," Pema said.

When Kai eventually emerged, Tao told him that he thought the blue dragon was a *naga*. Also that they had given him a name.

"I think Sunila is an excellent name."

"Is your meal ready?" Pema asked.

"It is."

Kai carried out three bowls of food on a tray and proudly sat them on a low table. Tao lit a small oil lamp. Pema and Tao stared at the food. Tao moved the lamp closer to the bowls.

"There are three courses," Kai explained.

"What are they?"

Kai pointed to one of the bowls. Tao peered at the watery grey liquid with feathers floating on top.

"Firstly, sparrow broth."

Kai picked up the bowl and drank some of the soup. "Very tasty," he said. "I first had this at an imperial palace in the presence of an emperor."

Then he pointed to the second bowl. "This is the main course. I created the recipe myself – baked field mice with worm sauce."

Tao could see the mouse tails and ears. Kai hadn't bothered to skin them.

"And finally, fried cicadas."

Kai stood back and waited for Tao and Pema to admire his creations. When they just stared, Kai pushed a bowl of sparrow broth towards Sunila. The *naga* sniffed it suspiciously, as if it might be poisoned. He wouldn't eat it. Kai offered him some of the main course. Sunila licked the worm sauce off the mice. He ate one fried cicada and then spat it out.

Mist streamed from Kai's nostrils. "This is good dragon food," he said, though Tao was sure that wild dragons didn't cook. "I do not understand why he does not like it."

Tao fetched a jar of honey and spooned a little over the mice and mixed some into the remaining sparrow broth. Sunila made a chirruping sound and buried his snout in the bowls, eating everything.

"It is a great shame that you cannot eat any of this food, Tao, because you do not eat the flesh of animals," said Kai.

He was about to fill Pema's bowl, but she stopped him.

"Thanks," she said. "I'm sure it's very tasty, but I'll leave it for you two dragons."

Tao went into the kitchen to cook some vegetables.

Sunila was pushing the bowls around the courtyard in his enthusiasm to lick them clean. Kai picked up some chopsticks, delicately selected a baked mouse and nibbled off its head. He chewed it thoughtfully.

"I think it needs a little more salt."

Chapter Fourteen
Moon Shadow

Tao needed a night of undisturbed sleep, but spending time with Pema had made his heart race and he lay awake. The moon was high in the sky and although it looked no bigger than a plum, moonlight flooded through the window, casting a soft shadow of the rock outside. The moon shadow was shifting slightly, rippling on the floor. There was no wind, even if there had been, it shouldn't have affected the moon shadow. Tao shut his eyes but opened them again immediately. He didn't like not knowing what the shadow was doing. Every tiny sound was amplified. There were creaks and bangs and a scratching sound.

Just as he was dozing off, a crash jolted him awake. The lamp next to the bed had fallen off the little table and smashed to pieces. He couldn't understand how that had happened. Fortunately, he hadn't left it alight or the spilled oil would have burst into flame and burned the house down. A night bird called, startling him and making his heart thud. He was becoming as frightened as a child.

Tao went out into the courtyard. He didn't want to be alone. Kai was asleep in his straw-lined hollow in the goat pen. His scales glowed softly in the moonlight. He had tried to make Sunila sleep somewhere else, but the *naga* had crept up after Kai had fallen asleep and was as close as he could get to him without actually climbing into the hollow. The blue dragon glowed too, but not as brightly as Kai.

Tao understood how Sunila felt. He wished he could lie closer to Kai. A dragon wasn't warm and cuddly, but even feeling his scales sticking into him would have been a comfort. Instead, he settled down on Wei's couch.

Kai had said he would sleep outside so that he could guard Tao. He seemed to have forgotten that his hearing was rather poor. He slept so soundly nothing disturbed him. He didn't hear the night birds or the howling of a wolf. Tao heard them all.

Darkness surrounded him. A current of cold air chilled his skin. He had been walking in the mountains and he had somehow wandered back into the underground passage again. Everything was black. He was searching for the glowing pool, but he couldn't find it. The gust of cold air grew stronger. Icy fingers dug into his arm. He opened his eyes, expecting to see nothing but darkness, but instead he saw mist issuing from the nostrils of a blue snout only a handspan from his face.

Sunila made a sad sound. He was hungry, and had been prodding Tao with his talons. Tao lay there, relieved to have left the nightmare behind.

"Thank you for waking me, Sunila," he said.

It was very early, and Tao still hoped he could go back to sleep, this time without bad dreams. But the *naga* was persistent. He grabbed the edge of the quilt with his teeth and pulled it off. Tao felt the morning chill on his naked body, and a dragon tail wrap around his ankle as Sunila tried to drag him out of bed.

Tao was fully awake now, and it didn't seem like the *naga* was going to leave him alone. He got up and put on his clothes.

"What do you want?" Tao said.

Then he remembered that the dragon didn't understand Huaxia. "Food?" he said in Sanskrit. "Grain?"

He wasn't sure he'd got the words right, but the dragon's blue eyes blinked at him expectantly. Tao didn't know the Sanskrit name for worms, but in any case he had no intention of going out looking for them so early in the morning.

"Honey?" he said.

Sunila put his paws up on Tao's knees and bumped Tao's nose with the end of his snout. It hurt, but from the loud purring sound he was making, Tao knew he'd guessed correctly.

"You are doing very well with communicating, considering the small number of Sanskrit words I know. You deserve a reward. We can walk over to the orchard and see if the bees will allow me to take some more honey."

Out in the courtyard, Tao almost ran into Pema, who looked like she was still half-asleep.

"You're up early," Tao said. "I'm taking Sunila to the orchard to get more honey. Do you want to come? It will wake you up."

"I suppose so."

Tao was about to go out through his tunnel.

"I'm not crawling through a hole in the ground and bramble bushes," Pema said. "I'll only come if we can go through the gate."

Tao didn't argue, but he couldn't bring himself to ask Pema to help him lift the bar. Fortunately, Sunila ran ahead and lifted the bar for them.

Pema yawned. "He's very different to Kai. Kai is like a dragon-shaped person, but Sunila is more like a very large blue dog."

It was a lovely morning. Sunila was leaping through the grass, enjoying his freedom. Pema stopped to collect windfall persimmons. She handed one to Tao and he bit into it. The sun shining on the dew, the sweet fruit in his mouth and Pema's chatter made the terrors of the night ebb away. He really had believed that he returned to the darkness and the ghosts were with him again. But that was a dream. Perhaps the moving moon shadow was a recurring nightmare that seemed real at the time.

He allowed himself to imagine a life like this – feeling free like the blue dragon – walking through the fields when he felt like it, growing his own food. With Pema. It was his family's land. He had every right to be here. Couldn't he be Kai's dragonkeeper here just as well?

Tao went to the pomegranate tree and waited for the bees to come and welcome him again. They buzzed around him. Pema stood back, afraid that she'd get stung.

"They won't hurt you," Tao said as he reached into the tree hollow and broke off another piece of honeycomb.

Sunila was trying to take the honeycomb from Tao's hand.

"You can't have it yet. This has to last for several days. I can't keep stealing the bees' honey. They need it to feed the baby bees."

Sunila tried again to grab the honeycomb, saliva dripping from his mouth.

"You didn't say it in Sanskrit," Pema said.

"Maybe not, but I'm sure he understood my meaning."

He put the honeycomb in his sleeve where the *naga* couldn't get it.

"You told him he could have some," Pema said. "He's been looking forward to it."

"I'm punishing him for his bad manners. He'll have to wait until the evening meal."

Tao repeated the words in Sanskrit, to make sure Sunila understood. Sunila made sounds like tree branches creaking in the wind and hung his head and his tail.

"The smell of the honey is making me hungry," Pema said. "Let's go and have breakfast."

They started to walk back to the compound, but a yelp made them turn round. Tao ran back to the pomegranate tree and found the *naga* shaking his left paw, which was covered with bees. Others were swarming around him, buzzing angrily and diving at his head.

Before Tao could get near the bees to calm them, Sunila had started running. He made a sound like howling wind. The bees were buzzing furiously after him, the whole hive. He was frightened, and with good reason. If so many bees stung him, he might die. Tao didn't know what to do.

Sunila stopped dead, stood up on his back legs and, to Tao's astonishment, unfurled a pair of small wings. He flapped them awkwardly from side to side, and took off, rising vertically. The bees seemed as surprised as Tao and Pema, and didn't follow him. When he'd reached a certain height, Sunila changed the angle of his wings, flew towards the compound and landed on top of the wall. They raced after the *naga*.

Kai was waiting for them at the gate.

"He's got wings!" Tao exclaimed.

Kai didn't seem surprised.

"Did you know?"

Kai looked away. "I have seen him flutter his wings before, but I did not know how close they were to maturing. This is his first flight."

"You should have told me."

Tao knew that wings were a very touchy subject with Kai.

"We can continue this conversation once we are inside," the dragon said, herding them back through the gate. "Can I remind you that we are supposed to stay hidden, and yet all three of you are trying to attract as much attention as possible, laughing and strolling around the countryside, with that beast making a din loud enough to be heard many *li* away."

Tao blushed. He had been enjoying Pema's company so much, he'd forgotten all about being cautious. He was annoyed that he'd allowed himself to be distracted by Pema. Kai was right; he'd hardly thought about his plans to help needy people since she'd arrived. And he'd risked revealing their hiding place.

Kai replaced the bar.

Pema was watching the *naga* up on the wall. "What's he doing up there?"

Bits of straw fell down.

"It looks like he's making a nest," Tao said.

"Not a very good one," Kai added.

"Perhaps he feels safer up there." Tao remembered his own experience in a dragon's nest. "*Nagas* might nest on high mountain ledges, or perhaps in tall trees."

Tao knew Kai was cross with him, but the dragon wasn't entirely without fault. He hadn't mentioned Sunila's wings. That was Kai's pride. Sunila had wings but he didn't.

"Dragons don't get their wings until they're at least a thousand years old, do they?" Tao asked, although he already knew it was true. "Sunila must be older than you, Kai."

Sunila flapped down from his nest. He had bee stings on his left paw and several on his ears, which had no scales to protect them. He was scratching the stings and making a high-pitched whining sound that was very annoying.

"I know they hurt, Sunila." Tao was now wishing he hadn't been so strict with the *naga*. "But you mustn't scratch them. I'll make you a bee sting remedy."

Tao went to the kitchen and mixed crushed garlic with vinegar and honey.

Pema was watching him. "It seems strange that bees' honey should be part of the remedy for their stings."

"My father always had a jar of this balm for when he got stung."

Tao dabbed some on Sunila's stings, which were starting to swell. But the *naga* immediately tried to lick it off.

"You need to bandage them," Pema said.

She went into Meiling's room and brought out one of Tao's sister's discarded gowns. The cloth was beautiful, deep maroon with a pattern of pink cherry blossom and blue butterflies. Pema unceremoniously ripped strips from the hem and handed them to Tao, who made Sunila sit on his haunches and hold up his foreleg. He bound the colourful bandage around Sunila's swollen paw. So that he could easily undo the bandaging and reapply the balm, he tied the strips of cloth with a bow. Then he bound strips around the *naga's* ears. Sunila inspected his paw, now adorned with a colourful bow. With the other paw he felt the bows on his ears.

Pema giggled. "He looks sweet."

Sunila didn't need to understand what she was saying. He was aware that she and Tao were chuckling, and that Kai was making his jingling-bell sound. This indignity wounded the *naga's* pride more than the stings had wounded his hide.

"Can't you give him some honey to cheer him up?" Pema asked.

Tao was about to fetch the honeycomb.

"You are treating him like a spoiled child," Kai said. "He must learn that honey is precious and he can only have a small amount each day. Then you must wean him off it, until he will eat whatever food is given to him."

"How are you going to explain that to him?" Pema said.

"Honey. Scarce. No eat."

That was the best he could do with his limited Sanskrit.

The painful stings, undignified appearance and lack of promised honey made the *naga* most unhappy. He stopped making the whining sound, much to Tao's relief because it was giving him a headache, and flew up to his nest on the wall.

"Now what's he doing?" Pema asked.

Tao looked up. Jets of mist were pouring out of the *naga's* nostrils.

"He's sulking. Kai also breathes mist from his nose when he's not happy."

Kai was watching too. Sunila was producing more and more mist. It was thick and dark grey, nothing like the fine white mist that curled lazily from Kai's nostrils when he was cross.

"I've never seen Kai make that much mist!" Pema said.

Tao could see threads of mist issuing from Kai's nostrils, though he knew that he was trying not to. Sunila's mist didn't thin and drift away like Kai's. It hung in front of the *naga* and collected into a cloud. Sunila continued to produce mist, but the cloud didn't grow bigger. Instead it became denser, darker. The mist stopped streaming from Sunila's nostrils, but he was still concentrating on the cloud, as if willing it to do something. It did do something. It rose a little and drifted away from the wall and into the compound. Tao, Pema and Kai, their heads upturned, watched this spectacle. The grey cloud stopped above Tao's head. Sunila opened his wings and flapped them so that they clashed together in front of him, making a sound like distant thunder. Then he stopped. The air was still and heavy. Sunila let out a screech. Suddenly, drops of water poured from the cloud. It was like a heavy shower of rain, but it fell only on Tao. It lasted no more than a few moments, but in that time Tao was drenched. The cloud became pale and thin, more like Kai's mist, and then faded away.

Tao stood there dripping. Pema applauded. Sunila seemed very pleased with himself, and Kai was trying not to look impressed.

"Can you make rain, Kai?" Pema said.

"The dragons at the dragon haven can make rain, but it is a long and exhausting process. It takes many dragons to produce a cloud that contains enough moisture to bring rain. Afterwards, we are spent and must sleep for several days."

"Sunila doesn't seem at all tired," Pema said.

Tao sat shivering in the courtyard. Pema had wrung out his dripping jacket and trousers and spread them on bushes, but the weak autumn sun had failed to dry them. He didn't have any other clothes, so he was wearing Meiling's cherry blossom and butterflies gown, which only came down to his knees because of the strips ripped from the bottom.

"I wish I could light a fire," Tao grumbled.

Pema was watching Sunila, who was flying around the walls, getting used to his wings, dipping and banking to one side and then flipping over.

"Look at that!" she said. "He can fly upside down!"

"We cannot let him fly around," Kai said. "Nomads might see him."

"How can we stop him?"

"We must lure him down and tether him," Kai said.

Tao didn't like the idea of restraining the *naga*. But he knew Kai was right. He fetched the honeycomb from the kitchen. Most of the honey had dripped out of it. He held it up and called out to the *naga*, who flapped down into the courtyard.

"Here you are, Sunila," Tao said. "You can have this. If you chew it, you'll get lots of honey."

The *naga* took it from Tao. Kai found a length of rope and slipped it over the *naga's* head. Sunila was too busy chewing the honeycomb to object. Kai led him to the goat pen and tied the rope to a strong pole.

"It's a shame to tie him up now that he can fly," Pema said.

"We have to," Tao said, though he felt the same way.

Tao spent the rest of the day in the garden and was glad when it finally got dark and he could light the fire, dry his clothes and begin preparing the evening meal. He opened one of his mother's jars of pickled vegetables, cooked some millet that he had found growing wild and steamed some greens. He also made a dish of stewed pears flavoured with ginger and honey.

He took the food out to Kai and Pema.

Sunila's meal was the same as theirs, but liberally sweetened with honey. He ate noisily. Kai complained that the *naga's* share of the pear dish was bigger than his. Tao enjoyed watching his friends as they ate the food he'd made, complimenting him on the flavours. For a boy who knew nothing about cooking, he thought he was doing a pretty good job of preparing meals for everyone.

When Sunila had finished his food, he started to whine and to pull at the rope around his neck. Tao went over and patted him.

"I'm sorry, Sunila. You must only fly at night when there is no moonlight." Tao patted the *naga* again, before leaving the goat pen and shutting the gate behind him.

"Nagas must have exceptional weather skills," he said. "Do you remember the sudden snowstorm on the mountain, Kai? I think he created that because he didn't want us to find the bodies of the Shenchi villagers. I have never heard of a dragon making snow."

Kai didn't answer.

"And the hailstorm, when the nomads were attacking him," Tao continued. "I heard a screech and a sound like thunder before the storm came."

A large spider was spinning a web in a corner of the pavilion. It was an orb spider, as big as Tao's hand, with bands of yellow on its body, and yellow stripes on its long legs. Pema refused to sit near it, but Tao wasn't afraid of it.

"Why are there so many insects?" Pema said, batting away mosquitoes.

"It's because my mother isn't here. She was always ordering the servants to kill all the *wuji*, though she knew Wei liked them. Not so much as an ant was permitted to live."

Tao turned towards the setting sun, feeling its golden light on his face. The mosquitoes flew towards him, circling around his head.

"And why are they biting me and not you?"

"I don't know. Perhaps your blood tastes better."

Moths started to gather around him.

"It's you, Tao," Pema said. "The insects are attracted to you."

"Pema is right," Kai said. "You refuse to kill insects

because of your beliefs, and Wei got great pleasure from observing insects. They are drawn to you because of your *qi*."

"No Buddhist would harm an insect. There's nothing unusual in that. Insects are creatures of the world that work hard all their short lives." Tao wasn't smiling. "Ants and bees never think of themselves as humans do. They are always working for the good of their communities. They are powerful in their own small way, and they teach us a lot, if we take the time to observe them. I am sure I have been an insect in a previous life. We all have. We should respect their place in the world."

"You love the insects," Pema said, "and they love you."

Pema lifted her feet off the ground. "Look! There are beetles too, all around your feet."

The beetles were small and shaped like miniature shields. They had dull brown shells and looked like tiny monks gathering around him, eager to hear his words.

Kai's jingling laughter rang out. "The insects are attracted to your *qi* – yours and Wei's." The dragon considered Tao for a moment. "This is your *qi* power."

"Don't make fun of me, Kai."

Pema couldn't interpret the dragon's sounds. "What's he saying?"

"That my *qi* power is attracting insects."

"What is *qi* power?" Pema asked.

Tao explained the ways that other dragonkeepers had concentrated their *qi* and transformed it into extraordinary skills – strength to lift huge stones, ability to hurl things a *li* or more, agility that enabled them to leap across rivers. He told her about Ping's power, and how she could make objects move.

"And yours is attracting insects?"

"It's Kai's idea of a joke," Tao said. "Not a very funny one."

"I am being completely serious," the dragon said.

"I haven't discovered my *qi* power yet."

Several moths settled on Tao's shoulders as if to contradict him.

"So you aren't Holy Boy any more," Pema said. "Now you're Bug Boy!"

Tao didn't like it when Pema laughed at him. He wished he could make objects fly across the room or lift heavy objects so that she would be impressed by him, instead of amused.

Was this really his *qi* power? An ability to attract insects?

Pema was chuckling. Kai was jingling.

Tao picked up his bowl of pears and stood up. He was still wearing his sister's gown. They laughed and jingled louder. Tao stalked off to Wei's room to eat in peace, slamming the door behind him.

Tao woke in the middle of the night as he knew he would. The moon shadow didn't even pretend to have the same shape as the rock outside. It disconnected itself from the shaft of moonlight and moved of its own accord. It rippled and stretched and lifted itself up from the floor. It had depth and shape.

Tao tried to shut his eyes, but he couldn't. He had to watch the moon shadow.

Gradually, the rags of moon shadow took on more shape. Some tendrils elongated and then twirled around each other, merging into two thicker appendages, one on each side. Others curled and twisted, radiating from a rounded shape at the top. Tao shivered. The resulting spectre looked as if it had a head with hair, and arms ending in long wavy fingers. Below, there was a rippling patch of shadow streaked with pale moonlight that resembled a billowing gown. The pieces of moon shadow kept drifting apart and reforming. Tao watched in horror as two circles of darker moon shadow collected on the dark head. They were eyes. The moon shadow held together. It had a human form, but it was transparent. The shadow eyes glared at Tao. He could no longer deny what he saw in front of him. It was a ghost.

Chapter Fifteen

ALONE

Tao wanted to shout out to Kai but he couldn't speak. And anyway the dragon wouldn't have heard him. The moon-shadow ghost seemed more solid, but as it drifted around the room, it passed right through a chair and a chest. He waited until it had drifted to the other side of the room before he ran through the shafts of moonlight and out into the courtyard. He leaped over the fence around the goat pen.

Tao found his voice. "Kai, there's a ghost."

The dragon didn't stir. Tao pulled his beard hard.

Kai woke, indignant. "Why are you doing that?"

"There's a ghost. In Wei's room. Come quick."

"You have been dreaming."

"No."

Tao kept tugging Kai's beard until he got to his feet, grumbling. He refused to hurry. The moon went behind a cloud. By the time they reached Wei's room, the ghost had gone.

The clouds had cleared by morning, and Tao didn't want to think about the ghost and darkness, he just wanted to be out in the sunshine. To take his mind off the terrors of the night, he had to keep busy. The first thing he needed to do was check on Sunila's bee stings and reapply the balm.

Kai was still curled up in his hollow, but there was no sign of the *naga*.

"Where's Sunila? I hope he hasn't escaped!"

The dragon yawned and stretched. "There is no need to panic. He was annoying me during the night. Before you were annoying me. He was trying to creep into my nest. I moved him to the stables."

The stable door was open. Inside, a loop of rope lay on the ground among a colourful tangle of torn bandages.

"He *has* escaped!"

Tao searched the compound from wall to wall, but couldn't find the *naga* anywhere.

"He must have flown away."

Tao was surprised to find Pema up already, eating left-over grain and pears in the peony pavilion. She hadn't seen the *naga* either.

"Perhaps he's made himself invisible."

Tao put out some grain mixed with honey, hoping that would attract the *naga*, but he didn't appear.

"What exactly did you say to him, Kai?"

"I … told him he was a pest … and I may have said that

I wished we had left him in the forest to starve."

"What a terrible thing to say!"

"But he would not have understood me. He cannot interpret my sounds as you can."

"Neither can Pema, but she can guess what you mean. Sunila can too."

"He'll come back when he's hungry, won't he?" Pema said.

When he hadn't returned by midday, Tao asked Kai to go and search for him.

"You can shape-change. No one will see you."

"What if he does not want to be found?" Kai said. "Searching for a dragon who can make himself invisible is a waste of time."

"We said we were going to help people. We should be helping all creatures, including *nagas*."

"He is free to go wherever he wants," Kai said.

Pema went back to the servants' quarters where she slept. Tao wondered what she did in there.

"This is your fault, Kai," Tao said. "You've been jealous of the *naga* ever since we captured him."

"That is not true."

"It is. He has the power of invisibility and he can fly. You've been like a child with a new baby in the family."

The dragon couldn't stop mist curling from his nostrils. "You have been treating him like a pet. He is a wild creature in need of … discipline."

"Well, if you won't go and look for him, I will."

Tao went out searching for the *naga*. Kai was right, of course. If Sunila didn't want to be found, he would make himself invisible. But Tao hoped the chunk of honeycomb he was carrying would attract Sunila. He tramped around the outside of the walls, walked through the abandoned fields. He searched and called all afternoon. He found some onions and three eggs laid by an escaped chicken, but there was no sign of the *naga*.

Tao went back to the walled compound. He didn't feel like crawling through the tunnel, so he thumped on the gate. He kept thumping until it swung open. Tao was mortified to see that it was Pema who had managed to lift the bar by herself.

"I couldn't find him." Tao looked around. "Where's Kai?"

"He's gone searching for Sunila too. He was pacing the walls for hours, worried about you out there alone."

Dusk crept over the hills to the west and the light faded, but Tao didn't light the kitchen stove.

"Aren't you going to cook tonight?" Pema asked.

"I'm not hungry."

Pema lit a small fire and cooked the eggs and onions that Tao had found.

"You can eat these eggs, Tao," Pema explained. "The chicken abandoned them. They would never have hatched."

Tao ate a few mouthfuls. As darkness fell, moths came to settle on his shoulders again. Pema smiled.

"Go on, make jokes about me and the way the insects are attracted to me," Tao said.

"I wasn't going to make a joke. It shows what a special person you are, Tao. Like no other. You have something in common with the insects. Everyone else thinks of themselves first. You never do. You are unique in these times."

She smiled at him again and took his hands. He didn't pull them away. A short while before, he had been annoyed with Pema. Now he couldn't bear the thought of her leaving. In Tao's daydreams of living in a walled community again, she had always been there. He was about to say that he wanted her to make her home in the compound, but she spoke before he had the chance.

"I'm leaving early in the morning, probably before dawn, so I'll say goodbye now."

Tao's dream disappeared like mist in sunlight.

"Kai will be back," Pema said, misinterpreting the anxiety on his face. He's a dragon. He can take care of himself."

Tao hadn't been thinking about the missing dragon.

"Where are you going?"

"I have things to do."

"What things?"

Pema didn't answer.

"Don't worry, Bug Boy," she said. "I'll come to visit you again soon."

Tao watched as Pema headed off to the hut she was sleeping in.

The moon wasn't quite full, but it was low in the sky and seemed huge. Tao climbed into Wei's bed and closed his eyes, but he could still see the light through his eyelids. He turned away from the window, but the moonlight reflected off everything – the wall, a painting, a bronze ornament.

The ghost arrived. This time it didn't form slowly from a shapeless patch of shadow. It was fully formed already, in the shape of a young girl. Her grey face, flecked with moonlight, had a melancholy beauty. Her eyes were dark and hollow, as if bruised by sadness. Tears of moonlight fell from them, but evaporated before they reached the path. The ghost girl didn't walk. She floated. Her body swayed, her arms fluttered, as if she was moving in water, not air. Though the night was still, the tendrils of her shadow hair were stirred, as if by a breeze. The folds of her shadow gown caught the moonlight as it billowed.

Tao knew he wasn't dreaming. And despite the fact that Pema had persuaded him that the ghosts in the cave had never existed, he was sure that this one was real.

Who was she? He thought back through his life, trying

to remember if any young girl had died within the walls. He couldn't recall one. The house had been there for many generations. Perhaps it was one of his ancestors, a child who had died before he was born and lost the way to her next life, but he didn't remember anyone claiming they had seen a ghost. Her pale face had a look of yearning. Her eyes were pleading wordlessly with him. She was stuck in the half-life between death and rebirth. Perhaps she had been content in that state while there were people who lived in the community, but now they had all gone and she was alone.

Tao wanted to help her, as he had the other ghosts, the ones in the cave that Pema had convinced him never existed. He remembered the way they had sighed when they were released from the world. In the dead of night, with the ghost girl before him, he begun to believe that they too had been real.

"I can pray for you," he whispered. "I can help you find your way into your next life."

The ghost girl turned to Tao. She was so small that she barely came up to his waist, but she drifted up so that her black eyes were level with his. A silver point of moonlight had formed in the centre of each eye, making her seem angry. Her tender shadow lips pulled back into an animal snarl, baring sharp, inhuman teeth. The waving tendrils of silver-tipped shadow hair writhed like a nest of snakes. Her delicate fingers bent until they were crooked and twisted like a crone's. Each one was tipped with a glittering claw, reaching out to Tao as if she wanted to rake them through his flesh and make him bleed. The ghost rushed at Tao, but her insubstantial claws and teeth couldn't harm him. He shuddered as she passed right through him, like a cold wind, taking his breath away. He turned around, but she was gone. The moon had disappeared behind a cloud. There was nothing but darkness. And he could breathe again.

Even if the ghosts in the cave hadn't existed, if he and Kai had created them in their minds from nothing more than a gust of cold air and some vague sensations, it made no difference. This ghost was real. He had felt her enter his bones, stop his breath. If she'd lingered in his body, he would have died, he was sure of that. As she'd passed through him, he'd felt her anger and sorrow, which was more tangible than her body. Grief, loneliness and her premature death had turned her into a hungry ghost. Whoever she was, Tao was convinced that she hadn't got lost on her journey into her next life. She had never begun it.

Tao didn't want to be alone. Not ever again. He needed companionship, someone to talk to and make the night terrors go away. He went outside. The moon came out from behind the cloud and flooded the courtyard with pale light, making angry crisscross shadows of bare twigs.

He didn't look back to see if the ghost had reappeared. He ran to the hut where Pema slept and knocked on the door. There was no answer. He went inside. Pema wasn't there and neither were her sword or her sleeping mat. It was still four hours or more till dawn, but she had already left.

Tao didn't want to go back to Wei's room. The feeling of safety he'd experienced each time he'd entered it had gone. Now, when he was in the room, all he felt was fear. He sat in the peony pavilion.

Although the ghost girl didn't trouble him again that night, sleep had deserted him. Thoughts and fears swirled in his head, fighting for attention. If the ghost had appeared the previous night, he could have discussed it with Kai. If she'd arrived a few hours earlier, he could have told Pema. But the ghost girl had waited until he was by himself to take on her full and undeniable shape. She hadn't uttered a sound, but Tao knew exactly what she wanted. She had left something inside him as she passed through him. A thought. A desire. She didn't want to begin another life. She wanted her previous life back. And if she couldn't have that, she wanted revenge for her untimely death. Tao was powerless to help her regain her old life, and he would have no part in revenge.

The orb spider was his only companion. It sat in its web, perfectly still, as patient as ever. But its calm stillness couldn't soothe the disquiet he felt. What had happened to Kai? He must be in trouble. Something must have gone wrong, otherwise he wouldn't have stayed away. Would he?

A few days earlier Tao had sat in this same spot sharing a meal with his friends and he had thought that his life couldn't be improved. He had felt safe in the compound, protected. The walls had done their job and kept enemies out, but they had not managed to keep his friends within. This was the first time in his life he had been completely alone.

Tao felt around by the side of the couch until he found his bag. He reached inside for the familiar shape of his dragon stone. His heart shrank inside him. For a moment, he'd forgotten that he no longer had the shard. Then his fingers brushed something else inside the bag. Something cool to the touch like the shard. But not smooth. Something with many facets and edges sharp enough to cut skin. It was the cinnabar crystals. Kai had gone out into the world alone without taking any cinnabar with him. The sharp edges of the crystals had scratched the tender hide behind Kai's reverse scales, so he had given them to Tao to keep in his bag. They had planned to stay together.

Tao struggled to stop his mind plunging into a whirlpool of panic. He pictured the shard in his mind – the lovely shade of purple, the milky white vein that passed through it, the faint threads of maroon that were only visible if you looked very close. Kai had used his own shard to find Tao. It had somehow led him to the monastery. Tao was sure the dragon stone would lead him to Kai. But he didn't have it.

Tao was the one who'd told Kai to search for Sunila. He'd expected that the *naga* wouldn't stray far from the food they had provided, that he'd be out in the fields and would come as soon as Kai called out to him. Tao had spent a lot of time fussing over the *naga*. If he was honest with himself, he had quite liked the fact that Kai was jealous of Sunila. His life had turned bad, like milk left in the sun. And it was all his own fault.

Tao got up as soon as the first hint of daylight gave vague shape to the familiar things in the courtyard – the ornamental cherry tree, the pavilion, the mountain-shaped rocks – but the morning light didn't weaken the power of his night terrors. Not this time. His belief in the ghost girl and his fears for Kai refused to fade.

He climbed the steps to the top of the wall, and walked around, searching the landscape in all directions for a dot of blue or green. There was no trace of Kai's voice in his head. The breeze brought no whisper of Sunila's cry. He didn't know what had happened to the dragons.

Tao couldn't sit and do nothing. He would have to go and search for Kai, though he had no hope of finding him. He wasn't hungry, but he forced himself to eat some cold rice. He filled his water skin and grasped his staff and, instead of rushing out and leaving the gate open, he carefully made his way through the tunnel. Without the shard he had no idea which way Kai had gone. He turned to the north. Three butterflies fluttered after him. Their ragged wings meant they were old and close to death, but they stayed with him and he was grateful for their company. He hoped it was a sign that he was heading in the right direction.

Tao spent the whole day searching for dragon tracks, calling out to Kai with his mind, but he didn't find him. Late in the afternoon, he returned to the compound. All day a realisation had been growing in his mind – without Kai, his life was meaningless. He was destined to become Kai's dragonkeeper. Being a novice monk had merely been preparation, teaching him to disconnect from his family, from the world.

He walked up the road to the compound, exhausted after a long day searching and a longer sleepless night. The gate was open a crack. His heart, already beating fast from the climb, beat faster. He made his tired legs run. Relief flooded through him. He wasn't even cross with Kai for forgetting to bar the gate.

He barely had the strength left to push the gate open wide enough for him to slip through. The compound was as quiet and empty as when he'd left.

"Kai." He didn't speak aloud. "Where are you?"

There were no answering words in his mind.

Then he heard a sound. It was the cheeping hiss of the *naga*, interspersed with happy flute notes. Tao's heart leaped. Kai had found Sunila! Tao discovered that he did have a wisp of energy left, enough for him to run into the courtyard.

He was about to call out to Kai again, but the words shrivelled in his mouth. Sunila was there. He was curled at the feet of someone lounging on Wei's couch. A hand was draped on the *naga's* head, tickling his ears. Sunila was purring. The shreds of hope fell from Tao like autumn leaves from a tree. The smirking face before him belonged to Fo Tu Deng.

Chapter Sixteen
TEA FOR TWO

"Tao, come and sit down," Fo Tu Deng said, as if he was welcoming an old friend into his own house. "I've made a pot of your excellent tea. I've been expecting you. Let me pour a cup for you."

Fo Tu Deng poured tea from a stout little teapot with a crabapple design etched on the lid. Tao's mother had taken the best bronze teapot with her to Jiankang. This little one, made from red clay, was the teapot she'd used whenever local elders called by. She had never wanted anyone to think that the Huans were wealthy.

Sunila was stretched out, purring at the feet of the monk who was chatting to him in fluent Sanskrit. The *naga* took no notice of Tao at all.

"This is my house. I want you to leave."

Fo Tu Deng smiled as he handed Tao a cup of tea.

"In these lawless times, I think anyone can take possession of abandoned property. This compound has such commanding views in all directions, and it's so comfortable. It will make an excellent base for my activities. I have settled myself into the charming room with the lacquered screen, the large bed and the cabinet painted with mountain scenes."

That was Tao's mother's room. She hadn't been able to take all her furniture with her.

The monk sipped his tea and patted the *naga*.

"One of my scouts told me he saw a young man wandering around near here with two dragons. It had to be you. Then this poor creature came to me distressed and malnourished."

He said something in Sanskrit to the *naga*, who purred in response.

"I know something about the dragons of Tianzhu. *Nagas* live in rainforests. Their main source of food is tree frogs, which the adult females collect. The males are rather lazy when it comes to food gathering. Their job is to keep away predators – tigers mainly, and humans of course." The monk smiled. "This fellow isn't much good at finding his own food. When my men encountered a shape-changing monster that killed with a venomous bite, I guessed it was a *naga*. I sent three of them to the mountains to find some decent-sized tree frogs so that I could test my theory, see if he would be lured by them." Fo Tu Deng chuckled. "Out on the plains, nomads don't have much experience of climbing trees. There was an unfortunate accident, but that encouraged the others to learn how to climb trees more skilfully."

Tao watched as the monk pulled a squirming green frog from a basket. It was as big as his hand. The *naga* snatched it from him and bit off its head. He crunched the frog's head and then ate the rest of the poor creature. It was a much more filling meal than the woodworm larvae Tao had provided.

"There are mango groves in the *naga* forest," Fo Tu Deng continued, "and the mangos are ripe for many months of the year. They are another important part of a *naga's* diet."

That explained why Sunila had such a sweet tooth.

"You did quite well, Tao, finding the larvae for this creature. That is what they eat in their home forest whenever the frogs are in short supply. The fallen trees become soft and pulpy and the larvae of certain beetles thrive in them." The monk drained his cup. "I'm sure this little lesson in the ways of the dragons of Tianzhu has been of great interest to you."

Fo Tu Deng poured himself more tea. Tao's was left untouched.

"He'll be very useful." The monk patted Sunila on the head. "I can train him to shape-change into a monster and bite on command; he could become a vital weapon to attack the enemy. And I can use him to threaten my men if they don't do as I tell them. And one day, when I finally get to build my own monastery, people will travel for hundreds of *li* to see the dragon from the land of the Buddha."

The monk sounded wistful, as if he wasn't entirely sure that day would ever come.

"Buddha has blessed me. First I found this creature and now you," the monk said. "You remember Jilong, I suspect?"

Tao nodded. How could he forget the cruel Zhao warlord who had subjected Pema to torture?

"Jilong is a demanding fellow. He wants me to look into the future and tell him how he can defeat his enemies. I do my best with the tools I have at hand, but I could do so much better with your skills."

"I'm not going to help you."

"That was not meant to be a request."

"You can't make me."

"I think I can." Fo Tu Deng put down his teacup. "Come with me."

He led Tao to the goat pen as if he owned the place. He opened the gate. Kai was there, slumped on the ground, shackled with iron chains, purple blood crusting around an ugly wound on his head.

Fear stabbed at Tao's heart. He couldn't hear the dragon in his mind. "Is he dead?"

"No, no," chuckled Fo Tu Deng. "If he was already dead, how could I use him as an incentive for you to … cooperate?"

Tao heard the awful scraping sound of a dragon in pain. Kai was stirring. Weeping iron sores were already forming where the chains made contact with his hide. But at least he was alive.

"Now then," Fo Tu Deng said pleasantly, as if they were bartering in a market. "Perhaps we can come to some arrangement."

Sunila grovelled at the monk's feet until he gave the *naga* another frog.

Tao sat with his head in his hands as Fo Tu Deng explained what he wanted.

"I have searched for weeks, but haven't been able to discover where Jilong's enemies are hiding. I thought they might be here in this compound, but I can find no sign of them."

The monk was trying to sound relaxed and in control of the situation, but it was obvious he was in a precarious position with the Zhao warlord.

"They pick off my men, so I know they must be nearby. They've disappeared like mist," the monk said. "At first we assumed they were the Zhao's old enemy the New Han, but every time they kill a Zhao soldier, they leave a token – a wooden disc with a black camel painted on it. I've tried torturing the citizens of Luoyang, but they don't seem to know who these people are. The men call them the Black Camel Bandits. That's why I need you. I must know what they are up to and how they can be defeated."

"But I can't help you," Tao said. "I've told you before …"

Fo Tu Deng held up his hand.

"You told me that you cannot summon a vision to help me. And yet, as I recall, somehow you managed it."

"I won't help you!"

Fo Tu Deng looked at Kai and smiled.

"Yes, you will. If you would like your dragon to be free of the hurtful iron chains, I suggest you start your summoning."

Fo Tu Deng's nomads arrived, weary and dispirited after another unsuccessful search for their enemies. There were about twenty of them, and they filled the courtyard and spread themselves around the house. They made a lot of noise, and built a large fire on the garden beds that Tao had dug over and reseeded. The nomads were unconcerned that the smoke could be seen for many *li*. They raided the food cellar, and wrung the necks of the few chickens Tao had been able to coax back to the chicken coop. They took enough food to last Tao and Kai for several weeks. And the nomads didn't even like it.

"Why are we eating grass seeds?" one of them complained as he stirred a pot of grain. "We can't fight if we eat nothing but food meant for horses and goats."

Another nomad prodded the chickens that were roasting in the fire. "And birds. All bones and pale flesh."

"We need something that bleeds," the other one said. "A goat or a deer."

"And *kumiss*. How are we supposed to fight with no *kumiss* in our bellies?"

They both sighed. Tao shuddered at the thought of the foul-tasting drink that nomads made from fermented mare's milk.

One of the nomads brought a bowl of food for Fo Tu Deng. The monk invited Tao to eat with him, but even if he ate meat, he couldn't have eaten the flesh of the chickens that had given him eggs. At least the nomads hadn't eaten the turnips and cabbages growing in the garden. They would sooner eat stones than vegetables. Fo Tu Deng shovelled down the food. For a small, skinny man he had a big appetite.

While the monk was eating, Tao went to Wei's room. His dream of the compound being a sanctuary where he and his friends could live in peace was shattered. But that wasn't his main concern. He could hear the faint sound of scraping blades coming from the goat pen. Kai was in pain.

When he'd discovered the solution to the iron problem, Tao had been so pleased with himself. He'd imagined that he'd always be at Kai's side ready to give him the cinnabar, if ever they were confronted with sword-wielding nomads. And then he had told Kai to go off alone and look for the *naga*, without a thought about possible danger. Fo Tu Deng's faith in Tao's ability as a seer was misplaced. He hadn't been able to foresee that he and Kai would be separated, and that Kai would need to carry cinnabar with him.

He took the lump of cinnabar from his bag, broke off two crystals and hid them in his sleeve. He went back outside.

Sunila was pawing the monk's gown.

"What do you want?" He kicked the *naga*. "Go away!"

"He's still hungry," Tao said.

"It's eaten all the frogs, the greedy beast!"

Tao remembered how much food Fo Tu Deng had just eaten. "He nearly starved. You can't blame him for wanting to eat as much as he can."

Fo Tu Deng called over two guards. "Chain this creature up with the other dragon."

All the nomads were watching as the guards brought a length of chain and warily approached the *naga*.

"It's a pity they weren't all wiped out in the fire," the monk muttered.

"What fire?" Tao asked.

"Back in Tianzhu. There was a forest where the *nagas* lived. The place was crawling with the beasts. I was spiritual advisor to the king of that region. He decided that his grand palace had to be on the very spot where the *naga* forest was. So he burned it."

Tao was horrified. "The whole forest?"

"Yes. It was quite a job. It's not easy to burn a rainforest."

"But what happened to the *nagas*?"

"Most of them died in the fire. This is the first I have seen in years."

"Years?"

"Yes, the fire was seven or more years ago. I don't know how he has survived."

One of the guards tried to put the chain around Sunila's neck. The naga bared his fangs and lunged at the man. The nomads who were watching took several steps backwards. They hadn't forgotten that the beast had killed their comrade.

Fo Tu Deng had run out of patience. "Kill it," he yelled, pointing at Sunila.

Sunila disappeared, startling the monk.

"You can't kill him!" Tao said. "He's one of the few of his kind left. And you said yourself he might be useful."

"I haven't got time to run around after dragons."

The monk leaned closer to Tao. "About this vision …"

Tao knew he had no choice. He would have to help the monk. "I will seek a vision," he said. "But first you must release Kai."

"I will do that when you have told me what I want to know."

"No. To seek a vision, I need to be calm." Tao might

be Fo Tu Deng's captive, but the monk needed him. "You must assure me that neither dragon will be harmed."

"You have summoned a vision before while in fear for your life."

"But Kai was not in pain then. He was weakened by the presence of iron weapons, but he was not shackled with iron chains as he is now. You don't understand the power that I have. I wasn't born with it. It only appeared when I met the dragon. It comes from my connection with Kai. If anything happens to him, my visions will disappear." This at least was not a lie. Tao was sure that was true. "And I cannot summon a vision if I can hear Kai in pain."

The dragon made a loud scraping metal sound to emphasise Tao's point.

Tao could see that Fo Tu Deng was wavering. Jilong might be hundreds of *li* away, but the monk was surrounded by a band of men loyal to the warlord. Fo Tu Deng wasn't free. The nomads would report back whatever he did, and Jilong was a ruthless man. If the monk failed to give the warlord the information he needed, he would kill Fo Tu Deng without hesitation.

"I will get the *naga* to show himself, and you can keep both dragons confined," Tao said, "but not chained."

Fo Tu Deng waved his hand impatiently. "All right."

Tao went over to the goat pen.

One of the guards brought the key to unlock the chains,

but wouldn't do it himself. Tao undid the chains and threw them aside.

He spoke to Kai with his mind. "How did they manage to catch you?"

"I was incautious," Kai replied. "The nomads captured Sunila, and I was hiding in the forest, waiting for an opportunity to free him. Although I was trying to aid him, he squawked like a chicken being attacked by a fox. A nomad crept up behind me and hit me on the head."

Tao inspected the dragon's head. "The blow has reopened the wound made by that large hailstone."

He had one of the crystals of cinnabar in his hand. He spoke aloud this time, so that Fo Tu Deng could hear him.

"Let me see your tongue."

The dragon poked out his tongue and Tao peered at it.

Tao had positioned himself so that Fo Tu Deng couldn't see what he was doing.

"The colour is slightly improved," he said, as he slipped the crystal under Kai's tongue.

Out of the corner of his eye, Tao saw some pieces of straw fall from the compound wall. He guessed that Sunila was up in his nest, still invisible.

"Now I will get the *naga* to reappear," Tao said.

He went to the kitchen, took the last remaining piece of honeycomb, and slipped the other cinnabar crystal into it. As he walked out into the courtyard Sunila reappeared at his side. Fo Tu Deng and his guards all jumped backwards a step. Tao went up to the *naga* who nuzzled his hand to find the honey treat. Tao stood with the *naga* at his feet, contentedly chewing the honeycomb, and allowed himself a small moment of triumph.

Chapter Seventeen
VISION OF DARKNESS

Sunila flapped back up to his nest on the wall and Tao turned to the monk.

"Now, tell me what it is you want to know."

Fo Tu Deng's eyes lit up as if Tao had already provided the answer to his problems.

"It is simple. I need to know where the Black Camel Bandits are hiding." He lowered his voice so his men couldn't hear. "They never make a proper attack, just lots of sneaky little raids. They kill my men, and demoralise those who remain. At this rate I'll have no men left. At first I thought they might be Di people or perhaps the Xianbei, but neither of those tribes use a camel as an emblem. They must be a new tribe, perhaps from the desert where they ride camels."

The monk needed some firm information to report to Jilong, something to prove that he was worth keeping alive.

"Would you like me to try for a vision now?" Tao asked.

"No, no," Fo Tu Deng replied in a low voice. "Wait until

my men have settled down for the night."

The Zhao soldiers drifted off to their quarters. Some of them had taken over rooms in the compound, others had put up tents near the horses tethered down by the gate.

Tao sat in the peony pavilion and invented a small ritual, as if seeking visions was something that he often did and a strict ceremony was required to achieve success. He washed his hands, sat cross-legged and took some deep breaths. He recited a sutra. Tao smiled to himself. Creating a performance in order to trick an audience was something he'd learned from Fo Tu Deng. He opened the vial and allowed the yellow oil to drip onto his palms, then rubbed them together until they were covered with a film of oil. He held up his hands as if accepting something from heaven. Fo Tu Deng stood back respectfully. Then Tao brought his hands down in front of him, cupping them together.

"Help me great dragon spirit." Tao was almost enjoying himself. "Hear your servant's request for knowledge."

He heard the jingling-bell sound of dragon laughter coming from the goat pen. He was glad that Kai had recovered quickly.

"What is the secret of the Black Camel Bandits?" Tao continued. "Where do they hide to evade the Zhao so successfully?"

He stared at his palms until his eyes became unfocused. The request had no connection with Kai, so Tao wasn't expecting a vision to come. It was no surprise, therefore, when all he could see on his palms was black. He took some deep breaths, and tried to invent a vision. He was about to give up, when a thought struck him. The other times he'd failed to conjure up a vision, he'd always found himself staring at the lines on his hands, not at blackness. It *was* a vision – a vision of darkness. After a while, his eyes adjusted and he could make out faint man shapes. They were almost as black as the darkness but not quite. The only features visible were their eyes. As they blinked, they almost disappeared. Tao's visions always contained other information, but no matter how close he peered, he could see no other clues. The blinking eyes reminded him of something, but he couldn't remember what. There was a faint smell of incense and the sound of bells, but he thought he must be imagining that.

Then he could see the lines on his palms again. The darkness had gone. He turned his hands over as if expecting to see another image on the backs of his hands, but all he could see was the dirt from the garden under his fingernails.

Fo Tu Deng had been standing quietly, but he couldn't restrain himself any longer.

"Did you have a vision?"

Tao made the slightest inclination of his head.

"What? What did you see? Tell me!"

Tao let his shoulders sag, as if the vision had exhausted him. He held up his hand to stop the monk talking.

"You must be patient. Deciphering a vision is like understanding a sutra. Sometimes, contemplation is needed."

Tao needed time to think about what this vision meant. There were no other elements to interpret as there had been in his previous visions. No puzzle pieces. There had to be a meaning to the vision, but Tao had no idea what it was.

"First you must tell me the truth. My vision has shown me that you are withholding information." That was a lie. "If you don't tell me the truth, I might give the wrong interpretation."

Fo Tu Deng was shifting uncomfortably from one foot to the other.

"Is Jilong pleased with your service to him? Is your position secure?"

This was a guess, but it made the monk flinch.

"I do not have to tell you anything!" he said.

"It's your question that I have asked, not mine. What I see is never straightforward. If you want me to interpret the vision correctly, you must tell me the circumstances that brought about your request."

Tao turned his most serene and holy gaze on Fo Tu Deng. "Did you choose to be in the service of Jilong?"

The monk's arrogant confidence had disappeared. "His men tracked me down. They came to the monastery and took me against my will to Jilong's headquarters. He said he needed a seer, because the Black Camel Bandits had taken back Jiyuan, a town he'd won no more than a month ago. I pretended to know the next town that Jilong would lose, and then tortured the citizens until someone confessed they were helping the bandits. Jilong believed that I had averted another defeat. Now he expects me to know everything – where his enemies are, what strategies to use, which jacket he should wear."

Tao nodded sagely as if this information was very useful – which it was.

"Then he wanted to know when the next bandit attack would be. I picked a vague time in the future, but the very next night they killed three of his men. I managed to explain it away, but he will not tolerate another mistake."

"I appreciate your frankness, Fo Tu Deng," Tao said. "It has helped me unravel the clues in my vision."

"Tell me. I must know." Fo Tu Deng had had enough of being polite. "If you don't, I will put your dragon back in chains. I will wound him with a rusty blade."

"I'll tell you," Tao said, but he didn't know the meaning of the vision until the words came out of his mouth. "The bandits only emerge from their hiding place at night. That is why you never see them." He remembered what the blinking eyes in the vision had reminded him of. It was the swallows in the cave. "They have a hide-out where they spend the daylight hours. It is underground or in some other dark place. When they come out at night, they are dressed in black from head to foot, just their eyes are visible."

Fo Tu Deng's eyes lit up. "Where is this place?"

"I don't know."

"Quick. Seek another vision."

Tao refused. "You must respect my gift and use it only when absolutely necessary, otherwise it will not serve you. Give your men this information. Send them out to find the hide-out!"

Fo Tu Deng hurried off to rouse his men, some of whom had barely laid down their heads. As soon as he was out of sight, Kai jumped over the fence surrounding the goat pen.

"Was that true?" he asked. "Or did you make it up?"

"I saw nothing but darkness, but I think I've interpreted it correctly. And there is something else that I learned from the vision. Something I didn't tell Fo Tu Deng. I've seen someone wearing black clothing like that before."

Kai nodded slowly. "Pema."

"I knew there was something she wasn't telling us. Pema is in the service of the Black Camel Bandits."

Chapter Eighteen
HAUNTED

The Zhao soldiers crowded into the courtyard. They were bleary eyed and unhappy that Fo Tu Deng had woken them after less than an hour's sleep. Tao was watching from the kitchen doorway.

The monk climbed onto Wei's couch so that they could all see him.

"We are the advance guard of the Zhao army," he said. "It is up to us to ensure that Jilong has all the information he needs to defeat the Black Camel Bandits."

The nomads were grumbling. Tao could tell Fo Tu Deng was losing what little authority he had over them.

"I have achieved our first goal by securing this compound for our headquarters. But we still do not know where the bandits are hiding. Finding them is our next task."

The soldiers' muttered complaints were getting louder. He wasn't telling them anything they didn't already know.

"And since you have failed to find our enemies, I have sought the help of Buddha." He glared at them all. "The

Blessed One has seen fit to give me a vision."

There was more muttering. None of the Zhao believed in Buddha. Some of them laughed – perhaps those who had witnessed the monk's previous failed attempts at being a seer.

"My holy vision has told me why we haven't been able to find our enemies." That got the attention of some of the men. "They have outsmarted us. They have evaded us because they only come out at night and they dress in black." He paused. "They have been right under your noses. You have been wandering around in full daylight, unable to find them because they are tucked up asleep in their hiding place. We have not been secretive. They easily found our encampments and murdered your comrades as they slept."

The nomads were all listening now.

"Our enemies have been cunning," Fo Tu Deng said. "Now we have to outwit them. Instead of searching during the day, we must seek them out in the hours of darkness. We must start tonight."

"Where is their hiding place?" one man asked.

"That is what you have to find out!" Fo Tu Deng exclaimed. "I'm not going to do all your work for you."

"Couldn't you have another vision?"

"No! The Buddha has more important things to be thinking about. This is a chance for you to show your worth. I will recommend that the man who kills the most bandits is promoted to Jilong's personal guard."

He glared at the men.

"The Black Camel Bandits have humiliated you. It is time to beat them at this game of night hunting and regain the honour of the Zhao."

Fo Tu Deng produced a skin of *kumiss* and the men's mood changed as they passed it around. The drink warmed their bellies and they were more willing to listen to the monk's plan.

"You must travel in twos and threes on foot. We need stealth."

The men talked enthusiastically among themselves. They had spent weeks searching for the bandits without any success. Now that they had a clue to help them find their elusive enemies, they forgot about their lack of sleep and were impatient to get after the bandits. The Zhao didn't have black clothes and hoods, but they smeared their faces with charcoal. Their captain divided them into two groups – one to search to the west, the other to the east – and they marched off.

Fo Tu Deng's authority over the Zhao was held by a thread. He needed an early success or Jilong would hear about his failure to locate the enemy, let alone come up with strategies to defeat them.

"We will find their hiding place and then we will crush them." He was talking to Tao, but it seemed as if he was trying to convince himself. "When we have reduced their numbers, I will send word to Jilong, so that he can come and finish them off. Then we'll have a celebration to honour his victory, some sort of ceremony. We'll need to round up an audience from Luoyang to witness his triumph. He likes a spectacle, as I'm sure you remember." The monk's eyes lit up. "I have an idea! After we capture the leader of the Black Camel Bandits, we will stage a public execution!" His smile faded. "All we have to do is find out who he is."

Six nomads remained in the compound. Fo Tu Deng ordered them to keep watch, in case the bandits attacked – or Tao and Kai tried to escape.

But the remaining men refused to go up on the walls.

"Take your positions!" Fo Tu Deng demanded, but they still didn't move. "What's wrong with you?"

"It's the *naga*," one of them said, glancing up at Sunila who was in his nest. "We don't want to go up on the wall while it's there. We're scared it will turn into a monster during the night and bite us."

"Scared?" the monk shouted. "You are scared of a small dragon?"

"It's quite big," one of the men said.

"It creeps up on us, invisible, and then reappears."

"And snarls."

"We can't concentrate."

"He only shape-changes when he's afraid," Tao explained.

"If you're nice to him, he won't harm you."

Fo Tu Deng's face was turning a shade of purple. "You're supposed to be warriors! Fearless."

"We aren't going up on the wall while the monster is there," the soldier said. The others nodded in agreement.

"I'll take care of the *naga*," Tao said.

He called to Sunila. The *naga* obediently flapped down and stuck his snout up Tao's sleeve, hoping to find honeycomb.

"I have something that will make him sleep soundly through the night. He won't trouble you again." He patted Sunila on the head.

The *naga* looked no more dangerous than a puppy. The guards climbed up to take their places on the wall.

"I want the dragons secured," Fo Tu Deng said. "Lock them in the stables."

Tao led the two dragons over to the stables. Fo Tu Deng watched as Kai made himself a nest with the straw. Tao made one for the naga and spread the remains of Meiling's gown over it. He still had some of the green water from the underground lake in his water skin. He emptied it into a bowl and stirred in a little honey. Sunila lapped it up, rearranged his nest to his liking, turned in a circle three times and settled down. He was asleep immediately. Kai curled up in his own nest. Fo Tu Deng watched Tao bar the door before he went to bed himself.

As soon as the monk was gone, Tao unbarred the stable door and let Kai out, glad that he finally had the opportunity to talk to the dragon in private.

"I'm glad the cinnabar has done its job," Tao said, leading Kai to Wei's room.

"Now is the time to escape," Kai said. "The guards have had no sleep. They will soon become drowsy staring into the darkness."

"Not yet. I have put Pema at great risk by revealing the bandits' secret. We can't leave her at the mercy of the Zhao. We must warn her."

"How can we warn her if we do not know where she is?"

"I don't know."

"If the Zhao capture Pema, they will not kill her. Not immediately," Kai said. "They will bring her back here to torture her and learn all they can about the bandits. Then we can free her." Tao winced at the thought of Pema being hurt.

"So we do nothing but wait?"

"Till the morning at least."

"I should have realised Pema was involved in something when I saw her dressed in black."

"Why did she not tell us she was working for the bandits?"

"She knew I wouldn't approve. I expect she is spying for them."

They watched the last embers die.

"Kai, there is something I haven't told you."

"What?"

"I've been visited by a ghost."

"There are no ghosts. Remember? It was the invisible *naga*."

"But this one isn't invisible like the ghosts in the cave. I can see her – the ghost of a young girl. She haunts me every night."

"I sensed there was something wrong with you. I thought you were ill, but it seemed odd since we were eating well and resting."

"I've hardly slept since we arrived here."

"It must be lack of sleep that is making you imagine you are seeing a ghost."

"I'm not imagining her. She is real. Or as real as ghosts can be. She appears when the moon is in the night sky. She is made of moon shadow."

"Let us leave Huaxia," Kai said suddenly.

"Now?"

"Now. Forget about Pema and Sunila and Fo Tu Deng. Leave them and your fears behind! It was wrong of me to delay. It will be hard work reaching the dragon haven, but we will never be safe while we are in Huaxia."

"You're ready to go to the dragon haven? Tonight?"

"I am. Immediately."

"If we'd done that when we left Yinmi, we would be halfway there by now," Tao said. "We wouldn't have met Sunila. I would've thought Pema was safe at Chengdu. But that wasn't what happened. You lingered. And now I can't leave until I have warned Pema."

The huntsman spider was walking across the wall. Kai saw it and was about to swipe it away with his tail.

"No, don't!"

"Another one of your *wuji* friends?"

"She is about to begin her night's work."

"But the spider must kill to survive," Kai said. "You must be prepared to do that too."

"I will never kill." He watched the spider. "I envy her. She doesn't question her purpose. She knows exactly what she must do – hunt for food, and protect her young until they are ready to make their own way in the world." There were fewer spiderlings on the ceiling. Some had already left. "I wish my purpose was as clear to me."

Tao took the lump of cinnabar from his bag and broke it into three pieces. "You must carry cinnabar with you at all times." He wrapped one of the pieces in a strip of silk from Meiling's gown. "That's so it doesn't scratch."

Kai carefully placed the parcel behind his reverse scales.

"I'll give some to Sunila and keep the rest," Tao said.

It was late. Tao was dreading sleeping alone. He couldn't keep his fear from Kai.

"You need sleep. We will both sleep in the peony pavilion tonight. I will be close enough to hear you if you cry out for help. There will be some explanation for the appearance of this ghost girl, as there was for the ghosts we thought were in the cave."

Tao took two quilts outside. Kai spent some time scrunching one of them into a heap before he lay down.

"We will have a full night's sleep," the dragon said. "And then we must plan our escape."

Tao lay on the couch. Moths hovered over him protectively, but they couldn't keep his fears at bay. Kai was snoring before Tao had even got comfortable. He would have given anything for the dragon's ability to fall asleep so easily.

He waited. The sky was dark grey and starless, but thin shafts of moonlight pierced the clouds here and there. The night air carried a faint smell of rotting leaves. The moon showed its face in a gap in the clouds and the ghost appeared. She drifted around the garden as if she was searching for something. She lingered by the pool, gazing at her reflection. Among the flowers, with her ghost gown billowing, she looked like a lonely little girl. But when she saw Tao she lost all trace of innocent sadness. Her dark eye sockets were like deep wells of misery, except for the small pricks of moonlight. She bared her teeth, which were small, sharp and tipped with silver moonlight –

more like a wolfcub's than a little girl's.

Tao pulled the quilt up to his chin like a frightened child, though he knew it would give him no protection. He was too far away from Kai to nudge him.

"She's here." His voice was no more than a whisper. The dragon didn't wake.

Tao felt the ghost girl's hand enter his body, reaching deep inside him. He could hear faint crackling as if his blood was turning to ice crystals. Her icy fingers found their way to his heart and closed around it. He couldn't breathe.

Tao tried to call out to Kai again, but his mouth was freezing too. His lips wouldn't move. The ghost girl was stopping him from speaking.

It was Tao's fear that woke Kai, but the moment the dragon opened his eyes, the ghost dissolved into a grey mist that wafted through the pavilion like smoke. Tao collapsed back on the bed, gasping air.

Kai sat up on his haunches and looked around. "What is wrong?"

"It was the ghost girl."

"I cannot see anything."

"She's gone."

"It was the wind," Kai said.

The air was as still as a grave.

"What wind?"

Chapter Nineteen
THE GOLDEN-HAIRED DOLL

The ghost girl wanted something. What it was, Tao didn't know, but if he didn't find out, he knew she would kill him. If he could work out who she was, or rather who she'd been, it might help him discover what she wanted from him. He thought that she must be recently dead. Perhaps before his family moved south a child died at the compound, and in the rush to leave, no one had performed the proper ceremony for her burial. He could rectify that, as he had with the ghosts of Shenchi. First he had to find her remains.

Tao got up and stepped over the sleeping dragon before the sun rose. The guards on the wall were sleepy and, in the grey pre-dawn, Tao easily avoided being seen as he crawled out through his tunnel and ran into the fields beyond the walls.

Previous generations of his family were buried in the Huan ancestral tomb in the Mang Hills behind Luoyang, but out beyond the fields Tao found several tombs where farm workers had been buried. They were almost hidden by overgrown grass and brambles. Closer to the compound was the place where cremations took place for those who had accepted belief in the Blessed One. There was an ashy patch where a camphor wood pyre had recently been burned, but this wasn't where a child had been cremated. It was the remains of Wei's pyre. Tao knew his brother was in his next life, so he hadn't visited that place since he'd returned. Still, he lingered there for a moment.

Whoever the ghost girl was, it was Tao she had chosen to haunt. He must have some connection to her. Had there been another sister born before Meiling – a first child who died young? Her death so painful that his parents had never spoken of her? She might have been quietly haunting the compound for a long time, happy to drift unseen among the living members of her family, watching her parents, her brothers and sister live their lives. Tao had never been aware of her before, but perhaps that was her choice. That would explain why she had focused on him, the remaining member of her family. Whoever she was, she had been left behind and she was furious.

Tao felt a lance point in his back. The nomads were returning after searching all night for the bandits.

"I'm not trying to escape," he said. "I was visiting the remains of my brother."

The Zhao soldiers hadn't found any of the Black Camel Bandits. They were dejected and exhausted. Tao was relieved that they hadn't captured Pema. As they marched him back to the compound, he thought about how he could get the trust of the ghost girl, this shadow sister.

In the daylight, Pema's explanation that there had been no ghosts of the Shenchi villagers made sense. No spirits had followed them into the underground cave. It was the invisible *naga* who had touched him in the dark, whose cold breath had chilled him. But it didn't matter how much Tao reasoned with himself, he still remembered the sensation of the ghosts departing when he'd finished his inscription, their sigh of release when he recited a sutra for them and they'd passed into their next lives. He hadn't imagined that. He hadn't imagined the ghost girl either. She was a child without knowledge of spiritual matters. Perhaps she didn't understand why she had been left behind. Tao had to help her let go of her past life and begin a new one.

Tao thought about what he would've done if he'd had a real little sister who he wanted to please. He would probably have given her a gift. He remembered the toys his father had made for him and Wei when they were children. For Tao, he'd carved a horse and a little cart with wheels that turned, some *liubo* pieces, a small bow and arrow. For Wei, he'd made animals – a monkey, a bear and a tiger – and hung them from the rafters where Wei could see them.

Their father had made all those things from wood, using just his knife and chisel. Tao decided he would make a toy for the ghost girl. None of those toys were suitable for a girl, but Tao remembered that when Meiling was young dolls were all she was interested in. Hers were made from baked clay, but there was no reason why he couldn't make a wooden doll.

When he got back to the compound, Kai was waiting for him.

"Where have you been?" The dragon sounded like a mother berating a wandering child. "We were supposed to talk about our plans when we woke this morning. It was dangerous for you to go out. The guards on the wall could easily have shot you to relieve their boredom."

"I was looking for the remains of the ghost girl."

Mist streamed from the dragon's nostrils. "Put this ghost girl out of your mind. She does not exist!"

Tao ignored Kai's comment. "Before we leave, I must do this one thing – I have to help her move into her next life."

He went to open the stable door, and Sunila bounded out, refreshed and full of energy.

Fo Tu Deng emerged. "What are these dragons doing loose?"

"I let them out," Tao said. "They will be powerful allies if you treat them well."

The monk made the exhausted nomads assemble and

started admonishing them for their failure to find their enemies.

"You're useless," he shouted. "You don't deserve to call yourself Zhao!"

The nomads were too tired to react to his jibes. As soon as he finished, they stumbled to their quarters to sleep.

"You must find out more information," the monk said to Tao. "I need to know exactly where this bandit hide-out is."

Tao bowed politely. "In the evening, before the men go out again, I will seek another vision."

"Do it now!" Fo Tu Deng ordered.

"First I must meditate to prepare myself," Tao said.

"I am going to ride into the city. I have to seize provisions."

Tao thought of the hungry inhabitants of Luoyang having to give up their meagre food stores.

"I expect a vision when I return," the monk said. "And make sure the *naga* doesn't escape. I've sent men to get more frogs."

Fo Tu Deng rode off with a guard of six men, none of who were happy that they were again denied sleep.

There was still grain in the cellar, and vegetables in the earth. When Tao had fed himself and the dragons, he went to his father's workshop. He spent some time selecting the right piece of wood, settling on a block of pale poplar. He knew it would take most of the day for Fo Tu Deng to ride to Luoyang and back, so he fetched his father's carving tools and settled down on a garden seat in the sunshine.

Sunila had found a grasshopper and was amusing himself making it jump. Tao was worried that the *naga* would unintentionally kill it.

"What are you making?" Kai asked.

"Something for the ghost girl. I thought if I gave her a gift, she might be willing to move into her next life."

"The ghost girl does not exist, Tao. Except in your imagination."

"I know you think I'm imagining her, but I'm not. And I am sure this will make her happy."

"Forget about this foolish enterprise." Kai looked around the ramparts. "There are just six men awake. Now is the time to escape."

"The only way you can get out is through the gate. The guards would see us and raise the alarm. The rest of the Zhao would be roused and they would haul us back again. They might be bad tempered enough to kill us."

"So we sit and wait? Is that your great plan?"

"I will not leave until I know Pema is safe."

Kai stalked off.

Tao gave Sunila the job of keeping birds off his newly sown garden beds. It took him a while to explain to the *naga* that he couldn't hurt them. Once he understood, Sunila made himself invisible and whenever a bird came near the garden, he reappeared with a squawk.

With his father's knife, Tao fashioned a head and a body from the piece of wood. He carved delicate features on the doll's face – downturned eyes, a small smile, a pretty little nose. He shaped arms from a smaller branch, drilled a hole through the body and threaded a length of string through it to attach an arm to either side. He cut another strip from Meiling's abandoned gown. He'd always mended his own robes when he was a novice, so he was quite good with a needle and thread. He made a tiny version of the gown from the cloth, tying it around the waist with a length of ribbon. Finally, he carved small feet at the end of the piece of wood, so that they peeped out from under the gown.

He needed something for hair, and after searching the entire house he could find nothing suitable. He was watching Sunila startle a blackbird when he realised that he had exactly what he needed at hand. Sunila's mane grew in a narrow band from the base of his horn to his shoulder blades. Kai's mane consisted of coarse brown hair like frayed rope, but the *naga's* was the colour of wheat, and the hair was as fine and soft as strands of silk. It was quite pretty.

When the *naga* settled down for an afternoon nap, Tao crept up to him and cut off a lock of his mane with the knife. He punched small holes in the doll's head and pushed a few of the dragon's hairs in each hole. He glued them in place and pulled the hair back into a tiny plait, tying it with some coloured thread. It was an unnatural colour for human hair, but it was the best he could do. Finally, he painted the doll's face. He made a sort of ink by grinding charcoal into water and outlined the eyes. He used the juice of a wolfberry to colour the lips. He found a little pot of blue cream that his sister had used to colour her eyelids. He painted blue dots in the centre of the doll's eyes, so that they were the same colour as Pema's.

Kai had been sitting, watching the process suspiciously from a distance. "Is it a Buddhist figure?"

Tao laughed. "No. It's a doll."

The dragon made an impatient sound, like someone banging a spoon on a bowl. "Even if this ghost did exist, she would not be able to hold a doll. How could she take it with her?"

Tao looked at the doll. It wasn't as pretty as Meiling's. His confidence in his plan was fading.

"I know she can't take it into her next life, but I thought if she saw that someone cared about her, she might stop being angry."

"That would make her want to stay here even more." Kai shook his head. "I do not know why we are having this discussion. There is no ghost girl!"

Tao didn't argue with Kai. He knew that the ghost girl existed. And he knew that she needed something.

As night approached Fo Tu Deng returned, saddle weary and bad tempered. The Zhao soldiers were waking up and they filled the courtyard with their bodies, their chatter and the smell of meat cooking. The monk drank some *kumiss* and shouted at the men, threatening them with punishment if they didn't bring back news of the Black Camel Bandits that night. He was so tired, he forgot that he'd asked Tao for another vision. He ate some food and went to bed.

Tao made a meal of grain, bean curd and mung beans for himself and the dragons. He mixed a spoonful of honey with Sunila's portion. The naga reached behind one of his reverse scales and pulled out some grubs that he'd found while Tao was weeding. He sprinkled the grubs on the food and ate it, leaving the beans licked clean in the bottom of his bowl.

Tao waited until the last of the Zhao had left on their night patrol before he carried out his plan.

He propped up the doll on one of the rocks, picked a few of the blue crocuses that were growing around the peony pavilion and arranged them with a sprig of bamboo in a little jar. He brought a half-burnt cone of incense from the kitchen altar, lit it and placed it next to the doll. He also found a scrap of paper.

"I need a poem, Kai. Something that a young girl would like."

Kai didn't want to take part in what he considered to be a foolish exercise, but in the end he couldn't resist the opportunity to compose a poem. He walked up and down the garden path, searching for inspiration. Finally, he made a sound like wind chimes in the breeze.

"Your young life ended too soon.
Do not weep for the past.
Illuminated by the moon,
Make your way at last."

"That's perfect!" Tao said. "The best poem you've ever composed."

Tao copied the words neatly onto the paper – or as neatly as he could using charcoal ink and a brush made by chewing the end of a twig. He placed the scrap of paper under the doll.

"What do you think, Kai?"

The dragon snorted. "I think this is nonsense."

Fo Tu Deng hadn't ordered the dragons to be locked up, so Kai went off to his hollow in the goat pen and Sunila flapped up to his nest on the wall. Tao was left to keep the vigil by himself. In the moonlight, the doll seemed a little sinister.

Tao lay on the couch and felt sleep pulling on his eyelids.

A gust of wind roused him from a dreamless sleep. The full moon was high in the sky. The bright moonlight had bleached the colour from the garden. The ghost girl was there already, storm-cloud grey and fully formed. Streaks of silver gathered in the folds of her gown. Tao watched as she drifted around the garden. She was no longer transparent. It was hard to believe that she wasn't made of something solid. From a distance, she was almost beautiful, like a dark *deva*, like a bad fairy. She stopped when she saw his gift and moved closer, her shadow eyes on the doll. He hoped his plan was working, that the gift would dissolve her anger. But the shadows around her hollow eyes deepened, and she bared her sharp teeth. Tao felt the cold points of her silver-white pupils bore into him like needles. He wanted to run away, but he couldn't move. The ghost girl whirled around him. Tao remembered how the Shenchi ghosts had circled him, creating a wind before they disappeared with a sigh. Had she accepted his gift? Was she getting ready to journey into her own next life? He muttered a sutra to help her on her way. She circled faster and faster. He waited for her to whirl into the air with a sigh, as the other ghosts had. But she didn't.

The ghost girl picked up speed until she was a grey blur trailing silver. Moon shadow couldn't produce wind, and yet she was making the air move somehow, swirling fallen leaves, tearing petals from flowers. The cone of incense tipped over and set light to the paper with the poem on it. But it was the doll that she was focusing on. The ghost girl's swirling fanned the flame. The doll's golden hair caught fire. She created a small whirlwind that lifted up the doll, spinning it round and round. The flames glowed brighter and burned off all the hair. And then the doll was thrown out of the vortex, hurled against a tree with such force that it smashed to splinters.

But the ghost girl's anger wasn't spent. She rushed from the garden into the house. Tao heard things crash and clatter, but he was too terrified to follow her to see what was happening.

Sunila fluttered down from his nest on the wall. Like all dragons his hearing was bad and he was unaware of the uproar. He scrabbled through the remains of the food left by the nomads. He was just looking for a snack. He glowed softly in the moonlight.

"Sunila," Tao hissed, but he didn't hear him.

Too frightened to run across the courtyard to warn Sunila, Tao picked up a rock from the garden and hurled it at the *naga*. His aim was bad, his strength pathetic. The rock fell on the path with a thud, well short of its target, but the vibrations from the impact reached the *naga*. He looked up, his blue eyes bright in the moonlight. That was when the ghost girl surged outside again and saw the *naga*. She let out an unearthly howl, high-pitched like the cry of a wild animal. It was the first time the ghost girl had made a sound. Howling with fury, she flung herself towards the *naga*. Sunila leaped to his feet and turned into a seven-headed snake. The ghost girl stopped in her tracks. The jewelled crests on the snakes' heads glittered in the moonlight. For a moment she wavered and her moon-shadow body began to disperse. But the *naga's* teeth snapped on nothing. The ghost girl's fury returned. She rushed at him and he transformed into his half-human form, but the writhing snakes growing out of his shoulders didn't deter her. Then, just as she reached the shape-changed *naga*, he winked out like someone blowing out a lamp. The ghost girl howled again.

Not a breath of air stirred. The ghost girl seemed calmer, as if her anger was dissipating. Tao wondered if her strength was fading, but the full moon was still in the sky and there were no clouds to hide it. It would be some time before she faded. She drifted over and hovered in front of Tao, motionless apart from the gentle rippling of her shadow gown. Her silver needle-prick eyes pierced him and, though he wanted to run, he couldn't move. He tried to call to Kai with his mind but no words would form. Close up, he could see that the ghost girl wasn't beautiful at all. Her coiling hair was in knots. Her skin was pockmarked and decaying. There was no ghost flesh on the fingers of her right hand. It had fallen away completely, revealing bones and clots of black blood. The tip of her little finger was missing.

She slipped into Tao, but this time she didn't pass through, she stayed inside him. She wasn't calm at all. Her fury was held in, like water inside a leather skin. But the skin burst, and her wrath poured into him. Tao gasped as it filled his body like icy river water. There were no words, but her anger was more eloquent than words. She didn't want Tao's gift and she didn't want to leave this world.

An image of a small cairn of stones formed in his mind. He suddenly realised who the ghost girl was. He understood why she was so angry.

Tao tried to breathe but he couldn't. While she was inside him, his lungs wouldn't expand. He tried to stir his *qi*, but it was thick and slow like freezing water. As his panic grew, he felt her rage turn to pleasure. Sparks of light appeared before Tao's eyes. His ears rang as if crazed monks were ringing temple bells. She was killing him.

Tao saw Kai bound across the courtyard. He knew the dragon was speaking to him, but he couldn't hear his words. Kai took in the ruined garden, the smashed and smouldering doll. He ran towards Tao, but stopped as if an invisible barrier blocked his way. Tao had given up any thought of breathing. He saw a burst of light, like a holy vision. He thought it was the Blessed One come to guide him to his next life. He had not avoided death at all.

But the ghost girl left Tao's body, and he collapsed, gasping for air. The bright light was still in his eyes. He realised what it was – not a holy presence, but the first rays of the sun appearing over the wall. The sunlight had taken away the power of the moon, reduced it to a faint shape in the dawn sky. The rays of light had dissolved the ghost girl.

Kai was leaning over him anxiously. "Are you all right?"

Tao could feel the dragon's breath on his face, smell his fishy, over-ripe plum smell.

"It was the ghost girl. I know you don't believe me. But she was here and she tried to kill me."

"I saw her," Kai said. "I saw the ghost girl. I am sorry I doubted you."

"I know who she is, Kai."

"Who?"

"It's Baoyu, the granddaughter of the old man from Shenchi."

Kai didn't argue this time. He inclined his head.

Sunila reappeared right next to them, making concerned cheeping sounds. Tao pointed at the *naga*.

"I made the doll's hair from his mane. I gave her a gift made with the hair of the creature responsible for all her grief, the ruin of her village, the loss of her family. The creature whose bite killed her."

Chapter Twenty
UNEXPECTED GUESTS

"I understand that the ghost girl is angry with Sunila," Kai said. "He was responsible for her death. But why does she wish to kill you?"

"I told her grandfather that she was at peace, and she isn't. I sent her remaining family members far away. I was the one who found food for Sunila. I saved him from starvation and I cared for him. Then, the final insult, I gave her a gift made of his hair."

"It is not your fault she died." Kai glared at the *naga*, who was trying to hide behind the couch. "Our problems started when the *naga* appeared. He is the one who killed her."

Tao couldn't blame the *naga* for Baoyu's death; he'd been mad with hunger when he crashed through Shenchi village. But it was true – since Sunila had entered their lives, nothing had gone right.

Baoyu had swept through Wei's room and knocked the precious things from the shelf. Those fragile mementos of the outside world that Tao had brought back for his brother had sat undisturbed for years, but now they were broken, smashed by the ghost girl's force. The baby spiders were all gone. Baoyu's fury must have frightened them away. She knew all the things that were dear to him.

Outside, Tao could hear the sounds of the Zhao soldiers returning from their second night of searching for the Black Camel Bandits. From the way they trudged silently to their quarters, he guessed they'd still had no success. Fo Tu Deng would soon be awake and Tao would have to face the monk and his demands.

In the kitchen, pieces of the red clay teapot and broken bowls littered the floor. Tao knew he hadn't seen the last of the ghost girl.

"It is time to go," Kai said.

The thought of leaving all his problems behind was tempting. The Zhao knew all about his secret places – Yinmi Monastery and his family home – neither provided sanctuary any more. But there was still something holding him back.

"Not yet."

"If we leave this place, you will be free of the ghost girl."

"No, I won't. She's been haunting me ever since we left her grandfather. I thought if I could convince her to move into her next life, then all would be well. But she won't go. There's something I have to do to appease her."

"What?"

Tao sighed. "I don't know."

"We cannot stay here."

"I know that. But I can't leave until Baoyu's ghost is at rest. I must find out what it is she wants."

"A ghost must stay near its remains," Kai said.

"So how can she continue to exist in ghost form when she is so far from her grave?"

"It seems a long way to you because we had to walk up and down hills and around mountains to get here. And we travelled at human pace. But her grave is not far away – as the dragon flies. If we travel further from her grave, she will not be able to follow us."

"Then she will haunt someone else."

"I suspect that it is not the ghost girl you are concerned about leaving behind, but Pema."

Tao felt his cheeks warm.

"It's true I am worried about her, but I will happily leave her behind if she has a safe place to live, and she has chosen a peaceful way of life."

"Huaxia is in chaos, Tao. You cannot save everybody."

Tao knew he couldn't save everyone. But he wanted to save Pema.

"Your duty is to be a dragonkeeper as Wei told you. You cannot allow these two girls – one dead, one alive – to shackle you to your past."

Tao's brain agreed with Kai though his heart disagreed.

"If you refuse to leave. I will go alone."

Tao couldn't let that happen.

"You're right, Kai. We must go."

Once Tao had made the decision, he wanted to leave immediately. He found a leather bag in a storeroom, the sort that goatherds carry on their backs when they take their flocks up to the mountain pastures in summer. It took him no more than a minute or two to collect his few possessions and put them in the bag. He looked at his toes poking out from his sandals. He needed more substantial footwear, warmer clothing. He wasn't sure how he would endure the winter months, but that was a problem for later.

Kai composed a poem to reassure him about the cold weather that lay ahead.

"Winter is a lovely season,
When cleansing winds do blow.
There is not a sensible reason
To dislike it because of a little snow."

"That isn't your best poem." Tao managed a smile.

Kai didn't have to pack. Everything he owned fitted behind his five reverse scales. Tao went into the kitchen, bundled up as much grain, dried fruit and nuts as he could fit into the bag and slung it on his back. He picked up his staff with its new dragon head.

Kai nodded approvingly. "It is good. Fitting for a dragonkeeper."

They walked towards the gate. "You go out through your tunnel when the guards are on the other side of the wall," Kai said. "I will use my mirage skill."

"What about Sunila?" Tao said. "We can't leave him here."

"We cannot take him to the dragon haven. He is a *naga*, not a dragon of Huaxia. The other dragons will attack him."

"Then we must take him back to Tianzhu."

They were still arguing about this when someone started thumping on the gate. The guards, who had been dozing in the morning sun, jumped to their feet, grabbed their weapons and peered down from the wall to see who was there. One of them gasped in horror. The thumping continued, accompanied by impatient shouting. Fo Tu Deng came out of Mrs Huan's room, bleary eyed.

"Are we under attack?" he called up to the guards. "Are our enemies at the gate?"

"No," one of the guards shouted back. "Not our enemies." From the tremor in his voice, it sounded like whoever was there was worse.

Someone lifted the bar and opened the gate. A pack of Zhao soldiers astride black horses was crowded outside. They wore leather armour and red plumes on their helmets.

The horses were snorting and sweaty after a long ride. At the head of the group was a handsome young man wearing a crimson jacket, shiny metal armour and a white fur hat. His leather boots were the same colour as his jacket. His black horse reared up, as if angry at being stopped from galloping, and then strode into the compound.

Tao groaned. "It's Jilong and his personal guard!"

"We should have left at dawn," Kai said. "The delay has cost us dearly."

Tao couldn't believe his bad fortune. The moment he finally decided to escape was the very moment Jilong arrived unannounced at the gate. Kai was right. They should have left as soon as they'd made the decision.

"I kneel before you, Langhai," Fo Tu Deng said, sinking unsteadily to one knee.

Tao had not heard the term before. It meant wolf child. He guessed it was the title given to the man next in line to be Chanyu – the leader of the Zhao.

"You should have sent word you were arriving," Fo Tu Deng said. "I would have arranged a welcome feast."

The monk's hair was standing on end, his outer robe thrown hastily over his shoulders, scarcely covering his skinny body. He was too busy bowing to Jilong to notice that Tao had a packed bag and was ready to leave.

"Where are my men?" Jilong asked.

"They are sleeping, Langhai."

The warlord glanced at the sun, which was almost halfway along its journey to midday. "At this time of day?"

"We have been up all night," the monk said. "Searching for the Black Camel Bandits."

"I have ridden all through the night," Jilong said. "But I am not asleep. No one else should be."

"I will rouse them immediately." Fo Tu Deng waved over a blinking Zhao soldier who had got up to pee. "Wake the men. Get someone to prepare food for the Langhai."

The man scurried away.

"I will explain our new tactics, but first you must have food and refreshments."

The warlord got down from his horse in a single smooth motion. He glared at Fo Tu Deng, who hadn't stopped bobbing and bowing since Jilong arrived. Then the warlord's eyes fell on Tao and Kai. He sneered at them as if he'd discovered not one but two cockroaches in his food. "What are they doing here?"

"I have captured them to serve you, my lord." The prospect didn't seem to please the warlord. "Or to dispose of, if that is your wish."

"Is the girl here too?" Jilong asked.

He meant Pema, who had tried to kill Jilong's uncle, Shi Le.

The warlord scowled at Tao and Kai. "If it wasn't for these two, that murderous little savage would not have escaped my punishment. Kill them both."

Fo Tu Deng had a problem. The monk needed Tao alive.

A young nomad, no more than a boy, was so tired he'd fallen asleep on his horse. He slid to the ground with a thump.

"The Langhai did not give any orders to stand down!" the captain of the guard snarled. He was a huge man with muscular arms and one ear missing. "Put that man in irons and give him no rations." The lad was hoisted up and taken away.

Jilong surveyed the compound. "This place will make a good headquarters."

He went over to the peony pavilion and sat on Wei's couch, leaning back and putting his red-booted feet on the cushions. He called for some *kumiss*.

But Jilong and his men weren't the last visitors to arrive. No one had bothered to close the gate. A covered carriage drawn by four horses came into the compound. Tao recognised it immediately. It was the same carriage that he'd seen at the horse-riding contest outside Luoyang. Then it had contained beautiful young ladies, favoured by the warlord, whose job it was to flatter him and look attractive on his arm.

Tao remembered the last time he'd seen that carriage, when Pema had stepped out, almost unrecognisable in a fine gown and with painted lips and eyelids. Tao's stomach clenched as the carriage door opened. He was half expecting Pema to emerge again among a chatter of ladies, wreathed in perfumed silk. But just one woman stood at the carriage door and waited as servants rushed to place steps for her to climb down. It wasn't Pema, and this woman was no court beauty. She was short, fat and old. Her hair had been tied up inexpertly in the style of Huaxia women, and had fallen to one side. She wore a creased and ill-fitting gown that was an ugly shade of green. She struggled awkwardly down the three steps. Jilong hurried over to give her support as she descended.

The woman stood in the compound, cooling herself with a bamboo fan. Her face was red from the effort of climbing down the few steps. Her brow was deeply wrinkled from scowling; she had an enormous nose, and the lines around her mouth turned down as if she'd never smiled in her life. She reminded Tao of a painting of a demon at Yinmi. The compound fell silent. Jilong bowed low before her.

"Mother," he said. "What are you doing here? Quarters have been prepared for you at Luoyang."

"I spent last night there. I didn't like it. The bed was uncomfortable. There were rats. And I couldn't see the stars." She spoke with a harsh accent, unlike Jilong whose Huaxia was perfect. "I was hoping for one of those imperial palaces I've heard so much about, but they were all in ruins. Your men told me you were here."

"As soon as I have defeated the Black Camel Bandits," Jilong said, "my first task will be to build a grand palace for you."

The woman grunted. "In the meantime, I will stay here."

Jilong turned to Fo Tu Deng. "See to it that the best room in the compound is prepared for Lady Wang," he said. "Unless I am mistaken, that will be the one *you* are currently using."

"I will do it immediately, Langhai." Fo Tu Deng backed away to Mrs Huan's room, bowing as he went.

Jilong took his mother's arm again and led her to Wei's couch.

Tao didn't recognise the kind and caring person that Jilong had transformed into.

"I am honoured that you have made such a long and uncomfortable journey to visit me," he said, stroking her arm.

"I want food," she said, whacking his hand with her fan.

Tao waited to witness Jilong's anger. Surely this woman would be executed for such disrespect. But the warlord's features rearranged themselves. His eyes filled with tears, his mouth turned up at the edges, his teeth were revealed. Something unfamiliar appeared on his face. It was a smile – not the mean sneer Tao had seen before, but the sort of soft smile women wore when admiring babies. It was like watching a tiger roll over to have its tummy tickled.

Jilong shouted orders at his personal cook. "Prepare a meal for Lady Wang immediately!"

"Get my chest," the old woman snapped. "I don't want one of your stupid men carrying it. They'll probably drop it."

"Of course, Mother."

Jilong scurried back to the carriage and hauled down a huge chest, like a child proud to be asked to do a task beyond his age. Some of his men went to help him.

"I'll carry it!" he insisted, though his knees were buckling under the weight.

Jilong staggered to Mrs Huan's room. Lady Wang followed.

Tao and Kai glanced at each other. It seemed there was one person in the world who had no fear of Jilong. His mother.

Chapter Twenty-One
THE ORB SPIDER

The Zhao troops were gathered around the peony pavilion where Jilong and his mother sat framed by its delicate carvings and double roof with the turned up corners. It was the sort of setting that the young warlord liked – something that made him look imperial. He stood up to address his men and they fell silent.

"You have heard the news," he said. "Our enemies have the upper hand. They have taken back Jiyuan, which I won less than a month ago."

He made it sound like he'd done it single-handedly.

Lady Wang sat on the couch, her knees apart, her feet dangling. Next to her were the remains of a small feast of four courses – roast deer, rabbit stew, baked pangolin and pickled eggs. She wasn't listening to the speech. She was still pushing food into her mouth.

"They attacked at night wearing their black clothes," Jilong said, "sneaking up on our comrades and killing them silently in the darkness."

"Cheats," the men muttered. "Cowards."

"They have no pride in battle. They will use any means to beat us."

Tao and Kai were watching from the kitchen doorway.

"Remember the tactics the Zhao soldiers used in the contests at the White Horse Temple?" Tao said. They had been prepared to do anything to win.

Kai nodded. "And that was when they were pitted against their comrades."

One minute Jilong was shouting that the nomads were useless soldiers, not fit to clean his boots, the next he was describing the wonderful victory they would have because of their superiority over their enemies.

"It is up to you." He left them to imagine what would happen if they failed. "Even I cannot defeat the Black Camel Bandits alone. You must find strength and fight with me. Your hearts must be filled with hatred for these spineless thugs. We fight for the honour of the Zhao!"

The men cheered and clashed their weapons. The warlord didn't need to give them *kumiss* to win them round. They were ready for a fight.

Jilong helped Lady Wang get down from the couch. She wiped her mouth on her sleeve and put her arm through his. The men were still cheering their leader as Jilong turned and walked straight into the orb spider's web. The sticky threads clung to his face and his crimson jacket.

The more he tried to free himself, the more entangled he became. The huge spider crawled out of the vine that wound around the pavilion. It descended on a lengthening thread of silk until it was dangling a finger-width from Jilong's nose. A look of horror spread across the warlord's face. The spider was reaching out to him with several of its yellow-striped legs. Jilong seemed unable to move. Tiny Lady Wang tried to bat it away with her fan. The spider stepped delicately onto Jilong's nose. The warlord screamed. Lady Wang hit his nose so hard it started to bleed. The spider, meanwhile, descended on its thread and sat on Jilong's hand. He jumped into the pool to wash it off, but the water barely came up to his knees. He slipped on the slime in the pond and fell on his bottom, still waving his hand to try to dislodge the spider.

Kai's jingling laughter rang out. "Did you make the spider do that?"

"No. At least not intentionally."

Tao wondered if his *qi* power really had influenced the spider. He moved forwards and bowed. "If I may assist, General."

Tao stepped onto a rock in the pond and reached out to the spider, which climbed onto his hand. He stepped back off the rock. The men were biting their lips, trying not to laugh. Jilong got up and stalked off to his quarters, leaving behind his mother and a trail of wet footprints. Tao put the spider safely back among the vines.

Fo Tu Deng grabbed Tao by the arm and pushed him into the peony pavilion.

"Quick," he said. "I need to know what advice to give Jilong. You must seek another vision."

"But …"

"I haven't got time for your excuses. I need a vision now! He hates to be humiliated. At any moment, one of his men will make a comment or a small mistake and Jilong will have him executed on the spot. I have seen it before. And then he will attack some unfortunate town and kill the inhabitants, just to improve his mood." The monk put his arm around Tao's shoulders. "You can stop people from dying."

That was the one thing that would convince Tao to help Jilong. Kai made a deep rumbling sound.

The courtyard was quiet. The soldiers had all gone to their quarters to sleep. Jilong was still sulking in his room. Tao had no distractions. If he could save people's lives, it was his duty to try.

"Tell me what Jilong wants to achieve."

"The Zhao have been victorious for more than ten years under Shi Le's leadership." Fo Tu Deng was whispering, though there was no one around to hear him. "Jilong isn't content to leave a trail of destruction behind him – though he has a talent for that. He is planning to take over from his uncle. He wants his own empire. He dreams of rebuilding Luoyang and making it his capital. The recent setbacks don't help his cause. Shi Le will not hand over the reins of power to Jilong while he is losing towns to bandits."

"It makes no difference to me which band of nomads is in power," Tao said.

"If you do not value the lives of your fellow Huaxia, it comes down to whether you value your own life and that of your dragon. If you don't seek a vision, I will see to it that you are both tortured."

Kai looked at Tao. "You may as well try." Tao heard the dragon's voice in his head. "If no vision comes, make one up. We have nothing to lose but our lives."

"I need to know as much about the situation as possible before I seek a vision," Tao said. "Tell me about Jilong's mother."

Fo Tu Deng didn't argue. He sat down on an embroidered cushion.

"Lady Wang is not his natural mother. She is his uncle Shi Le's mother. When Shi Le took Jilong in when he was a boy, she adopted him as her son. He became devoted to her, as you see."

"How is Shi Le?" Tao ventured.

"He lives, but the wound that wretched girl inflicted has left him unable to walk. Or so he says. Anyway, he rules from his bed, which he never leaves. Jilong still answers to him, but he would like to be the one they call Chanyu."

Tao shuddered at the thought of Jilong's ruthless uncle who had killed Pema's family. She had tried to seek revenge and kill the Zhao leader herself, but had failed. She was wandering around the countryside somewhere. If Jilong's men found her, they would recognise her and take her to Jilong.

Kai's voice echoed in Tao's head again. "You must invent a vision. Something that will enable us to escape."

Tao's head was spinning as he tried to come up with a plan. What could he make up to convince Fo Tu Deng that he'd had a true vision? He needed something that would be an advantage to the monk, but at the same time help them escape.

Fo Tu Deng put a cushion on the floor for Tao to sit on. The monk was impatient for him to start. Tao removed the oil from his bag.

"I must calm my mind," Tao said.

"Do you want some incense?" the monk asked. "Should I recite a sutra?"

Kai made his jingling-bell sound, amused by the monk's eagerness to help.

"Ah, good," Fo Tu Deng said. "The dragon is providing bell ringing. That always helps to create a holy atmosphere."

Tao smiled to himself. That brief moment of lightheartedness calmed him. Sunila had come down from the wall to watch, as if he thought this was an important moment. He helped add to the sense of occasion.

It gave Tao an unfamiliar, malicious pleasure to see the monk squirming with impatience. He slowly rubbed the oil into his hands and stared at them. He was thinking about a way to escape the clutches of the Zhao, not a vision he was certain would not appear. He examined his palms, mirror images of each other, except for a scar on one and a splinter in the other. The sun was making him drowsy.

He was stifling a yawn when a small moth landed on his palm. The intricacy and beauty of each individual insect always fascinated Tao. This one had four brown wings with orange markings. Such a small creature, so vulnerable, and yet each leg, each feeler, was perfectly made. It brought tears to his eyes. The moth flew off. His palms blurred. He wasn't expecting a vision, so he hadn't thought about letting his eyes go out of focus. He was astonished when an image appeared on his palms.

He saw a booted foot in a leather stirrup. It was a distinctive boot – red, with a scorpion tail attached to the toe. The colours were muted, as if seen at night. But Tao knew that boot. He'd seen it just a few minutes ago. It belonged to Jilong. There was something else – the owner of the boot was astride a creature and it wasn't a horse. His boot dug into the animal's flank, which was covered in silver scales.

Tao gasped. The vision disappeared. He didn't want to tell the monk what he had seen – Jilong riding a dragon. He didn't want to tell Kai either. For once, Tao knew the meaning of the vision immediately.

"Well?" the monk said. "What did you see?"

Kai was staring at Tao. He knew he'd seen a real vision.

The monk leaned forwards, eager to hear what Tao had to say. "Tell me!"

Tao was in no hurry to tell the evil monk what he had seen. "Jilong is a vain man. He is not used to failure. The loss of Jiyuan and his inability to find the Black Camel Bandits has wounded his pride."

"You are right. He would never admit it, but I suspect his recent defeats have diminished his confidence."

Tao tried to keep his thoughts from the dragon, but he couldn't. Now Kai knew what he had seen in his vision.

"Do not tell him!"

Tao ignored Kai. "You must provide Jilong with a dragon," he told Fo Tu Deng. "It will give him back his confidence. His men will see him as a strong leader, and it will intimidate the Black Camel Bandits."

Kai made a deep rumbling sound, like someone beating a copper drum.

Fo Tu Deng's eyes lit up. "Why didn't I think of that? Remember how keen he was to ride that yellow beast? Except that one was deranged. It threw him off." The monk glared at Kai. "Can you assure me that this one will not do the same?"

Tao glanced at the angry dragon. "He doesn't like the idea, but I will convince him this is the only way."

Fo Tu Deng sagged with relief. "Jilong needs something to make him feel like he's in control. A dragon will be an advantage in battle – as long as it is at the Langhai's command."

"He will be."

Chapter Twenty-Two
THE HOARD

"I will not submit to Jilong!"

"You won't be submitting, you'll be pretending to submit."

"It will seem the same. Now I am free of the iron sickness, we can escape."

"I can't ignore this vision. This is not a trick to impress the monk, not a street performance. This is the result of my second sight, which has come from my connection to you. It will benefit you. It has to."

"How could it possibly help me?"

"I don't know yet."

Steam issued from Kai's nostrils, like a boiling kettle.

Fo Tu Deng waited for Jilong to wake. When he emerged after a few hours sleep, the monk bowed down to him.

"I have had a vision, Langhai."

Jilong glared at Tao. "Didn't I order that he and his dragon should be killed?"

"You did, Langhai," Fo Tu Deng said. "And I was about to attend to it when I was struck by a vision!"

He sent Tao to make tea. Jilong sat in the peony pavilion and listened as the monk recounted Tao's vision. The warlord didn't like the plan any more than Kai.

"With a name like yours, it is your destiny to ride a dragon!" Fo Tu Deng was saying.

The name Jilong meant "young dragon".

"It is an omen, Langhai," the monk persisted. "And luckily, I didn't have the boy killed as he is the only one who can communicate with the dragon."

Tao brought out the tea on a tray. He had made it in the apple blossom teapot which, thanks to the ghost girl, was lacking a lid and most of the spout. He poured the tea, but not much ended up in the cups. The warlord's brow was creased. Tao thought he was probably remembering how Sha had thrown him off, leaving him lying in the dirt in front of all of his men.

Fo Tu Deng also guessed the warlord's thoughts. "It will not be like the last time, Langhai. The yellow dragon was a wild beast, crazed, but this one is more civilised."

"And the boy can communicate with this dragon?"

"Yes, Langhai."

Jilong picked up his tea, sipped it and burned his tongue. He glared at Tao.

"I did like riding a creature that could fly, surveying the

battle as if it were drawn on a strip of hide. But I do not want to be subjected to any indignity like last time."

"That will not happen, General," Tao said. "Kai can't fly. He has no wings."

Jilong turned to him. "No wings? What good is a dragon without wings?"

"He has sturdy legs. He can run fast for many hours without tiring. And you have seen his fighting skills."

Sunila chose that moment to flutter down from his nest up on the wall. He landed with a lot of flapping.

"Are you collecting dragons?" Jilong asked Fo Tu Deng. The monk smiled modestly. "It is my holiness that attracts them."

Kai was making a rumbling sound. Tao was worried he might be about to attack Fo Tu Deng, but Jilong had lost interest in Kai.

"What about *this* dragon?" Jilong was studying Sunila. "It has wings."

"He's too small," Tao said. "And I can't communicate as well with him. He—"

Fo Tu Deng cut him off. "Do not speak unless you are addressed! I am the one who has had the holy vision."

Jilong turned to the monk. "What exactly did you see?"

Fo Tu Deng blinked. "I saw …"

Tao was tempted to let the monk find a way to wriggle out of the predicament, but then he remembered that somehow the vision was to Kai's benefit. If he wished to call himself a dragonkeeper, he had to heed the advice of his second sight.

Fo Tu Deng was staring into the distance as if trying to recall the details of his vision. Tao could remember clearly what he had seen on his palms.

"It was wrong of me to question you, reverend brother," he said. "Now that I think of it, you did say that the dragon's hide was silver in the moonlight. The dragon in your vision could have been blue."

Fo Tu Deng looked relieved. "Exactly! And this creature is a *naga*, a dragon from Tianzhu. I have studied them in their natural habitat, Langhai. They are excellent fliers and what they lack in endurance they make up for in agility."

Sunila flapped his wings again. They didn't look strong enough to support his own weight, let alone a rider as well.

"You will need a bridle, Langhai," Fo Tu Deng said, "and a saddle."

Jilong scowled. "That was not sufficient when I rode the yellow beast."

"If I could have permission to speak, General," Tao said.

Jilong gave a curt nod.

"As well as fitting a bridle and a saddle to the *naga*, you could perhaps use a harness that would keep you securely seated, should he … swerve unexpectedly."

Jilong agreed to a test flight. "I'll wait until this evening."

He didn't want his men to witness it in case anything undignified happened.

"But that will be after dark, Langhai." The monk glanced at the *naga*.

"If it can't fly at night, it will be useless," Jilong snapped. "All our clashes with the bandits will be at night."

"Of course. But it might be wise to have your first flight in daylight, Langhai."

Tao fetched a bridle, a cart harness and a saddle blanket from the stable. "I'm sure we can fashion something from this."

The monk spoke to Sunila in Sanskrit, explaining what they wanted him to do, telling him how honoured he was, while Tao put the saddle blanket on the *naga* and secured it with straps. Sunila was smaller than a horse, so the bridle needed adjustment around his snout before it fitted. Tao used part of the cart harness to cross over the rider's shoulders, fastening them to the straps that held the saddle blanket in place. Sunila was ready for a test flight. Tao held out the reins to Jilong.

The warlord hesitated. "If the beast does not behave, I will personally slay him."

"He'll be very good, General," Tao said, hoping that was the case.

Jilong carefully mounted the naga, whose legs were so short that the warlord's feet almost touched the ground.

Sunila took a few steps backwards, like a skittish horse. Tao whispered reassuring words in Sanskrit and Jilong tightened his grip on the reins as Fo Tu Deng passed the harness straps over his shoulders, crossing them at the back and buckling them securely. Tao fitted a pair of stirrups.

"Tell the beast I am ready to fly," Jilong said.

Fo Tu Deng said something in Sanskrit.

The blue dragon didn't move. The monk flicked his rump with a strap.

"Just one circuit around the walls, Sunila," Tao said.

The *naga's* wings didn't stir.

"He needs some encouragement. Kai, do you have any sweetie berries?"

The dragon shook his head.

Jilong had his own ideas about encouragement. He dug the heels of his red boots into Sunila's sides. The *naga* sat down.

Fo Tu Deng taught the Zhao general a few commands in Sanskrit and Jilong repeated them. His pronunciation was poor, but Sunila responded by unfurling his wings. They were so delicate, Tao was sure he could see through them. Sunila flapped them, but his paws remained firmly on the ground.

"I don't think his wings are strong enough to fly with a rider," Tao said.

As if to contradict him, the naga flapped his wings. It

was hard for him to get off the ground, particularly with a human on his back. Unlike a bird, he didn't launch himself forwards and gradually gain altitude. He angled his wings so that he could flap them sideways, and took off vertically with his tail hanging down. Jilong would have slipped off if they hadn't put the straps across his shoulders.

"Don't worry, Langhai," Fo Tu Deng called out, over the noise of flapping wings, though he sounded worried himself. "That's the way *nagas* always take flight, because they live in dense forest."

"I hope he will drop Jilong from a great height," Kai said.

When Sunila had risen to about the height of the wall, he lifted his tail, changed the angle of his wings and started to fly horizontally. Then his flight was graceful and seemed to take less effort. He took advantage of wind currents and glided like a hawk. Tao watched anxiously as the *naga* made a circuit of the compound – once, twice, three times. Jilong gave the command to land, but Sunila took no notice. The sun was low in the sky and moths were gathering. He suddenly went into a dive. Jilong gripped the reins. Tao was convinced the naga was about to crash-land, but he pulled out at the last moment with a snap of his jaws. He had a particularly large moth between his teeth. Then he changed the angle of his wings, flapped them from side to side, hovering in the air before descending vertically and landing with a thump.

"The beast is in need of some training, Langhai," Fo Tu Deng said. "But I think that went well for a first flight."

Tao nodded his agreement. "Very well indeed."

"It is like a horse," Jilong said. "It needs breaking in."

The only creatures in the world that Jilong had patience with were horses. Tao had never seen him abuse a horse, and he seemed to have respect for them and treated them well. Tao wanted to make sure that he had the same attitude to the *naga*.

"If I might suggest something, General," Tao said, "I have observed that Sunila is fond of shiny things. These creatures collect them like certain birds do. I think if you offer him small gifts that are appealing to him, he will respond to you. Also his preferred food is tree frogs. If you provide him with rewards, I am sure he will obey you."

Jilong nodded thoughtfully. "We will resume the training tomorrow. Now I must join my men."

"You're going out?" Fo Tu Deng said. "But you've had so little sleep. You must rest, Langhai."

"I will rest when we have defeated the Black Camel Bandits," he said.

Jilong called for his stableboy. It was the lad who had fallen asleep on his horse. He had been forgiven for his lapse. "Take this beast away and bring me my horse."

Sunila made an unhappy creaking sound as the boy gingerly led him away.

Tao was hoping to get a few moments to speak to Kai alone, but the Zhao were waking up. And Lady Wang, who had spent the entire day in her new chamber, waddled over to the peony pavilion, hoisted herself onto the couch and demanded food. Tao couldn't make an evening meal for himself and the dragons because Jilong's cook had taken over the kitchen to prepare another feast for her.

While the men were eating, Tao went to the stables. The twelve stalls were occupied – eleven with horses, the twelfth with the *naga*. The stableboy had given them all a bucket of grain. Sunila was looking unhappily at his. The boy was grooming the horses, keeping a nervous eye on the *naga*.

Kai had followed Tao into the stables. "This is not right. We should be fleeing from the nomads, not helping them with their cause."

"Be patient, Kai. We cannot question my visions. They have never led us astray before." Tao had niggling doubts himself, but he hoped Kai wouldn't hear them in his thoughts.

The stableboy had finished grooming the horses. He stood with the brush in his hand, staring at the *naga*.

"Should I brush him?"

Kai had calmed down, but he was still unhappy. "He

would appreciate a little juniper oil rubbed on his wings."
Tao heard the dragon's voice in his mind.

"Do you have any juniper oil?" Tao asked the boy.

He shook his head, trying to keep an eye on both
dragons at once.

"His wings are new and delicate," Kai said. "They will
need some sort of balm if he is to avoid them getting too
dry and cracking."

Tao thought for a moment. "There is some sesame oil in
the kitchen. Will that do?"

The stableboy looked confused, as he only heard Tao's
side of the conversation.

Kai nodded.

Tao fetched the sesame oil and rubbed it into the *naga's*
wings. Sunila flapped them happily.

"And he likes his grain cooked," Tao told the stableboy.
"He is also fond of tree frogs and woodworm larvae, but he
might settle for a bowl of whatever you're having tonight."

Tao had weaned the naga off honey, and he was much
less fussy about what he ate.

After the Zhao had marched off, Tao made a pot of
lentil soup and shared it with Kai.

"I will stay with you tonight," Kai said to Tao. "In case
the ghost girl tries to attack you again."

"Thank you."

Tao was glad that no one had commandeered Wei's

room. Kai scratched up the spare quilt on the floor next to Wei's bed, turned around three times and settled down without complaint. Tao climbed into bed. He was exhausted and with Kai so close, he wasn't afraid. In any case a thick layer of cloud had blotted out the stars and ... the moon.

Tao woke from a deep sleep and was enjoying the comfort and warmth of a good bed and a thick quilt. The sound of a dragon snoring close by reassured him, but something had disturbed his sleep. Back at the monastery he had often woken during the night. But here he was warm, with no bedbugs biting him and no homesick novices sobbing. It was still dark, but the pale shape of the moon was visible through the thinning clouds. As Tao watched, a shaft of moonlight stabbed through and shone down on the garden.

"Something's wrong," he said, but Kai didn't hear him.

Tao knew what had woken him – a smell. It wasn't pleasant. He was reminded of a time when a mouse had died behind a wall. There was also a sickly sweetness like decaying fruit. A screeching sound, something like a chicken whose neck was being wrung, set his teeth on edge. It was coming from the stables. Something had happened to Sunila. He got up and went outside.

There were no horses in the stable. Just the *naga,*

tethered to the side of his stall.

And Baoyu.

The ghost girl was hovering above Sunila, snarling, her snake hair coiling. It was her smell that had woken Tao. He realised he had smelled it before when she appeared, but had thought it was the decaying leaves in the garden. It was the sweet, rotten reek of death. She was paler than the previous night, but still terrifying.

Baoyu wasn't interested in Tao any more. She had turned her wrath on the *naga*. Tao looked up at the night sky. There would be no help there, the clouds had melted away. The ghost girl wasn't trying to kill Sunila. Not yet. The *naga* breathed out mist in an attempt to create his own cloud to cover the moon, but Baoyu circled around him, causing a wind so cold that his mist turned to ice crystals and fell to the ground like a tiny shower of snow. She entered the *naga*. Tao remembering the awful sensation of having the ghost inside him, and being unable to breathe.

Kai came into the stable. Tao's fear was so strong it had woken him.

"We must do something!" Tao said. "She will kill him."

Baoyu didn't stay inside the *naga*. After a few heartbeats, she drifted out and away. The *naga* took a shuddering breath of air and let out an anguished cry. To Tao's surprise he strained to go after the ghost girl. Tao untethered him.

"She has learned something from him," Kai said. "Stolen one of his thoughts."

They followed Sunila into what had been Meiling's room. Baoyu was there, hovering next to a curtain covering an alcove. Sunila rushed up to the ghost girl and shape-changed into a seven-headed snake, roaring at her, but she was not disturbed by the apparition. She created a gust of wind and the curtain blew aside, revealing an untidy clutter of what looked like rubbish. The moonlight was stronger now. Tao pushed open the shutters and pale light flooded in. The pile contained a shawl and some jewellery, a silver bowl, and the head from the broken statue of the kitchen god. There was a ripe pomegranate and some wilted chrysanthemums.

"It is a dragon hoard," Kai said. "Sunila has made a new one."

Kai was right. Tao recognised the length of blue ribbon that had been in the *naga's* hoard in the cave.

Baoyu moved closer to the hoard, swirling around it, creating a draught of air which blew the lighter things from the pile – feathers, scraps of silk gauze, a gold earring. She whirled faster, until she was a blur of grey, sparks of silver streaming in her wake. Heavier things were lifted into the air – a hair comb, a bronze incense burner, a piece of a broken vase – and then they were flung against the wall. Sunila made a screeching sound as he saw his hoard destroyed, but he did nothing to save it.

Kai pointed at something in the hoard that was reflecting the moonlight.

Tao caught his breath. The object had a purplish colour. He could see what it was now. His dragon-stone shard. His heart sang to see it again, but Baoyu's icy blast grew even faster, until it picked up the shard and spun it in the air. That wasn't what she was interested in. Tao gasped as she flung it aside. He dived to save it, but was too slow and it hit the corner of a chest. Tao snatched it up, cradled it in his hands, tracing the creamy white veins, feeling its cool, smooth shape. Tao ran his finger over the unfamiliar sharp edge of a chipped corner and it cut through his skin.

"He must have gone back for the ribbon and the shard after we left the cave, " Kai said, "and brought them here."

"I didn't lose my shard." Tao glared at Sunila who hid behind a screen. "You stole it from me."

The ghost girl's wind had died to nothing more than a draught of cold air. Tao thought that everything in the pile had been dispersed, but Baoyu was still circling slowly. He looked closer. There was one small item left that hadn't been scattered. The ghost girl hovered over it. Her sadness filled the room like fog. The object wasn't shiny or sparkly like the other things in Sunila's hoard. It was black, and no bigger than a soya bean.

Tao moved closer but he still couldn't make out what it was. "What is it? A pebble?"

Kai's dragon eyes were focused on it. "It is a small bone."

"What sort of a bone?"

Kai pointed a talon at the ghost girl's right hand and the little finger with the tip missing.

"It is hers," he whispered. "It is her finger bone."

Chapter Twenty-Three
EARTHLY REMAINS

Baoyu circled the bone and held up her fleshless fingers. Each one was made up of three blackened bones – except for the little finger which had only two. Tao now understood why she was so angry. When Sunila had attacked Shenchi village, starving, looking for food, he had bitten Baoyu, who had just happened to be in his way. His fangs had dug into her flesh, but he had sunk them so hard he'd bitten off the end of her finger. That was what she'd been searching for – her missing finger bone. The *naga's* venom had entered her body. It had slowly eaten away the flesh of the little girl's fingers, and then spread to the rest of her body, poisoning it day by day until she died.

The ghost of that young girl turned to face her killer. Her still sadness disappeared. She snarled and her sharp little teeth glittered in the moonlight like deadly pearls. She had found her missing bone, and now she was ready to kill the *naga*. Sunila turned into his half-human, half-snake shape. The snake heads growing from its shoulders reached out to her and spat venom, but it couldn't hurt her now. He turned into his snake form and slithered from the room. She followed him.

Outside, he flashed from one shape to the other and shrieked, but that didn't deter Baoyu. She entered his shape-changed body and the illusion was broken. Frost formed on his scales, so thick he looked like a silver dragon. He was frozen, unable to make any movement, not a blink, not a twitch. Tao knew what Sunila was experiencing – a desperate desire to suck in air, yet an inability to make his lungs work. He remembered that terrifying feeling, knowing that his body was healthy, uninjured, and yet he was about to die. There wasn't a single cloud in the night sky, no hope that the moon would be obscured. And it would be several hours before it set.

The *naga's* blue eyes were frosted over, but Tao was sure they were pleading with him.

"She's going to kill him. How can we stop her?"

Kai roared and ran at the silver dragon, but he stopped dead before he reached him.

"I cannot help him," he said. "It is as if there is a wall of ice surrounding him."

Tao and Kai had some impressive skills, but none that were of any use at that moment.

Tao knew that after the ghost girl had killed Sunila, it would be his turn.

"Tell me what it is that you want."

The ghost girl emerged from Sunila's body. The *naga* collapsed to the ground, sucking in breaths quickly, afraid that she would attack him again. But she didn't.

Tao could feel the yearning emanating from Baoyu's body. She reached out her poor blackened hand as if she longed to pick up the bone. Moonlight tears fell from her hollow eyes. It made Tao's body crumple with sadness, and salty tears filled his own eyes. He tried to swallow them, but couldn't stop them from brimming over. The ghost girl was so close to him that the icy chill radiating from her froze the tears on his cheeks. She was a child who had experienced the pain of losing her family. He remembered how miserable he had been the first year in the monastery when he was seven. He had missed his family so much – his father's quiet calmness, his sister's carefree happiness, even the stern presence of his mother, but especially Wei. He had never felt such an empty feeling before or since, such sorrow. And yet his family had been alive and he was able to visit them twice a year.

The ghost girl had lost her parents, but she had still continued to care for her grandfather and little brother after her body was poisoned.

"You have family, here in Huaxia," Tao said. "Your grandfather and brother are travelling to the southern city. Do you want to go to them? To be near your living family?"

Baoyu snarled and raked her silver claws through him. They couldn't wound his body, but they left tracks of cold pain inside him. He hunched over, unable to speak. Kai moved closer so that he could support him.

The dragon made an anxious sound. "I told you before, a ghost cannot stray far from its grave. She cannot go south."

"I'm sorry. You can't follow your family. Forgive my ignorance."

Baoyu's ice-cold presence had slowed Tao's brain. His Buddhist teachings mentioned ghostly spirits, but had not given him any useful knowledge about what to do if confronted by one. Baoyu was hovering in front of him, her ghostly anger contained, but threatening to burst out. He couldn't understand why she was now focusing her anger on him. He was not responsible for her death.

"Perhaps she wants her bones to be with the remains of the other villagers in the cave," Kai said. "Or with her mother's."

Tao shook his head. "She knows where those graves are. If she wanted to return to them she would have already. There is something else, some reason why she followed us."

The ghost girl circled the tiny finger bone, her moon-shadow fingers elongating and reaching out to it. There had been women living in the compound who still followed the old ways. They used to visit their family tombs in the fields every year to sweep them and leave fresh food offerings for the dead. They went out even when nomads had been seen in the area. They considered hungry ghosts to be a threat worse than armed soldiers. Tao's mother had never quite let go of the old ways, so she used to send someone to the Mang Hills once a year to do the same at the Huan family tombs.

Tao remembered the image of Baoyu's burial cairn that the ghost girl had left in his mind when she passed through him. He suddenly understood the ghost girl's yearning.

"You want all your bones to be together! You want your finger bone to be returned to your cairn."

Baoyu stopped circling. She faced Tao, but this time she was not radiating anger. Tao's sluggish brain was trying to think how he could achieve this.

"We'll have to escape from the compound and find our way back to her cairn."

As the words came out of his mouth, Tao realised how difficult that would be. It was a long way to walk, and it was in the opposite direction to the dragon haven. They would risk running into nomads again.

Kai was following his meandering thoughts. "There is an easier way to achieve this."

"How?"

"I can take it. I know where the cairn is. I can run there."

Tao looked at the moon. "No. It would take too long. Sunila should take it. He can fly."

Kai made an angry rumbling sound. "His wings are small, meant for flapping up into trees, not flying long distances! My legs are powerful. I can run faster than he can fly!"

Tao was sure that Kai was exaggerating. "But he can fly straight from here to there. You would have to run up and down mountains."

In his stumbling and inadequate Sanskrit, Tao explained their plan to Sunila, but the *naga* was learning the language of the Huaxia. He already knew what Tao wanted. The ghost girl also understood what they were saying, though in life she had never heard a word of Sanskrit. Sunila reached out to pick up the finger bone in his talons. Baoyu swept back to him, ready to enter his body again.

"No. You don't trust Sunila," Tao said. "Why should you?"

Tao could feel the ghost's cold breath on his face. He tried to keep his voice calm. "We understand. Sunila is the one who brought about your death, though he didn't mean to. But he will return your finger bone to the cairn. And if he doesn't, you have the power to kill us all."

Baoyu circled Tao. She was paler and less substantial. He could see through her.

"I think she has stayed away from her remains too long," Kai said. "She has used up her strength and now she is too weak to make the journey back."

"What will happen to her if she doesn't return to her grave?"

"She will lose her ghost body."

Tao shivered. "Perhaps there's a place in hell for bodiless ghosts."

Neither of them suggested just letting her fade away.

Silver tears fell from Baoyu's eyes.

"I understand your unhappiness. You grieve for your dead mother, like I did for my dead brother who was so close to me it was as if he was my own flesh. My parents and my sister have moved south, the same as your grandfather and brother have. It is unlikely I will ever see them again."

He had never really considered that before. The thought did make him sad, very sad.

"If you were my sister, I would be praying for you to begin a new life as I did for my brother. Please, let me say the words to release you."

Baoyu was still for the first time. Her grim face softened. She shook her shadowy head as she lingered to gaze at her ghostly reflection in the pool, causing a small breeze that made leaves fall gently from the cherry tree and float on the surface of the water.

"She likes it here," Tao said.

Raucous laughter from up on the walls cut through the silence. The guards, cold and bored with staring into the darkness, had lit a fire in a brazier on the ramparts and were drinking hot *kumiss* to warm themselves. The courtyard was hidden by trees and the guards weren't doing their duty anyway. They were amusing themselves by hurling the Huan cups and bowls they'd been using from the top of the wall. They found the sound of the pottery smashing on the ground outside hilarious.

"I wish I could get the nomads out of here before we leave," Tao said.

"If Baoyu had more strength," Kai said, "she could frighten the Zhao away."

"That's the answer!" Tao couldn't believe it hadn't occurred to him before. "That will solve both problems."

Neither Kai nor the ghost girl understood what he meant.

"If Baoyu is happy here, she should stay. She can haunt the Zhao so that they leave. If anyone tries to live here who she doesn't like, she can scare them away. It will be known far and wide that this place is haunted. She can protect my home."

"But she's fading, you can see that," Kai said.

"Then we will bring her cairn here. Sunila, you must go to the grave in the mountains and bring back all Baoyu's bones. We will rebury them here!"

"But how will Sunila carry her bones?"

Kai didn't trust the naga to collect every bone and bring them back safely.

Tao's brain had finally woken up. "He won't have to. I'll go with him. I'll carefully collect all her bones and carry them back."

Specks of moonlight erupted from Baoyu's hair like sparks from a fire. Tao was sure that this was a sign that she was happy with his plan.

"Will you do it, Sunila? Will you take me to Baoyu's grave?"

The *naga* didn't need words. Tao could tell from the way his blue eyes shone that he was keen to help. Kai didn't need words either. He couldn't hide his envy.

"While we are gone, Kai, you must dig a grave, a deep hole somewhere within these walls, a place where Baoyu's bones will be undisturbed forever. I'll say a sutra. If ever she decides she's ready to leave and start a new life, she can."

Moths had gathered around Tao, hovering above him, as if they approved of the plan.

"And the insects will help keep intruders away." Tao wasn't sure how he knew that, but he was confident it was true.

Baoyu's tears stopped falling. She turned in a circle, her shadow gown billowing. She was happy.

"It is not safe," Kai said. "You have no control over Sunila. He might fly anywhere. You might fall off."

Tao would not be dissuaded. "I'll use the harness. And he'll keep me safe, won't you, Sunila?"

The *naga* stood upright and unfurled his wings. He looked as pleased and proud as the ghost girl did. They were both glad to be given a task, to be useful.

This time it was Tao who could hear Kai's thoughts. Tao's safety wasn't the dragon's only concern. This would be Tao's first dragon flight, but it would not be with him. It would be hundreds of years before Kai's wings grew. Tao wouldn't live long enough to fly with him.

"I'm sorry, Kai, but I have to do this," Tao said. "Then Baoyu might forgive Sunila for her death, and she will be at peace."

Tao fetched the harness and saddle from the stables and fastened them onto the *naga*. He climbed onto his back and buckled the straps across his shoulders. He'd found an empty rice sack in which to bring back the bones.

"The moon is out. Sunila will glow," Kai said. "The nomads on the wall, those out searching in the darkness, they will see him. They will shoot him down."

Tao thought for a moment. He remembered a sutra about the *devas* who could not be seen by humans. He spoke to the *naga*. "Invisible!" he said in Sanskrit. "Make yourself invisible."

The *naga* vanished. Tao looked as if he were suspended in midair.

"*You* are still visible," Kai said.

"As you explained to me, he hasn't really disappeared.

He has taken on the same colour as the sky. Once Sunila is in the air, no one will see me from below."

The *naga* made his ungainly vertical take-off. Tao held the reins tight and felt the narrow leather straps strain as they took his full weight. He gripped the *naga's* flanks with his knees.

Below, Kai was making anxious scraping sounds. Tao called down to him, wishing he didn't have to leave the dragon behind.

"Try not to injure worms and beetles as you dig the grave." He could hear the tremor in his voice as Sunila flew up to the height of the top of the wall.

The *naga* changed the angle of his wings, levelled his body and flapped off into the darkness. Tao hunched down as they passed over the guards on the wall. Despite the moonlight, they didn't see the dragon.

Tao settled his weight into the saddle. He felt secure now that they were flying horizontally. This was his first, and probably his last, dragon flight. He wished it was daylight so he could see the land stretch out below him. All he could see were the black shapes of treetops. Above him were the stars. The moon was getting low. They didn't have much time.

The flight was not the exhilarating experience Tao had imagined. The night air was freezing as it rushed by him. He could tell the naga enjoyed flying, but he wasn't as fast as expected. Just as Tao was thinking that he might freeze to death before they reached the cairn, the *naga* started to circle, descending as he did. Like all dragons, Sunila's eyesight was excellent, even in moonlight. He was looking for their destination, and when the *naga's* hind paws touched the earth, they were right next to the small pile of rocks that was the resting place of Baoyu's earthly remains. Tao remembered the exhausting journey to the compound, clambering up and down mountains that had taken almost a full day. Although the *naga* didn't have great speed, this journey had taken less than an hour.

Tao warmed his hands in his armpits before he could get his fingers to undo the straps. He climbed down from the *naga's* back, his legs stiff with cold.

"Well done, Sunila." He patted the *naga*. "You did a good job. You fly well."

The *naga* made a chirruping sound.

Tao carefully removed the stones from the cairn that he had rebuilt, and uncovered the remains of the little girl. It didn't take long. He was expecting to see a whole skeleton laid out, recognisably human. Instead there was a jumble of bone fragments mixed with damp ashes. Tao had been present at two cremations, his brother's and that of an old monk who had died at the monastery, but he had only concerned himself with the souls of the dead, not their remains. The bone fragments were shades of pale grey.

The heat from the fire had made them brittle and they had cracked. He picked some up and they broke in his fingers. He rinsed the bones with water from a nearby stream to clean off the wood ash, carefully scooped them up with a piece of bark and put them in the sack. There were slivers of bone from an arm or a leg, and larger curved pieces that must have been parts of Baoyu's skull. He saw one little tooth, white and neat, not sharp like her ghost teeth. Tao had been expecting the sack of bones to be almost as heavy as the child would have been when she was alive, but Baoyu's bones only filled one corner of the sack and weighed no more than two handfuls of rice.

Sunila was sniffing the breeze and shifting impatiently from one foot to the other. Then he suddenly unfurled his wings and took off.

"Wait!" Tao shouted. "Don't go."

The *naga* disappeared into the darkness above.

"Don't leave me!"

Tao let the sack fall from his hands. The fragile bones made a clinking sound as they fragmented even more. The cold was penetrating his own bones. He thought of the long walk back to the compound – if he could even find his way without Kai to lead him. He felt the panic rise in his throat, and Kai wasn't there to reassure him, to guide him, to protect him. He thought of Pema. If Jilong's nomads captured her he hoped she would die swiftly.

But after a few minutes, Tao heard a flapping sound. The *naga* was descending again. He landed next to Tao, who was about to hug the *naga* with relief until he saw that he had a large tree frog in his mouth and one in each forepaw. They were all squirming, struggling to escape.

"I'm glad to see you, Sunila." He ruffled the *naga's* golden mane instead. "I should never have doubted you."

Before his wings had grown, Sunila had passed the same way and nearly starved. Now that he had wings, he could fly up into the trees and find frogs. Tao looked away. He didn't want to watch the creatures' death throes as the *naga* ate them alive.

Tao picked up the sack of bones, muttering a sutra for the souls of the frogs.

"Now we must go," he said.

Tao tied the neck of the sack with two lengths of vine and secured it to the harness. Then he climbed onto the *naga's* back and strapped himself on. Sunila flapped his wings. Tao clung on.

The journey back to the Huan compound seemed much longer. The *naga's* small wings weren't meant for long flights. They flapped slowly. Tao could hear rasping breath and feel Sunila's great heart beating fast. The naga was tiring, and Tao hoped he had the strength to make it back to the compound. Tao was so cold, he could no longer grip the reins. He was glad he'd secured the sack of bones well. He wouldn't have been able to hold onto them with his frozen fingers. The moon was almost at the horizon.

At last, the glow from the fire that the guards had built on the compound walls came into view. Sunila made himself invisible. Kai and Baoyu were waiting, their faces upturned. Sunila landed in the courtyard. Tao's hands were too cold to unbuckle the straps, but Kai managed to undo them with his talons. Tao climbed down from the *naga's* back and Kai supported him as his frozen legs gave way.

"Well done, Sunila," Tao said.

Baoyu was hovering anxiously.

Tao had thought that Kai would dig the grave in the furthest corner of the compound, but instead he'd dug it in the garden, right next to the rock whose shadow had caused Tao so much night-time fear.

"This is the busiest place," Tao said. "You've put her grave at the heart of the compound."

"I know, but this is her favourite place. She will be happy to be buried here, and no one will dig up this little patch of garden."

Tao smiled. "You're right. It's a good choice."

Baoyu watched as Tao climbed down into the grave and emptied the sack. Kai made a sad sound like a cracked bell ringing when he saw the small pile of bones.

Something was still troubling the ghost girl.

"You have forgotten this," Kai said.

He held the tiny finger bone clasped between two of his talons. He placed it in the grave. It was black from the *naga's* venom and was the only bone that was whole. Baoyu drifted into the grave to examine her bones. She shed a few moonlight tears and then left the grave. She was content.

The two dragons scraped earth into the grave to cover the bones. Sunila made low musical sounds as he did his work. Tao remembered the way Sha had made a similar deep, humming lament. There wasn't a suitable Buddhist sutra for such an occasion, since hungry ghosts were from the old beliefs. Instead Tao made up some words of his own.

"May Baoyu's bones rest here undisturbed forever. And may she eventually attain a state of peace so she can begin a new life and live long and happily."

The dragons tamped down the earth with their paws. Tao couldn't risk making a commemoration. He didn't want anyone to know where the grave was. He replanted the crocuses and the chrysanthemums that Kai had dug up. The dragon pushed the rocks back into place with his tail.

Baoyu circled around the grave. The sky to the east was tinged with pink. The ghost girl's mouth turned up at the edges in the slightest smile, before her shadow body dissipated in the first rays of sunlight.

"Tomorrow night she will be stronger again, now that she is near her remains," Kai said. "I hope that is something we will not regret."

Chapter Twenty-Four
AWAKENING

The *naga* had gone to sleep in the stables. Tao lay down on Wei's bed, exhausted. He didn't bother to take off his clothes, he just pulled the quilt over himself. Kai curled up on the floor at the end of the bed.

Tao was woken by Fo Tu Deng shaking his arm.

"Jilong is furious. They still haven't found the Black Camel Bandits' hide-out. You must seek another vision. He will kill us all – you, me and the dragons. And it won't be a slow death. You know what he's capable of."

Tao sat up. The sky was still tinged with pink, so he knew that what his body was telling him was right – he'd only been asleep for a few minutes. He felt more tired than when he'd fallen into bed. But the monk's words gave him a gleam of hope. If the nomads hadn't found the bandits hide-out, then Pema was still safe.

Out in the courtyard, Jilong was pacing back and forth. He was exhausted too, and angry, which Tao was sure was a bad combination. The warlord marched over and poked

Fo Tu Deng in his scrawny chest.

"I need something else from you, seer." He snarled the word like an insult. "If I don't find the Black Camel Bandits tonight, by this time tomorrow you will be dead. They are close. They kill my men, and yet I have not seen a single one of them. Where do they hide? It is a simple request. That is all I need to know from you. I can do the rest. Prove to me that you really are a seer and not a fraud."

Jilong took a few steps towards his quarters and then turned back.

"And my mother has decided she likes this place and wants to make it her home. If you survive the night, you and your assistant will be moved to Luoyang."

Tao certainly didn't want to die, and he didn't want to go back to Luoyang either, but it was the thought of Lady Wang taking over his family home that finally strengthened his resolve.

He spoke to Kai with his mind. "It's time to reclaim our freedom."

Fo Tu Deng hopped about, insisting that Tao have a vision immediately.

Kai came into the courtyard. "You may as well," he said. "If we are going to escape the clutches of the Zhao, we could use some advice."

Tao was so tired, this time he really did need to prepare himself to find the mental energy to concentrate and seek a vision. He sat cross-legged and recited a sutra. Then he smeared the oil on his hands and stared at them. He could see nothing. Lady Wang was shouting at her servants somewhere in the house. The men were arguing over whose fault it was that they hadn't found a single bandit. Someone building temporary stables was hammering. Tao needed peace and quiet. He tried to picture a tranquil scene – a view from a mountain, a lake, a garden in summer – but his mind wouldn't focus. He concentrated on the birdsong and the buzzing of insects, but that made him drowsier still.

A slap across the face woke him. He'd fallen asleep and Fo Tu Deng was standing over him.

"A messenger from Shi Le has arrived. Whatever was in the message has put Jilong in a worse mood. He's gone to rest. I must have something to tell him when he wakes."

"It's no good," Tao said. "I can't do it."

"You have to or we'll both die," Fo Tu Deng said.

"I want to summon a vision as much as you do," Tao said. "But I can't. I haven't got the energy or the concentration. I must sleep. Just for an hour or two."

Fo Tu Deng reluctantly agreed. Tao went back to Wei's room, only to find some men carrying the bed out through the door.

"Where are you going with my bed?"

"Lady Wang wants it out of the room," one of them replied.

Inside he could see Lady Wang sitting on his mother's favourite chair. Her servants were fussing around her, applying cosmetics to her jowly cheeks and sagging eyes, and trying to comb the knots out of her coarse hair.

"Go away, boy," she said. "This is my dressing room now."

Tao grabbed the quilt from the bed as the men passed him.

Kai found an empty farmer's hut and Tao didn't object as the dragon made him a bed of straw on the earthen floor. Tao collapsed into it and felt Kai spread the quilt over him. He breathed in the familiar and much-loved smell and sank into the open embrace of sleep, like a baby in its mother's arms. He didn't really care if he never awoke.

Tao did wake, about an hour before midday. It was a pleasant sunny day and there was no noise from the compound to disturb the peace. The nomads were all sleeping, and fortunately so was Jilong. The few hours sleep had refreshed Tao. Kai was curled up next to him, breathing evenly, his snout buried under his tail. Tao got up and crept out of the hut so as not to wake him.

He was surprised that Fo Tu Deng hadn't woken him earlier, but one of the guards told him that Lady Wang had wanted to be carried out in a palanquin to admire the autumn leaves in the orchard, and she had insisted that Fo Tu Deng escort her.

Tao made himself some rice porridge and took it out to the peony pavilion. He had the garden to himself. He could see where the earth had been disturbed to dig Baoyu's grave and that some of the plants were in different positions, but the Zhao had no interest in gardening and he was sure they wouldn't notice.

Tao needed to seek another vision. He had some time before the men woke and started preparing food. But Lady Wang would return soon and Jilong could wake at any moment. Once that happened this peaceful state of mind would desert him. The guards on the wall had their heads together, leaning over a game of *liubo*, so Tao was able to wriggle out through the tunnel and run into the fields without anyone noticing. Once outside, he heard a flapping sound and felt a current of air. Sunila materialised. He had flown over the walls while invisible.

"You can come with me," Tao said, "but you must behave."

He knew exactly where he wanted to go. He gave the orchard a wide berth and walked to the stream. He sat on the grass. It was the spot where he had come with Wei and Kai and Pema. The sun warmed his back. The willow tree had lost all its leaves, but its naked branches trailed in the river. He sat with his back against the trunk and stared up into the branches. He could make out the bird's nest where Pema had restored a baby bird to its family. The nest was abandoned. The birds would have flown to somewhere warmer.

The *naga* waded into the water and splashed around. Tao's duties were pulling him in different directions. He had to be useful to Kai, to keep an eye on Sunila, to ensure that Baoyu was content, and there was a vaguer sense of duty to his family and the memory of Wei. Then there was Pema. If only he'd been able to convince her to live a simple life somewhere out of danger. And while he was trying to achieve all these impossible things, he had to live like a good Buddhist.

Near where he was sitting, the river was disturbed by a scatter of rocks in its path and it changed from quiet and serious to cheerfully foamy as it rushed around the rocks, before settling down to continue more sedately on its way. He poured a few drops of oil on his hands and carefully rubbed them together to distribute the oil evenly. He felt so peaceful it wasn't necessary to recite any sutras. He remembered the last time he had sat on that riverbank. It seemed like such a long time ago. The image of Wei, still alive and smiling, and of Pema splashing in the shallows as Kai taught her to fish, made him realise that day had been one of the happiest of his life. His eyes filled with tears, not from sadness or regret, but from gratitude that he had been fortunate enough to have those precious minutes, before the chaos of the world intruded. He put his hands together. The tears blurred his sight as required.

Solitude and inner peace were the perfect conditions for receiving a vision, and yet no vision came. Tao couldn't understand it. He had been drawn to this place and his mind was completely focused on the task. He had brought the shard of dragon stone with him in case it could enhance his visions somehow. His finger felt the new chip, but it was the cool smoothness of the rounded edges that he loved to touch. He had always been drawn to the shard, ever since his great-grandfather gave it to him – long before he met Kai. He placed it in his lap and tried again for a vision. Nothing happened.

Tao felt the knot of *qi* inside him, solid and unmoving. When he'd tried to explain the sensation to Kai, the dragon said it sounded like indigestion. But it wasn't painful or uncomfortable. It was part of his beloved brother. It was beyond words. He began to understand the connection between the *qi* and the shard. The characteristics of a dragonkeeper had been passed down from the Huan ancestors in equal measure to Tao and Wei. The brothers were the same in every way, or at least they had been until the moment of Wei's birth. Alone, neither of them could have been a dragonkeeper, but together they could. It wasn't until Wei had poured his *qi* into Tao that the skills of a dragonkeeper had woken inside him.

The *qi* began to stir. The shard was awakening it. It was a wonderful feeling, like warmth from a fire, the touch of a loved one, and a smile all merged together. He felt the *qi* power within him, but still didn't know how it would manifest.

Dragonflies that hovered over the river flew towards him. Beetles and slaters gathered around his feet. Spiders dangled from trees. Worms appeared. All the *wuji*, were drawn to him as if to witness the awakening of his *qi* power. It was his connection to these small creatures. He couldn't deny it, but how this ability could serve any useful purpose, he didn't know.

There was something else. Tao could feel another power stir within him. The knot of *qi* seemed to unravel. It didn't snake along his arms and try to burst out of him. It spread from his heart and found its way into his mind. He heard a sound, nothing more than a whisper. He held the shard with both hands; the voice became clearer. It was coming from inside himself, but it was not his own voice, not that inner voice that berated him if he didn't try hard enough, or if he was forgetful or clumsy. It was another voice – gentle, reassuring – one he had never heard before, and yet was so familiar to him. The voice didn't use any language spoken by mouth. It was wordless, not heard but experienced. It spoke in emotions, sadness and joy together. It was Wei.

His brother was speaking to him. Not from his next life. Tao had no connection to that new version of his brother, whoever and wherever he was. This was something that remained of the old Wei, his unique and silent empathy. Tao had been able to understand it when Wei was alive and he could understand it now. He could translate this inner language, as he could translate Sanskrit into Huaxia or Kai's sounds into words.

You are the dragonkeeper, the voice was saying. *Not for one dragon, but for all.*

Chapter Twenty-Five
TRUST

"Where have you been?" Fo Tu Deng shouted when Tao wandered back into the courtyard.

The monk had only just returned from his own outing in the countryside with Lady Wang.

"I have been meditating," Tao said.

"The *naga* is Jilong's now. You shouldn't take him out without permission."

Tao was about to escape to Wei's room, but he remembered that Lady Wang had taken it over.

"I have chained up your dragon!" Fo Tu Deng's eyes were blazing with fear and anger. "If you don't seek a vision immediately, I will fetch extra chains so that he will suffer even more."

Fo Tu Deng sent for the stableboy and ordered him to chain up the naga as well. Tao tried to appear anguished. He could hear Kai groaning plaintively from the stables, but it wasn't the sound he made if he was really in pain. Kai and Sunila both had a supply of cinnabar. They were immune to the effects of iron.

"You must seek a vision and tell me how we can find these Black Camel Bandits. Jilong will be awake at any moment."

Nothing the monk said could disturb the calm that Tao's communion with Wei had left within him. There was something else too. He felt powerful. Tao couldn't help smiling.

This infuriated the monk. "How dare you! I will order the chains on the dragons to be doubled!"

Fo Tu Deng turned and found himself face to face with Jilong, who had stepped out from behind the peony pavilion. The monk's body crumpled. Jilong towered over him, hands on hips. He was a slender young man, but he seemed twice the size of the monk.

"I knew you were a fake. You will regret deceiving me."

The warlord signalled to the captain of his personal guard. "Shackle the monk in the goat pen."

The guard hauled the monk away. He whimpered, but didn't bother to protest.

Jilong walked over to Tao. He had the swaggering gait of a man used to absolute power, a bully who knows he always has at least ten men at his back.

"So, boy," he said. "You are the one who has the visions."

Tao wasn't smiling any more. "Yes, General. But it is not something I have control of. Visions come or don't come, and often I can't interpret their meaning."

"But a vision told you that the Black Camel Bandits hide in darkness during the day and don't come out until after nightfall?"

"Yes, General."

He didn't mention that his visions only served dragons.

"When you have sought a vision for me, I will unshackle your dragon."

Tao had made so many mistakes since leaving Yinmi. He had wandered around, thinking he could fill his days with boyish adventure with Kai at his side. He had believed that it was his duty as a Buddhist to help everyone in need that he came upon – Pema, the old man, Baoyu. He had wandered like river water flowing around rocks, following the course that required the least effort. The purpose of his life was clear to him at last. He didn't need a ceremonial mirror to prove it. He was a dragonkeeper. It was his family heritage, taken up for the first time in two hundred years. He felt privileged to be the chosen companion of a dragon, but it had brought responsibilities that he would never have dreamed of when he was a novice.

He couldn't concern himself with Pema or Baoyu. His duty was to protect the dragons. He should have left the compound earlier, but deep down he knew that wouldn't have been right. Everything that had happened was part of his journey to this new knowledge. And yet, here he was with his home full of enemies and a Zhao warlord menacing him. He knew his destiny, but he had no map to follow. There were still rocks to negotiate before his life flowed smooth and straight. Each step he had to take was a mystery, but he was beginning to feel confident that he could find the way. He had his brother to help him.

"The Langhai does not like to be kept waiting," the captain of the guard said.

Tao and the warlord were in agreement about one thing. He needed to seek a vision.

The men were waking and making their usual clamour.

"My vision will be more accurate if I have quiet," he said.

At a signal from the captain, the Zhao soldiers fell silent.

"And Kai and Sunila must be released from their chains."

The captain looked at the warlord for his approval, but Jilong was reluctant to free them.

"Both dragons are part of the ritual," Tao said. "They will not try to escape."

At a nod from Jilong, one of his men went to the stables, and the stableboy brought out the two dragons, tethered with rope. They both went to Tao and he touched their heads as if he was administering blessings.

Kai was making his impatient dinging sound. "We must take the first opportunity to escape."

"This vision will show us the way." Tao spoke to the dragon with his mind.

"We should have left before. If we had …" The dragon's voice in Tao's head paused. "Something has happened to you. Your mind is different."

"I have accessed my *qi* power at last. It has not given me unusual strength, I have no special skills that will help us in a battle. I will explain it to you later. You must help me convince Jilong and his men that I am a seer."

"You are a seer."

"Yes, but we must put on a performance."

With his back to Jilong, Tao slipped the vial of oil behind one of Kai's reverse scales.

The Zhao gathered to watch as Tao sat cross-legged on a cushion and the dragons crouched next to him, one on either side. He closed his eyes and chanted part of a sutra. Then he held out his hands to the dragons. Kai took out the vial and placed it in one hand. Sunila seemed to understand what he was required to do. He reached behind one of his reverse scales as well, pulled something out and solemnly placed it in Tao's other hand. When Tao saw what it was, he almost burst out laughing – it was a frog's leg. A frown formed on Jilong's brow. Tao had to think quickly to work it into his little ceremony. There were some large ants hurrying in and out of a hole in the earth nearby. He concentrated on his *qi*. He needed the help of the ants.

"The ways of the universe are a mystery, O Blessed One," he said, placing the frog's leg on the ground. "The life of our earthly flesh is fleeting." The ants diverted from their path to examine the frog's leg. "It dies, it decays, it is consumed." The ants managed to lift the leg and carry it to their hole, which others were busily enlarging so that it would fit. "Our souls though, last forever, thanks to your grace."

All of the Zhao were watching with fascination. He was half-expecting Buddha to descend from the sky and turn him into a pile of dust for spouting such nonsense. Now he had to concentrate. He had to summon a vision. Not for Jilong, but for himself and Kai.

Carefully removing the stopper from the vial, he allowed four drops of the yellow oil to drip onto his palm. He rubbed the oil into his hands, drew them together and let his eyes lose focus. He peered at his cupped hands. This time he had no doubt that a vision would appear. It did. But Tao didn't like what he saw.

Jilong had seen the moment of hesitation on Tao's face. He moved closer.

"What do you see?"

All eyes were on Tao. No one doubted his ability as a seer.

"I need time to decipher my vision," he said.

"Tell me, boy!"

Tao was still staring at his palms, hoping for a different interpretation.

"You must have patience, General."

Tao heard the intake of breath around him. None of the Zhao would dare speak to Jilong in such a way.

"Every detail is crucial. If I miss something, it could mean the difference between victory and defeat." Tao studied the image laid out on his palms until it faded. "I saw men wearing black hoods and masks. They were outside a city gate. They had fear in their eyes. Moonlight illuminated characters carved on a yellow earth wall."

"Is that all?"

"That is all. I told you my visions need interpretation."

Jilong had leaned so close, Tao could see the hairs of his beard.

"So what does it mean? The bandits will attack, that much is clear, but when? Where?"

For once, Tao knew exactly what the vision meant. But the information seemed to benefit Jilong, not the dragons.

"The masked men represent the Black Camel Bandits, as you say. The moon was low in the sky, newly risen. The attack will take place tonight, not long after midnight. And I know the carvings. They are on the walls of Luoyang near the West Brilliance Gate."

As well as seeing these images, Tao had also felt afraid and anxious and lonely. He didn't mention those things to the warlord.

"But are the bandits inside the city or will they attack it from that direction?"

"The carvings are on the inside of the wall. The bandits will attack that gate intending to take the garrison."

The carvings were insults the citizens of Luoyang had crudely carved on the walls. Jilong was the only Zhao in the city who could read Huaxia. The characters were small, ill-formed and below a man's line of sight, so there was no chance that the warlord would ever notice them. It was a small rebellion from the downtrodden people of Luoyang.

"Are you sure that they will attack this one gate?"

"Yes," Tao said.

The nomads muttered to each other. Tao could tell they were impressed by the way he'd interpreted these few signs. Jilong was not used to trusting anyone. He stared at Tao as if he was trying to see through his skull and into his mind. Tao had described everything that he had seen in the vision, so he looked the warlord in the eye, knowing he would see no deception in his face.

"You must trust me, General."

"Then I will station my men inside the gate, ready to ambush the bandits."

Tao glanced at Kai. Had his visions really turned to the service of Jilong? He couldn't believe that. He had to trust his second sight. This latest vision was of benefit to Kai, how he didn't know. He was troubled at the thought of the

Black Camel Bandits being slaughtered because of him. But mostly he was concerned about Pema.

"If we could kill them in their hide-out before they attack, that would be better," Jilong said. "Are you sure there is no clue as to where the bandits are hiding?"

"I am sure. This is the place for the confrontation."

Tao was glad the warlord wasn't looking at him now. This time he would have seen the lie in his eyes. Tao remembered there had been smell and sound in a vision, not this last one, but the vision of blackness when Fo Tu Deng had wanted to know where the bandits were hiding. He had smelled incense and heard bells, prayer bells. Now he knew. The bandits were hiding in the cellars of the White Horse Temple.

Jilong ordered his men to prepare for battle.

"I will ride the *naga*," he said. "Leave six men to guard the boy and his dragon."

"That won't be necessary," Tao said. He had seen one other thing in the vision. He hadn't realised its significance until that moment. "In my vision I saw my own fingers brushing the carvings. I must go with you."

He couldn't bear the thought of returning to Luoyang, but if he went with Jilong, he could go to the White Horse Temple and warn Pema.

"And your dragon?" Jilong asked.

Tao remembered the emotions he had felt – fear, anxiety,

loneliness. That could only mean one thing.

"He was not in my vision."

Kai let out an angry roar.

"I'm sorry, Kai." Tao spoke to the dragon with his mind. "I must be true to the vision. I don't understand it, but it was clear. I felt my anguish, my separation from you. I was alone."

"This is part of the plan, isn't it? I will shape-change and come with you in secret."

Tao shook his head and turned to Jilong. "You must lock him in the cellar so that he doesn't try to follow me."

This was the second time Tao's visions had made Kai angry. Tao prayed he hadn't made a mistake in trusting them. They had told him to leave Kai behind, and he was leading the Zhao straight to Pema.

Chapter Twenty-Six
BETRAYAL

Tao was riding behind one of Jilong's soldiers, bouncing around like loosely tied baggage.

"Don't sit there like a bundle of firewood," the soldier said. "Move with the horse."

Riding was so natural to the Zhao, the nomad couldn't explain how to do it any more than he could instruct someone how to breathe. Tao clung to him, even though he smelled like sour milk and burnt meat.

"And let go of me."

Tao released his grip on the nomad's tunic and held on to the saddle blanket. That only made him more unstable.

They had waited until after dark to leave the compound for Luoyang. There was a risk that the Black Camel Bandits might attack before they got to the city, but Tao had told Jilong the exact position of the moon in his vision, and he took the chance that the attack would be after midnight. That gave the Zhao the advantage of arriving at the city under cover of darkness.

Jilong had flown off on Sunila. He would have reached the city in minutes. For those on horseback it took hours. The sound of Kai's anguished cries as Tao left the compound still rang in his ears.

They were close to Luoyang. It was too dark to see it, but Tao could feel the hulking ruin of the city in front of them. He'd been trying to get away from Luoyang for months, and now here he was riding towards it.

Tao had hoped he would somehow be able to escape as they passed the White Horse Temple, but Jilong had told his men to ride in a wide arc around the city's eastern wall, to avoid any possibility of ambush. They didn't go near the temple.

The nomads turned their horses again and the walls finally loomed before them. They entered the city through the northern Broad and Boundless Gate. Tao got down from the horse, stiff and sore, but he would have climbed back on without complaint if he could have ridden away from that hateful city.

Tao walked through the gate with a sinking heart. Luoyang hadn't changed. The yellow earth walls were still crumbling. The gates were still missing. Weeds and thorn bushes grew in the streets. The few inhabitants kept out of the way of the Zhao, slinking into the shadows, sneering and muttering when they thought they were out of earshot.

The city had a bad smell. There was no waste in

Luoyang, so it wasn't rotting rubbish that made it smell bad. It was an animal smell – sweat, urine, excrement – and the animals were human beings living in the worst possible conditions. Tao saw some people cooking their evening meal – two rats on a skewer.

Tao made his weary legs follow the Zhao soldiers down the narrow street towards the garrison in the north-west corner of the city. But before they reached the garrison, Tao's traveling companion jabbed him with the end of his lance.

"The Langhai wants to see you," the man said.

He led Tao to the palace ruins where Jilong had taken over a large room that would have once been grand, but it had been stripped of its fine furniture and decorations long before. There was a painting on the ceiling. It might have been the Seven Sages in the Bamboo Grove, but it was hard to tell as it was now black with soot, thanks to a fire that was burning in the middle of the room. Tao had been expecting the Zhao leader to have a high chair and a bed with elegant carvings, but all he had was a felt rug and a straw mattress, as if he was out on the plains not inside a palace. Jilong told Tao to sit with him and offered him food, but it was all meat and *kumiss*.

"I need more information about these Black Camel Bandits," Jilong said. "Who are they? Where are they from? And where are they hiding?"

"I have given you all the information I have."

"It is not enough. Seek another vision."

"You must treat my second sight with respect, General, if it is to serve you."

The guards in the room moved forwards, eager to punish the impudent young man, but Jilong waved them away.

"If you want me to seek another vision so soon after the last one, I must have solitude where I can meditate to regain the mental concentration I require. And I need food that does not contain meat."

Jilong made a small movement with his hand, and two nomads took Tao to another smaller room with no roof. After a while one of them brought him grain and some sad wilted green vegetables, which Tao suspected had been snatched from one of Luoyang's inhabitants.

There wasn't much time. The moon would soon be rising. Tao had to escape and find Pema. But first, he would seek a vision.

The vision came quickly, and it was in shades of black and white. He saw someone lying in a puddle. He knew it was one of the Black Camel Bandits because of the black clothing and the masked face. He peered at this new vision, but could see nothing that told him more than he already knew – there would be a battle and it would be at night. He had hoped the vision would tell him how to escape and warn Pema, how to stop the battle, but it didn't.

His visions were to aid dragons, not nomad girls. And yet he couldn't stop doubt creeping into his mind. His visions had separated him from Kai, and everything he had seen seemed to benefit Jilong.

There were no other clues, apart from a vague feeling in his fingertips, as if he was running them over silky material. He didn't know what that meant. Tao was about to lower his hands and wipe them on his trousers, but the image on his palms became clearer as if the moon had appeared between clouds. The vision was now tinged with colour. The puddle was dark red, and there was a purplish bruise on the bandit's forehead. And the staring eyes were blue. It was Pema lying dead in a pool of blood.

Tao jumped to his feet. What had he done? He had told Jilong to come to Luoyang for the express purpose of engaging the bandits in battle. He always imagined that, because she was a girl, Pema would be a spy or a messenger for the bandits, not a fighter. But there she was bleeding on the battlefield. The image faded, but in his mind he could still see the pool of dark red blood and Pema's unblinking eyes. It was the look of someone who had died in terror and pain. Tao had given Jilong the advantage in the coming battle. And he had sentenced Pema to death.

He recalled all the visions he'd had. He must have misread one of them. Surely his second sight, which sprung from his connection with Kai, wouldn't have told him to leave the dragon behind and to endanger Pema's life? He wished Kai was with him. He would have stopped the panic rising. He had to go back to free the dragon. The image of Pema was still clear in his mind. His faith in his ability as a seer was fading. Before he could free Kai, he had to warn Pema.

Tao banged on the door. He took a deep breath and tried to calm himself. He didn't want the guard to know how terrified he was. The door opened.

"I need to pee," Tao said. "It's urgent."

The guard held a bone in one hand and a cup of *kumiss* in the other. He pointed the bone towards the latrine. Tao hurried along the corridor. The guard drained his cup before following him. Tao turned a corner, broke into a run and lost the man. He wasn't going to the latrine. He had to get to the White Horse Temple and stop Pema from taking part in the battle. On foot it would take too much time. He didn't have a horse, but somewhere in the garrison there was a dragon. A dragon with wings.

Tao found where the horses of Jilong's personal guard were stabled. Sunila was there too, but while the other horses each had a bucket of dry grass, the *naga* had a bucket of tree frogs. He was no longer starving, so he was enjoying the game of waiting until they tried to escape before he pounced and ate them.

"Sunila, I need your help. I have to get back to the

compound. If you make yourself invisible, we can escape before the moon rises. Will you take me?"

The *naga* was wearing a new harness. There was a red diamond-shaped jewel on his forehead. Smaller jewels studded his breast harncss. Hc sat up as if to display this finery.

"Please, Sunila. Pema will be killed if I don't do something."

Tao was about to remind the *naga* how they saved him from starvation, when Sunila speared a frog that was trying to escape, using one of his sharp middle talons. Tao knew he was wasting his time. He had told Jilong that he would gain Sunila's allegiance if he provided his favourite food and gave him gifts of shiny things. The warlord had taken Tao's advice, and the *naga* was now loyal to him.

It was almost midnight. The battle would begin shortly. Pema's life was in his hands. Tao had wasted valuable time trying to get Sunila to help him. The moon would be rising above the city wall at any moment. The nearest gate was the Great Xia Gate, but that was right alongside the garrison. He couldn't risk running into Zhao soldiers who knew him. Images of the city before it was destroyed floated up from his memory. The houses around the palace ruins were where rich people had once lived. The Huan house was a few streets back from that area, but Tao had played in those streets as a child, wandered the alleyways behind the grand houses while his mother visited friends.

Those mansions were now in ruins, the alleyways littered with rubble, but Tao knew the way. He zigzagged through the back alleys towards the West Brilliance Gate without being seen.

There were no more guards patrolling the wall than on any other night; Jilong didn't want the Black Camel Bandits to suspect that there was an ambush. The two guards were peering into the darkness, looking for any sign of attacking bandits, straining their ears for the sound of galloping horses, the whistle of speeding arrows. But crouched behind the parapet were other Zhao soldiers, waiting to spring up when the bandits approached. More soldiers were stationed out of sight inside the gate. Just as Tao had hoped, these were soldiers from the garrision who didn't know him. They had been waiting for hours, and they were getting restless. They were sitting down, passing around strips of dried meat and a skin of *kumiss*.

Tao slid along the crumbling yellow earth wall, towards the gateway. In his worn clothes and straw sandals, he could easily pass as a citizen of Luoyang. He smiled when he came to the carvings he had seen in his vision. *All Zhao are stupid melons. Jilong is a pig-faced son of a rabbit.* The darkness gave him cover and he silently slipped out through the gate.

Then he was outside the city. The rim of the moon appeared over the wall. Tao broke into a run, still hoping no one had noticed him. He couldn't see the White Horse Temple, but he knew that it was not much more than a *li* to the west. He hurried in that direction, aware that he was still in arrow range of the men on the wall. But before he had gone more than fifty paces, he heard galloping horses behind him. The guards on the wall were more vigilant than usual. Of course they had seen him escape. He ran, although it was pointless. He stumbled over a rock, fell, got up again and continued to run. Moonlight illuminated the white walls of the White Horse Temple that were now only a few *chang* away. He stopped dead. He realised he had led the Zhao right to the Black Camel Bandits' hiding place.

A Zhao commander behind him shouted an order. "Halt!"

The sound of the galloping horses stopped. Tao couldn't understand why he'd been given this reprieve, but he was going to take it with thanks. He started running again. His rasping breath hurt his throat. But then in front of him he saw a line of about fifteen foot soldiers, dressed in black, their faces masked by black cloth, all but their eyes. Tao couldn't see how many ranks of men were behind this frontline. Pennants with the black camel emblem fluttered in the moonlight. He'd only seen them in a vision before, but now the Black Camel Bandits were there in the flesh. At the sound of a command, they drew their swords. Tao turned to flee, but behind him the dozen men of the Zhao detachment sent to capture him were in battle formation. There weren't many of them, but they had an advantage. They were on horseback. The bandits, who were prepared for a fight within the city walls, were on foot.

Orders to attack rang out from both sides. The men, whooping and shouting, leaped forward at the same moment, one side on horseback, their opponents on foot, rushing headlong towards each other. Tao was between them, but no one was interested in him. He looked to the right and to the left for a way to escape, but there wasn't time to get out of their way. The night air was suddenly full of arrows. The horses and men were closing in on him, and he would surely be trampled.

Chapter Twenty-Seven
TRAITOR MOON

The enemy forces met with a clash of weapons. Tao was surrounded by chaos. Swords slashed through the air and sliced through limbs. Lances dug into flesh. Bodies fell all around him. Horses' hoofs stamped the earth. One horse stepped back, rammed its rump into Tao and kicked him in the chest, bruising his ribs and knocking the breath out of him.

Tao had brought about this confrontation. Men would die tonight because of him. He remembered the visions that led him to this point, trying to think how he had misinterpreted them. Arrows whistled past his ears. He fell to his knees and folded his arms over his head, as if they could protect him from the shower of arrows. A thought hit him like a blow to the head. He hadn't misinterpreted his visions. They had kept Kai safe, away from the conflict. Tao had made the mistake of trying to use the visions for the wrong purposes. He still was, though deep down he knew it wasn't possible. If he didn't get to the White Horse

Temple and warn Pema, she would die.

He crawled towards a clump of trees, away from the fight. He had no interest in the battle, if it could be called that. He could see now that there were no other ranks behind that first line of bandits. It was an insignificant skirmish that would soon be forgotten. If the two bands of men chose to kill each other, it was not his concern. He had no allegiance to either of them. His focus was on saving his friends. If he reached the trees, he could skirt around the fighting men and make his way to the temple. He could warn Pema and then return to Kai and beg his forgiveness.

Tao was almost at the trees. Apart from the kick in the chest, he had managed to get away unscathed. There was still time to put everything right.

Then he heard a voice, a familiar voice. Moonlight was filtering weakly through clouds. When he struggled to his feet he could make out a small figure on a horse, shouting orders at the Black Camel Bandits. It was Pema. He couldn't understand why she had the authority to give orders. Zhao soldiers were galloping towards her, their swords glinting in the pale moonlight. Tao called out to her, but his chest hurt and his feeble voice couldn't be heard above the noise of the battle.

Tao had no weapons, not even his staff to fend off blows. But Wei's *qi* was ready, as if waiting to be summoned. He closed his eyes and felt the *qi* surge inside him. At last, it was at his command. He couldn't kill people with it, but perhaps he could disarm those who were trying to kill him. He thrust his arms into the air and felt the *qi* radiate from him. For the first time in his life, he felt strong. But the *qi* didn't explode from his fingertips in powerful bolts. Instead, it gently drifted up into the night air in slender threads and seeped down into the damp earth through the soles of his feet. Those thin strands didn't have the power to rustle leaves, let alone disable a nomad soldier.

The Zhao had almost reached Pema before she saw them. She called to the bandits for help, but they were struggling against the mounted soldiers. Tao ran into the path of the Zhao to slow them, but they didn't notice him. A horse knocked him to the ground. He lay there, winded, horses' hoofs thudding all around him, churning up the earth.

But his *qi* was still flowing out of him.

Where his cheek lay against the ground, he noticed crumbs of churned-up earth start to shift a little, as if something below was stirring. Lumps of soil were pushed aside and crawling insects emerged from the ground. Just a few at first but then there were more – slaters, huge ants with snapping mandibles, cockroaches, and stag-beetles as long as his finger. There were huntsman spiders as well, emerging from under rocks. Soon there were hundreds of *wuji.* They were responding to the gentle strands of his *qi*.

The insects were crawling up the horses' legs and onto their riders. Moths were gathering above them, some no bigger than a fingernail, others with a wingspan as wide as a spread hand. They flew at the soldiers' eyes. A cloud of mosquitoes descended on the men, sucking blood from any exposed skin. On threads of spider web carried by gusts of wind, hundreds of spiders drifted from the surrounding trees, settling on the nomads' faces and hands. There were fat-bodied black spiders, green ones with spiky legs, and the familiar yellow-striped orb spiders. The Zhao soldiers stopped their attack. In fact, all fighting ceased as men from both sides furiously tried to brush off the insects that were crawling inside clothes, into mouths and up noses. They yelped and scratched at bites. Despite the pain in his chest, Tao smiled. This was his *qi* power, effective but not deadly.

Something swooped down from the night sky. It was Sunila with Jilong riding him, a plumed helmet on his head. Jilong was yelling, Sunila was roaring. Together they made a terrifying sound that made the bandits turn and run. Tao would have expected stronger discipline from the men who had won back towns from Jilong, but he hoped Pema was retreating with them. Sunila's scales glowed pale silver and his mane streamed behind him, a shade of grey in the weak moonlight seeping through the thinning clouds. His huge horn was the most luminous part of him. Jilong, in his metallic armour, was like an extension of the *naga*. He yelled at his men, directing them where to attack so that they could kill more effectively. Sunila was flying too high for the winged insects to reach Jilong as he fired arrows down on his enemies, most of whom had dropped their weapons as they tried to rid themselves of the *wuji*.

Then the traitor moon moved into a break in the clouds. It was past full, but it seemed huge. A shaft of moonlight shone right on the spot where Tao was crouching. Jilong saw him. He wheeled Sunila round, fitted an arrow to his bow and aimed it at Tao. The warlord hesitated for a moment. He might have been weighing up whether he needed a seer or not. One of the Black Camel Bandits rode up, stopping between Tao and Jilong. The moonlight shone on the rider. Blue eyes glared down at Tao.

"Get on the horse," Pema shouted.

Jilong recognised her. The hatred in his eyes was visible, even from that distance. He let loose his arrow, but it wasn't aimed at Tao. He would deal with him later. Pema tried to get her horse to move, but it reared up, startled by Sunila. The arrow dug deep into the horse's thigh and it fell to the ground. Pema managed to leap clear. She scrambled over to Tao, grabbed his hand and pulled him to his feet.

"Get away, Pema," Tao shouted. "I can take care of myself."

"It doesn't look like it."

Sunila had circled wide, and was too far away for the warlord to get a good shot. While Jilong was struggling to get the *naga* to turn and dive at them, Tao and Pema ran. The warlord slung his bow over his shoulder and, drawing his sword, dug his heels into the *naga's* flanks and leaned forwards to make him dive. Sunila swooped above Tao's head. Tao caught sight of something he'd seen in one of his visions – a red boot clamped to a dragon's silvery hide, and on the toe of the boot a scorpion tail. He only glimpsed it as it flashed past, but it looked as if the scorpion tail was moving, crawling off the boot and onto the *naga's* scales. Sunila let out a screech. He broke out of his dive and soared up steeply again, swerving from side to side. Something had spooked him. He looped above the battleground. Jilong clung to the reins and the straps held him fast. Sunila swooped down again, still screeching. While everyone else was watching the aerial antics of the *naga*, Tao and Pema kept running.

Something dropped from the air and lodged in Pema's hood. Tao stopped to pick it off. It was a huge centipede. He realised that he hadn't paid enough attention to the vision that had told him Jilong would ride a dragon. The warlord had worn scorpion tails on his red boots as decorations before, but now they were unadorned. What he'd seen in the vision was a centipede. It had responded to the call of his *qi* and crawled onto Jilong's boot before the *naga* took off. Like all dragons, Sunila was terrified of centipedes. Unaware that it had been dislodged, he was still streaking through the air, shaking each leg in turn, which made him pitch from side to side. He shook his head furiously, no doubt imagining the centipede was crawling into his ear. And then he turned upside down. Jilong clung to the reigns as his arrows and sword fell to the earth. One of the harness straps holding Jilong broke, but his grip on the reins and the other strap across his shoulder stopped him from falling.

Tao held up the centipede for Sunila to see. With his excellent eyesight, the naga saw the creature in the moonlight. Jilong was berating him, but Sunila was calmer now. He reached up with one of his back paws and with his dextrous three toes he managed to undo the buckle securing the remaining strap. Then he did a backflip. Jilong plummeted headfirst to the ground and landed with a thud. Sunila righted himself and flew towards the rest of the Zhao. They fled as he chased them away.

Tao let out a whoop of triumph. "Sunila is still with us!"

The ten members of Jilong's personal guard galloped onto the battlefield. Without the advantage of winged steeds they had lagged behind their leader. Astride their black horses, with red plumes rippling, they looked as magnificent as ever, but their faces were grim and pale.

They had seen Jilong fall from the *naga*. Their job was to protect him, and they had failed. They left fighting the bandits to the other Zhao soldiers and turned their attention to Tao and Pema. Word had spread quickly that Tao had betrayed the Langhai, and they all remembered the girl who had tried to murder their Chanyu.

Zhao reinforcements also arrived, at least forty of them. The bandits were now completely outnumbered. Sunila wheeled above them, breathing mist and creating a cloud that covered the moon. He screeched and then torrential rain fell from the sky. The battlefield was soon a sea of mud. The bandits, almost invisible in their black clothes, had the advantage as they ducked around the Zhao horses, which were struggling in the mud. But one of the Zhao was swinging something around his head. It was a length of rope with two metal balls on the ends. He let it go and the balls flew through the air and the rope wrapped around the *naga's* feet. This threw him off balance. His flimsy wings couldn't compensate and he tumbled to the ground. Tao couldn't see where he fell.

The rain stopped, the cloud dispersed and the moon lit the muddy battlefield. Tao saw how few bandits there were, no more than fifteen, and some of them were wounded.

The Zhao were riding towards them.

"Call for reinforcements!" Tao yelled to Pema.

"There are no reinforcements."

"But there must be more." He couldn't make sense of this.

"I have to stand with them," Pema said.

Tao held her back. "They can take care of themselves."

"No, they can't. When I returned from Chengdu, the Zhao had a tighter grip on the city than ever. I couldn't go back to my home. I recruited my own band of soldiers from the boys of Luoyang."

"So you are their leader?"

"Yes. It was my idea to wear black, and we met in a house in Bronze Camel Street. That's how I came up with the name."

Pema shook off Tao's hand and ran towards the bandits. The moonlight revealed Tao alone and exposed. Jilong's personal guard were the most disciplined Zhao soldiers, the best trained. Their moon shadows led the way as they galloped towards Tao and formed a circle around him.

"It's his fault," one of them said, unsheathing his sword. "It was his idea that the Langhai ride that creature. And now he's dead."

"The Langhai wouldn't have wanted him to die quickly."

"That's right. He would've made him suffer."

The circle of horses around Tao tightened. There was no way for him to escape.

But Pema had managed to regroup the bandits. They

might have been afraid of flying dragons, but they bravely charged at Jilong's men who were surrounding Tao. In the confusion, one of them tried to attack Tao, mistaking him for one of the Zhao. His mask had fallen from his face and Tao could see that he was just a boy, no older than himself.

The Zhao reinforcements had scattered when they heard that Jilong had fallen, but one of their captains had rallied them. Pema braced herself to fight as they galloped towards her. She and her Black Camel Bandits were outnumbered at least four to one. Tao had to do something. He felt the *qi* stir within him and then flow out of him, as it had before.

The air was suddenly full of buzzing. Tao thought he was imagining it. He knew for certain that bees never came out at night, but there they were, hundreds of them, buzzing furiously, attacking Jilong's guard and the Zhao reinforcements, stinging their faces. The horses were unfazed by the battle, but they were frightened by the bees. They reared and whinnied and shook their heads, trying to dislodge them. The soldiers were waving their swords, though they were useless against the bees, which were only stinging the Zhao, not Pema's bandits.

"The bees are on our side!" Pema said. "I'll never tease you about your *qi* power again."

But each bee had just one sting, and once it was delivered, all it could do was fly away and find a place to die.

Jilong's guard were the first to recover from the bee attack. One of them urged his horse towards Tao. He had lost his sword, but as he dismounted he pulled a dagger from his belt and lunged at Tao. Before the guard could stab him, there was a disturbance among the horses. Something else was unsettling them.

A moon shadow that had frightened the horse. Men cried out as the grey apparition passed among them, trailing specks of moonlight in its wake. Tao almost smiled. It was Baoyu. The man with the knife had his eyes on her. Tao had the chance to escape. The Zhao, who had stood firm when then had been attacked by the *naga*, fled at the sight of the ghost girl. She had regained her power, just as Kai said she would, and Tao had no regrets.

Baoyu turned her hollow eyes on the Zhao soldier in front of Tao. He stabbed his dagger into her shadow body again and again, but it passed through air. The points of silver in her eye sockets held his gaze. She bared her sharp teeth as she circled him, and then she disappeared inside him. Frost formed on his beard and on the dagger blade. He opened his mouth, trying to gasp in air, but his insides were already frozen. Pema ran over and knocked the dagger from his hand. It fell to the ground and smashed into pieces as if it were made of glass.

Those men who hadn't fled were staring in terror and disbelief as the ghost girl wreathed around them, frightening their horses.

Pema was staring too. "Is that …?"

Tao got to his feet. "A ghost. Her name is Baoyu."

"You have the strangest allies."

Tao didn't have time to explain. A black horse with a jewelled bridle and breast harness and a red plume on its head galloped onto the battlefield.

Tao couldn't believe his eyes. "It's Jilong!"

The Zhao leader's face was bleeding, his helmet dented, but he was still very much alive. His astonished men cheered and called his name. His personal guard, though their faces were swollen with bee stings, regained their deadly calm and rallied at the Langhai's side.

Then the moon disappeared and so did Baoyu.

The remaining Zhao were still fighting Pema's bandits, who had no military discipline but were using their sly street-urchin skills to deceive and confuse the Zhao. Jilong had lost interest in the Black Camel Bandits.

"Kill the traitors," he shouted.

He looked from Pema to Tao, trying to decide which of the two to kill first. It didn't take him long to make the decision. Pema had tried to murder his uncle, but

Tao had betrayed and humiliated *him*.

"I will take care of the seer."

Jilong divided up his personal guard. He sent five after Pema, but he led the remaining four against Tao. As Tao turned to run, he stumbled over a body, slipped in the mud and fell on his back. The warlord jumped down from his horse and stood over him. There was an orb spider crawling up Jilong's sword arm, but he brushed it away. He had conquered that fear. Pema was too far away to help. And in any case, she was fighting off her own pursuers. Time seemed to slow. Jilong's sword moved towards him in a gentle arc. He noticed that it wasn't the bronze sword the warlord had when he rode Sunila, but a simple iron weapon with a rusty hilt, the sort of weapon used by common nomads. Its blade was sharp though. Tao gasped as it plunged deep into his shoulder.

He heard Pema scream. She had seen him wounded. Tao covered his wound with both hands and watched the blood seep through his fingers. The Zhao, who had paused to watch their leader kill the seer, turned back, swords at the ready, but the surviving bandits had melted into the darkness. Pema hadn't escaped though. She was still fighting off four Zhao horsemen.

Tao had fallen on a slight rise in the ground. He watched as his lifeblood ran down the slope and pooled in a shallow depression.

One of the four Zhao horsemen now lay dead on the ground. Pema somehow managed to get past the others. She ran at Jilong, ready to plunge her sword into his heart, but another horseman caught up with her and knocked the sword from her hand. She kept running at the warlord, even though she was weaponless. Jilong stood still and waited for her to come within range of his sword. She ran right up to him until she was breathing in his face. Jilong lifted his sword, but before he let it fall, Pema raised her knee and kicked him in the groin. He crumpled to the ground. One of the other horsemen galloped up to aid his leader. He took a weapon from his belt, a blunt club, and swung it at Pema. She instinctively raised her hand for protection. The club hit her arm. Tao watched as her forearm bent the wrong way and she fell, screaming with pain.

Tao managed to raise himself on one elbow. Before him was the scene from his vision – Pema, her eyes frozen in terror, lying in a pool of blood. But it wasn't hers. She had fallen where his own blood was soaking into the ground. She was staring at him, white-faced apart from a bruise on her forehead, wide-eyed. She wasn't dead, and it wasn't the prospect of her own death that was terrifying her. Her sword arm was broken, but she would live to be taken prisoner. Tao was the one with the fatal wound. As his consciousness faded, he saw the captain of Jilong's guard, the man with arms like hams and an ear missing, pull Pema to her feet and drag her away.

Tao was overwhelmed by grief and anger. He couldn't save Pema. He was going to die. His visions had betrayed him.

Chapter Twenty-Eight
LAST HOPE

But the knot of *qi* inside Tao was not ready to give up. Despite the fact that so much of his lifeblood had leaked from him, Wei's *qi* was determined that he would live. His allies had fought bravely, but their strength and powers were limited. Though he rejoiced that Pema was alive, she was a captive of the Zhao, and that could be worse than death. He had to save himself so that he could fulfil his destiny. But first he had to rescue Pema.

Tao remembered his last vision. There was one other element that he hadn't interpreted – the sensation of touching silken cloth. The meaning was suddenly clear to him. He reached inside his jacket and felt a band of silky material that was tied around his chest. It was a strip of his sister's gown. His shaky fingers undid the knot and pulled it out. He could just see the apple-blossom pattern in the moonlight. Something was wrapped in a fold of the silk – his dragon-stone shard. When Tao left the compound, the only thing Jilong had permitted him to take was his vial of oil, but Tao didn't want to be parted from the shard again, so he had bound it to him. He held the piece of dragon stone in his hand. Warmed by his body heat, it didn't have its customary coolness.

His body was weak, but his mind was still strong. With every *shu* of his strength he focused the *qi* inside him. When he'd practised controlling his *qi*, he'd tried to concentrate it into something small and dense that he could hurl as a weapon. That was a mistake. His and Wei's *qi* could never be used to harm anyone, but it could reach out as it had to the insects. Instead of trying to concentrate it, he drew it into a long, fine thread that drifted out from him, thin but strong like a strand of spider web. With the help of the shard, he stretched it further and he directed it toward his family home. He had one friend left that he could rely on. Kai was his last hope, but he didn't know if the *qi* could reach that far.

The Zhao took no notice of him, assuming he was dead. They were rounding up the remaining bandits. With one hand, Tao managed to bind the silk strip around his wound. A stillness had settled over the battlefield. But that calm was shattered by a terrifying roar. A huge seven-headed serpent streaked down from the sky. Each head was topped with a jewelled crest glittering in the moonlight. A split tongue protruded from each mouth, spitting and hissing. Each pair of eyes was full of hate and hunger to kill. The Zhao and the bandits alike fell to their knees at the sight of the monster. Those who made the mistake of staring into those eyes were frozen, unable to move. The *qi* might not reach the Huan compound, but it had reached Sunila.

Tao thought that Pema's knee had ended Jilong's part in the battle, but to his surprise the warlord galloped into view. His horse was momentarily startled by the monster swooping from the sky, but Jilong reassured it. He had seen dragons shape-changing before, and the men who had been with Fo Tu Deng had reported the *naga's* alarming transformations to him. He steadied his men, assuring them it was an illusion. The Zhao were well aware that, illusion or not, the naga could deliver a deadly bite. They didn't run, but when Jilong touched his horse's flanks and rode towards the spitting serpent, only the remains of his personal guard were at his side.

Shape-changed Sunila lunged at Jilong, his fangs bared, but a loyal soldier raised his sword to protect his leader and the fangs sunk into his arm instead. The *naga* managed to rake three talons across the warlord's chest, cutting through the metal plates of his armour. Blood oozed through the slits. Jilong, his hand clamped over his chest, screamed orders and his men showered the seven-headed monster with arrows. Wounded, Sunila couldn't maintain the illusion. He returned to his own shape. Most of the arrows had glanced off his tough scales, but three had found their mark in the unscaled parts of his hide – one in the pit of his left foreleg, the other two in the underside of his tail. He grasped the arrows and pulled them out. Purple blood oozed from each wound.

Sunila was almost spent. He didn't have the strength to shape-change or to create a storm. All he could do was breath mist. Zhao arrows had grazed his wings, but they had not been pierced, so he took off. A few Zhao had weapons left, but they were weary and their arrows fell back to the ground, unable to reach him. As the *naga* swooped above them, he exhaled again and again, and the cold mist sank to the ground, covering the battlefield with a white fog. The Zhao stumbled around, unable to see where they were going. Sunila retreated into his own mist.

Tao was sure his allies were all defeated, but the moon came out from behind the clouds and Baoyu reappeared. She was the only one who could not be harmed by the weapons of men. She swept over to the nomads, showing her decaying ghost face and leaving cold fear inside every man. She spooked Jilong's horse. It reared, threw the warlord off, and galloped away.

Tao managed to get to his feet. The wound in his shoulder was so painful that he thought he was going to pass out, but he gathered his remaining strength and searched for Pema. He found her bound together with some of her bandits. He cut them free with his wolf tooth.

Pema grasped his hand. "I thought you were dead."

"Not yet."

The sky to the east had turned pale grey. The sun would soon be rising.

The Zhao were reduced from more than fifty men to less than ten. Baoyu was continuing to terrify them, allowing the surviving Black Camel Bandits to escape. The battlefield was strewn with bodies ripped open by awful wounds or bearing the puncture marks of a *naga* bite. Riderless horses with wild eyes fled from the battleground. The wounded were crying out. This place was more like one of the realms of hell than anything Tao had experienced when he was trapped underground. And he couldn't imagine that hell itself could be any worse.

He smiled at Pema. She held her broken arm against her body. They were both injured, but they had survived.

An arc of brilliant sunlight appeared over the walls of Luoyang. Baoyu faded to nothing.

Jilong walked out of the shreds of mist, which were all that remained of Sunila's fog. The chest wounds the *naga* had inflicted had weakened him, but he was determined to finish off his two worst enemies.

Tao didn't have the strength to fight even a wounded Jilong. Instead, he gently put his arms around Pema, partly so that he could protect her from the warlord's blade, mostly because if he was going to die, he could think of no better way to depart this life than with her in his arms.

Jilong unsheathed his sword as he approached. "There's no escaping this time. A seer is no use if he's a traitor as well."

Two of Jilong's guards grabbed Pema and pulled her away from Tao.

The warlord examined Tao as if he was a freshly cooked haunch and he was thinking about the best way to carve it. Tao's *qi* was depleted. His allies were exhausted, wounded or dispersed by the sun. Dead *wuji* littered the battlefield, their short lives sacrificed for Tao's cause. Jilong smiled as he raised his sword.

And then a dragon leaped out of nowhere. Green, strong and proud, he looked bigger than he really was. With his tail, he knocked the sword from Jilong's hand. Kai had used his mirage skill to hide himself until he was almost upon them. He held Tao's staff in one paw and he threw it to Tao who caught it easily. The Zhao quailed when they saw yet another unnatural foe.

"Don't worry about the dragon," Jilong said. "He may seem fierce but it's an illusion. He is weak from being chained, and your iron swords will render him as fragile as a newborn foal."

The soldiers held back, unconvinced. As they turned to

run, Kai attacked them, raking their flesh with his talons. The sight of the dragon, fresh and strong, despite having run all the way from the Huan compound, gave Tao new hope. This was why his vision had told him to leave Kai behind! He was needed at the end of the battle when all Tao's allies were spent. Kai collided with Jilong, knocking him over. The Zhao leader was soon on his feet again with his sword drawn. But he had little strength left. And Kai was angry. Jilong's guard were reduced to six men. Pema took care of two of them. Tao could hold only one of them at bay, blocking his sword with his staff. The dragon head on the staff glowed in the dawn light, making it seem like more than a piece of wood.

The other four guards ran towards Kai, but the dragon swept them over with one stroke of his tail, as if they were pieces on a board game. They got to their feet, looking around for the dragon, but Kai had disappeared. He couldn't make himself invisible like Sunila could, but he could shape-change into something small that they didn't notice. Tao saw a mouse scamper behind Jilong and turn into a tiger. Kai's roar didn't sound like a tiger's roar, but it terrified the surviving Zhao soldiers. Kai turned into a monkey and then a vase of flowers. He was ready to have some fun with them, but Jilong didn't have a sense of humour. He took two steps forwards and ran his sword through the vase. Tao gasped. The dragon took on his true shape, purple blood seeping from a wound in his flank. The point of the sword had managed to slip between two scales. Kai groaned and staggered as if he was about to collapse. The guards moved to finish him off.

"Leave the dragon," Jilong said. "I wounded him with an iron weapon. He will soon die. Get the seer."

The sight of the dragon's blood reawakened the captain of the guard's lost courage. He strode over to Tao, who held up his staff, but even the thought of immediate death couldn't raise another *shu* of energy from his battered body.

Pema tried to come to Tao's rescue but she was still fending off one of the guards. The other lay at her feet. The captain aimed his sword at Tao's heart. Kai leapt at him. The cinnabar, Tao thought, Kai had remembered to eat more. He'd pretended the wound was serious. The iron sword had done little harm. Tao saw the dragon's eyes change from brown to red. Kai lowered his horns. The Zhao soldier tried to run, but Kai was at full strength and he could have outrun a galloping horse. It wasn't a fair contest, but at that point Kai had no interest in fairness. He was a beast, a wild animal intent on his prey. He reached for the nomad with the talons of his left paw and grasped him as easily as a tiger catching a rabbit. He tilted his head to one side, cold and calculating, and aimed his horns at the gap between the front and back panels of the captain's armour. Tao wanted to cry out to stop him, but his voice wouldn't come. The dragon's horns sunk deep into flesh. The captain was surprised to see his own blood pooling on the ground in the dawn light. But Kai hadn't finished. He thrust his horns in deeper so that they found the heart, lungs and liver. The soldier's legs crumpled as if he was made of nothing more substantial than paper. Kai pulled out his horns. The captain was dead before he reached the ground, a gaping hole in his side.

Kai turned on Jilong, blood dripping from his horns. He loped towards the warlord. This was no instinctive attack brought on by a rush of anger or fear. Tao could hear Kai's thoughts as he decided where to land a lethal blow. Jilong saw the dragon's red eyes. He whistled to his horse, which returned to his master, despite the fact that there was a dragon about to attack. Jilong swung up onto the horse as it passed.

"Death to all dragons!" he shouted before he galloped away with his three remaining guards. Kai didn't chase them.

Tao, Kai and Pema stood together. They had suceeded against all odds. Tao couldn't help smiling. His visions hadn't betrayed him. It was his own mind that had misled him. His visions had only ever told him the truth.

Chapter Twenty-Nine
DEPARTURE

Tao and his allies limped back to the Huan compound, and allowed themselves just one night to rest, one day to heal. All the wounds, dragon and human, were cleaned, stitched and treated with red cloud herb. Pema's broken arm was bound and strapped to her. Throughout that day and night Sunila and Kai took turns to pace the top of the wall, their dragon eyes piercing the surrounding countryside for any sign of a Zhao attack.

Darkness had fallen. Baoyu was drifting around the courtyard, her ghost gown billowing around her.

"I'm grateful that you are staying here to guard my family's home," Tao said to her. "You aren't my true sister, but you are my shadow sister. And now it is your home too."

Wuji circled Baoyu's head like a crown and crawled beneath her like a moving carpet. With them to keep her company, she wouldn't be lonely. Sparks of moonlight twinkled among the tendrils of her hair. Tao knew she was happy. And so was he. He had achieved everything he'd wished for. His friends were safe. All of them.

The ghost girl had begun her work before she left to assist them in the battle. She had thoroughly terrified Lady Wang. Judging by all the cockroaches, scorpions, ants and huntsman spiders they found in Wei's room, the *wuji* had also done their part in ridding the compound of the nomad woman. By the time Tao and his friends returned from the battlefield, wounded and weary, Lady Wang and her entourage had gone.

The goat pen was empty when they returned. Tao didn't know what had happened to Fo Tu Deng. He guessed that he had escaped to find a new place to taint, new people to exploit to his own advantage.

Tao had told the surviving Black Camel Bandits that they were welcome to make the compound their headquarters, but they had chosen to take off their masks and black clothing and melt back into life in Luoyang. They hadn't given up their resistance to Zhao oppression, but before they could defeat the Zhao, they needed to increase their ranks. Tao was relieved that Pema didn't go with them. She was too recognisable.

Tao said goodbye to Baoyu. They'd decided to follow the bandits' example and travel only at night. It was no longer safe for them to stay at the Huan compound. Jilong and his men knew where they'd be.

They waited outside the gate while Sunila dropped the bar in place and then flew over the wall to join them. Then they set off into the night, heading west. Tao was still too weak from blood loss to walk. He was sitting in the cushioned wheelbarrow once used to transport Wei. Kai was pulling it. If anyone had seen them, they would have seemed a strange travelling party – two dragons, a blue-eyed girl and a boy in a barrow. No one would have guessed that they were victors in a battle. But no one saw them.

Though their futures didn't lie in the same direction, they all wanted to get far away from Luoyang and the Zhao. Tao shivered as he recalled Jilong's parting threat. Tao had no doubt he would seek revenge for his humiliating defeat.

Despite the worsening weather, Tao wasn't cold. Lady Wang, in her haste to leave, had abandoned several boxes of clothing. Pema had gone through them and found fur-lined boots and coats made of squirrel and fox pelts for herself and Tao. He knew he would need them to survive the winter, so he'd said a prayer of thanks to the animals who had been sacrificed to help him.

Kai was leading them away from Zhao territory. Their first task was to escort Pema safely to Chengdu. Tao was looking forward to this journey. As soon as he was strong enough, he would walk at Pema's side, talking to her day after day. They would have to say goodbye eventually, but for now they had time together.

"I hope I will never see Luoyang again," he said.

He knew in his heart he wouldn't. That filled him with relief and anxiety in equal measure.

"It is a big decision to leave behind all human contact," Pema said. As happened so often, she had read his thoughts. "Are you ready to spend the rest of your life in the wilderness with dragons and no human companionship?"

"Yes." It was time to be honest. "There is only one human I will miss. And that's you."

It was a clear night. The moon lit Pema's face. Tao could see that she was troubled.

"I told those boys they would succeed against the Zhao and take back Luoyang," she said. "They trusted me. It was a foolish plan."

Five of the young bandits had died in the battle.

Tao reached out and took her hand.

"You didn't force them to join you. It was their decision."

"I have finished with revenge. It only brings more sorrow," Pema said. "I am beginning to understand your reluctance to end the lives of any creatures."

Sunila flapped down out of the darkness. He had been scouting ahead. The *naga* would stay with Tao and Kai for part of their journey, but he could not go with them to the dragon haven. He would struggle to survive in the cold mountains. Now he had wings, it would be easier for him to find food and, with luck, other *nagas*. But while his wings were still growing, he had decided to travel with them until they got to the northern borders of Tianzhu.

After that, Tao and Kai would leave the world of men behind. They would head north to the mountains where the dragon haven was hidden.

Sunila took a turn at pulling the wheelbarrow, and Pema kept him company. Kai dropped back to walk alongside Tao.

"I will lead us through valleys as far as I can," the dragon said. "But sooner or later we must climb to the snowy peaks. It will not be easy."

"I'd rather face any hardship that nature has to offer, than the suffering humans can devise."

"The conflicts of men are behind us."

"Jilong still lives," Tao said. "All I have done is turn him against all dragons."

"We have achieved many things. Firstly, none of us is a captive of the Zhao."

"I suppose so. And now I think Pema really has let go of her wish for revenge."

"You have unleashed your *qi* power. And your visions, though sometimes hard to understand, have never let us down."

Tao smiled at a dragonfly that was hovering over his head. His was a strange *qi* power, but it had proved useful. And his visions had all combined to give them success, to enable Tao to face his destiny.

"How long will it take to reach the dragon haven?"

"A long time."

"Is that a long time in dragon or human terms?"

"It will be months, but not years."

"But look at me. I can't even walk!"

"You are weak now, but I am strong. At times it was the reverse. That is why we need each other. We are opposites, you and I – beast and boy, impulsive and cautious, fast and slow, aggressive and passive."

"Arrogant and modest."

Kai's jingling laughter rang out in the night.

"Together we are whole. Most important of all, we are both ready to fulfil our destiny – me as leader of the haven dragons; you as dragonkeeper, not only to me but to all dragons."

Tao had told him about the *qi* message from Wei.

"There has never before been a dragonkeeper for all dragons," Kai said. "Are you ready for that burden?"

"It has taken me some time to break the bonds that I didn't know existed – leaving behind my home and any chance of seeing my family again, any possibility of returning to a monastic life – but I have."

"Life at the dragon haven will be more solitary than a monk's."

"But I will be in control of my own destiny. Being a novice meant that I had no responsibility. My life, every day of it, was laid out before me. I never had to make any decisions."

"Now you are facing an unknown future where you must be responsible for many dragons."

"I am ready," Tao said. "Are you?"

"I am. I left the dragon haven unintentionally, without a word. I acted like a dragonling. Before returning there, I was determined to achieve something that made me worthy to lead the other dragons. I wanted to be a hero. I did not wish to return with nothing but sore paws and drooping spines. I wanted to take back some knowledge or skill that would impress the other dragons."

"You *are* a hero. You saved us all from the Zhao, but I don't think that will impress wild dragons. And you're returning with nothing."

"I am returning with something that will be of great benefit to the haven dragons."

"What?"

"I am returning with you."

GLOSSARY

ALMS
Food or money given to the poor as charity.

BUDDHISM
A religion based on the teachings of Buddha, a man who lived in India in 6th century BCE.

CHANG
A measure of distance equal to about 2.3 metres.

CINNABAR
A bright red mineral whose chemical name is mercuric sulphide.

HUAXIA
An ancient name for the country we now call China.

JUJUBE
Another name for the fruit called the Chinese date.

KARMA
In Buddhist belief, the justice by which deeds done in one lifetime affect a person in a later lifetime.

LI
A measure of distance equal to about half a kilometre.

LIUBO
An ancient Chinese board game. Archaeologists have found *liubo* boards and pieces, but no one knows what the rules are.

NOVICE
A person who has been accepted for a training period before taking vows to become a member of a religious order.

PALANQUIN
A rectangular covered box for travelling in, carried on poles on the shoulders of four men.

QI
According to traditional Chinese beliefs, *qi* is the life energy that flows through us and controls the workings of the body.

REBIRTH
Buddhist belief that after a person dies they are born into another life.

SANSKRIT
A language used in ancient India.

SHU
A measure of weight equal to about half a gram.

SUTRAS
Buddhist teachings.

TIANZHU
What people in early China called India.

WUJI
The Chinese word for invertebrates. This is the term that covers all creatures that do not have a backbone, including insects and other creepy-crawlies such as scorpions, worms and snails.

PRONUNCIATION GUIDE

All Chinese names and place names are written in *pinyin*. These words aren't always pronounced the way you'd expect them to be pronounced. This is a rough guide to the correct pronunciation.

Baoyu	*Bow* (rhymes with "cow") *you*
Chang'an	*Chang-ann*
Chengdu	*Chung-do* (rhymes with "two")
Fo Tu Deng	*Foe too dung*
Gu Hong	*Goo* (rhymes with "too") *Hoong* (*oo* pronounced as in "look")
Huan	*Hwarn*
Huaxia	*Hwar-she-ar*
Jiankang	*Gee-en-kang*
Jilong	*Gee-loong* (*oo* pronounced as in "look")
Kai	Rhymes with "buy"
Luoyang	*Lwor-yang*
Pingyang	*Ping-yang*
Puqingshuo	*poo-ching-shwoar*

qi	*chee*
Shenchi	*Shen-chee*
Shi Le	*Shir Luh* (rhymes with "blur")
Tao	Rhymes with "now"
Tianzhu	*Tee-en-ju*
Yinmi	*Yin-mee*
Wei	Way
Wuji	*Woo-gee* (*Woo* rhymes with "too")

Afterword

Writing a sequel is both a pleasure and a challenge. I enjoyed continuing Kai and Tao's journey and discovering myself what happened to them next. Although I had a fair idea of the bones of the story when I start writing, as often happens the most interesting developments appeared during the writing process. It is a matter of faith that it will happen.

It was very convenient that I had an entomologist as a next-door neighbour. I'd like to thank Dr Sabine Peronne of Museum Victoria for answering my many questions about insects. Dr Jacqui Mulville of Cardiff University provided very helpful information about ancient cremation.

As always I couldn't have written this book without the support of my family, John and Lili, who helped me overcome my fears and doubts, put up with general grumpiness, and, in Lili's case, helped me fix major plot problems. Lili also lobbied for the "foreign" dragon to be a *naga* and I'm glad she did.

My thanks to Jess Owen for her thorough edit, which improved the manuscript no end, and to Nicola Robinson for a forensic proofread. Thanks also to Gayna Murphy for the lovely design and Sonia Kretschmar for another absolutely gorgeous cover illustration.

Finally, I am very fortunate to have Maryann Ballantyne as my publisher. My sincere thanks to her for her skill and encouragement throughout the writing of this novel – and for rescuing me from a tracking-changes induced meltdown towards the end (partly while she was boarding a plane). She has the unerring ability to put her finger on the very thing that needs fixing. Her help and support is invaluable.

Carole Wilkinson's Dragonkeeper series is loved by readers all over the world and books in the series have won both literary and children's choice awards. Carole embarked on her writing career at the age of 40, happily leaving behind her previous employment as a laboratory technician in jobs involving blood and brains. She has been making up for lost time ever since. She has a fascination with dragons and is interested in the history of everything. Her books are a combination of meticulous research and imagination.

Carole's website is carolewilkinson.com.au

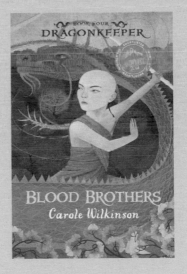